"You want to stay *here?*"

"Of course." Abbie's ex-husband shrugged out of his worn leather jacket and tossed it on the couch. She could see the muscles ripple along his forearms.

"Why? You're a cop. You should be out trying to find our son, not hanging around here."

His exasperation was evident. "And what if he calls and you can't find me? Or he's in trouble and I can't get in touch with you? Justin is the issue now. We don't have time for ex-wife and ex-husband problems."

For several moments she stared up at him, too aware of the weary lines around his mouth, too aware of his big strong body—and too conscious of a sudden and equally foolish need to have him hold her in his arms.

But he was right—Justin was the issue now—and she slowly nodded.

ABOUT THE AUTHOR

Dee Holmes, a much-published author of both fiction and nonfiction, won her first major award—a RITA—back in 1991 for her first published novel. Now, many awards and eight romance novels later, it's a pleasure to welcome Dee to Superromance! Her tenth romance novel is a very special—and emotional—one. It's the story of a missing son and a salvaged marriage, a new beginning and a reconciliation. Very happily married herself, Dee (who makes her home in Rhode Island) is the mother of a grown-up son and daughter.

Dee Holmes

HIS RUNAWAY SON

Harlequin Books

TORONTO • NEW YORK • LONDON
AMSTERDAM • PARIS • SYDNEY • HAMBURG
STOCKHOLM • ATHENS • TOKYO • MILAN
MADRID • WARSAW • BUDAPEST • AUCKLAND

ISBN 0-373-70699-5

HIS RUNAWAY SON

HIS RUNAWAY
SON

CHAPTER ONE

"MRS. WHEELER, I know you're upset, but if we're going to find your son, I need a few questions answered."

"Yes. I'm sorry." Abbie glanced toward the front door, as she'd done a dozen times in the past few minutes, hoping Justin would rush in with his usual teenage energy. But the only people to arrive had been some curious neighbors and the two police officers who'd come when she'd called less than an hour ago. She also wondered what was keeping Burke. It irked her that she needed him.

Then, as if thinking about her ex-husband had conjured him up, the door opened and he walked in. He stopped to say something to one of the detectives.

Abbie stood, suddenly wondering if Justin had contacted his father, but when Burke turned toward her, the grim expression on his face dashed that hope.

Their eyes met in the mutual realization that even though their marriage hadn't worked, their love and worry for their son was deep and strong. She watched him look beyond her toward Justin's room before they both gave their attention to the detective.

"Let's start with an easy question, Mrs. Wheeler," the young officer said. "When was the last time you saw him?"

She sat back down on the edge of her indigo brocade couch, her knees trembling and her shoulders aching. "This morning when he left for school."

"Anything unusual happen?"

She shook her head, tears welling up in her eyes. A thousand times since she'd found the note in his room, she'd rethought every moment of this morning and of all the recent mornings.

"No," she said. "In fact he seemed happy, and we laughed about a couple of comic strips in the morning paper." She used a wadded-up tissue to dab at her eyes. "I almost wish there *had* been something wrong, or at least some indication he was going to do this. Then there'd be a place to start looking."

She didn't have to glance up to know Burke was now standing a few feet from her. She could almost feel his concern, but also his expectation that she should have answers to why Justin had run away.

Despite their five-year-old divorce, his presence gave her, as it always had, a sense that he could somehow fix things, make everything right. With her fear for Justin crowding out rational thinking, she was grateful he'd come so quickly and even more grateful he was a cop.

His sable hair was thick, too long and barely combed. It fell over his forehead in a way that made her want to brush it back. Dressed in snug jeans, a dark olive green T-shirt and a leather jacket, he could have been a biker or a drug dealer, instead of an undercover cop. His body language was precise and confident. No missed signals, no hesitation, no mistakes.

Yet despite their twelve-year marriage and the son they'd had together, she knew little about Burke, the man. He'd remained an enigma to her, as if he'd chosen to keep distance between them, placing her in a compartment labeled wife and mother.

A long time ago she'd given up trying to bridge that emotional gap. While Burke might have cared for her, he didn't love and trust her in the deep abiding way she believed was fundamental for making a marriage work.

"Kids today have the damnedest reasons for doing things," the officer was saying. "In most cases they're home by night."

"Perhaps." Abbie nodded, but truthfully she had doubts. She knew her son. He wasn't the type of kid to run off for some silly reason. She realized, though, the young officer was trying to relieve her fears.

"Did he take the bus to school?"

"Yes."

"And you saw him get on the bus?"

"Well, no, actually. I said goodbye at the door and then went to get ready for work. Justin wasn't here when I got home, and I assumed he'd gone to play baseball. I did a few things and then took some clean clothes into his room. I think it was around three o'clock." It was only just after four now, but it seemed like hours had passed. "That's when I found the note."

She shook her head in despair. "All it said was, 'I have to get away from here. Don't worry about me.'"

The officer scribbled in his notebook. "All right, let me go back over this quickly to make sure we have it all straight."

Burke drew closer, stopping inches from where she sat on the couch.

Abbie looked up at him. "Hello, Burke."

"Abbie."

He reached down and took her arm, raising her to her feet. "Could you leave us for a minute?" he asked the officers, who nodded and exited the room.

Burke drew her into his arms, tucking her head beneath his chin. She was stunned by the gentleness of the gesture.

"How are you doing?" he asked.

"I'm scared. Worried. Frantic."

"Yeah. Me, too."

She slipped her arms around him, glad for his strength, his support, glad their personal differences were set aside for the sake of their missing son.

"I tried to call you," she said softly. "You weren't at your apartment, and when I contacted the department, they said they'd find you. I couldn't wait, Burke. I couldn't just sit here and wait for you to call. Time was of the essence. So I called the Walcott police. They came immediately."

"Shh, it's okay. You did the right thing." He tipped up her chin up. "You do believe I came the minute I got your message, don't you?"

"Yes. Justin's too important to you." She didn't say that she and their marriage had never been that important, and she had past experiences with Burke to prove it. Such as the night they were to meet to discuss their crumbling marriage and he hadn't showed up or called or even gotten a message to her.

"He's important to both of us, Abbie," Burke said, as if wanting to make sure she understood that this closeness was all about their son.

"Of course he is," she replied. She was honestly taken aback by his calmness. She and Burke had differed in the past about how Justin should be raised; she'd fully expected that in some way Burke would hold her responsible for their son's behavior. Or that he might not have taken Justin's running away seriously. She'd feared, in fact, that he would have given some logical explanation about how every kid runs away at least once.

Burke had never made a secret of the fact that he thought her views of parenting were too idealistic. That she didn't see the world as it really was. At the same time he'd thought her overly protective of Justin.

Perhaps she had been, she thought now. From Justin's early tearful days in kindergarten, when she'd felt as if she was abandoning him to an unfriendly world, to the time just a few years ago when a Halloween prank got him and three of his friends arrested, she'd feared for him. She'd envisioned a police record and the first step into a life of crime.

But Burke had shrugged off the arrest. Let Justin see at a young age that crime doesn't pay, he'd said, and it will keep him out of future trouble. That their son hadn't been in trouble with the law since was of little comfort to Abbie now.

She'd read Justin's note three times before it completely registered, before the words ''I have to get away from here'' made their full impact. What kind of trouble was her son in?

By her own choice, she'd seen little of Burke since their divorce. Justin saw his father almost every weekend, but Abbie had gone to great lengths to keep her distance.

Burke unsettled her, and in vulnerable moments, such as now, she recalled only the good parts of their marriage—which inevitably led to her having second thoughts about herself.

What if she'd been more understanding of what being married to a cop meant?

What if she'd been braver when he was off on some dangerous stakeout or drug bust?

What if she'd been more tolerant of his tendency to be a loner? That trait had attracted her in the beginning, but after they were married, it became a barrier so thick she couldn't penetrate it.

She sighed. Why wrestle with old questions now? What was the point? Maybe she *had* been a worrywart, but she'd never been able to treat Burke's job as if it was just an ordinary job, his risky undertakings merely routine.

Yet for Burke, his work was his love, his life, his mission. She thought she'd accepted that when she married him, but she'd soon realized marriage wasn't going to change him. At this moment, though, she appreciated the irony that it was the very fact that he was a cop that filled her with the hope, and indeed, the expectation that everything would be okay.

The officer who'd been questioning her returned.

Burke asked, "What have you got so far?"

"Not much. We contacted your son's teachers, but they said they didn't notice anything about his behavior that would indicate he was going to run away. We're in the process of contacting his friends."

"I'll be surprised if anything comes of that. Kids don't squeal as a rule."

"Still, we could get lucky."

Burke shrugged. "What's your name, Officer?"

"Larry Thompson."

"Haven't worked down in this part of Rhode Island for a while, but your name's familiar." Burke frowned, and Abbie could almost hear the spin of the memory file he carried in his head. "You pulled a baby girl out of that burning car a few summers ago, didn't you?"

Thompson looked stunned. "Yeah, but I'm surprised you remember that."

"Good heroic police work makes the rounds, Thompson. And that was quick and decisive thinking."

"Instinct, I guess. Have a little girl myself."

Abbie stepped away, intending to do something besides stand and listen to Burke chat with another cop. "If you'll excuse me, I'll just—"

Burke stopped her, taking hold of her upper arm so naturally it felt as if he did it every day. Abbie's insides leapt, and a shiver ran down her spine. He'd been hugging her tenderly a moment ago. Why should *this* gesture unsettle her so?

Pulling her against him, Burke said to Thompson, "I want you to do the same kind of work to find our son."

"You got it."

"Good. I'd like a copy of your notes and the preliminary report."

"I'll fax them to you in Providence—"

Burke shook his head. "I'll be here with Justin's mother."

Abbie's eyes widened. He was staying here? How was that going to get Justin home?

After the two men discussed how soon Burke could have the information, Thompson joined his partner outside and drove off.

Abbie pulled away from Burke, feeling as if she'd run out of oxygen. She studied him for a couple of seconds, then took a deep breath and asked, "Why are you staying here?"

He shrugged out of his worn leather jacket and tossed it on the couch. She could see the muscles ripple along his forearms. On his wrist hung the familiar identification bracelet he'd worn for as long as Abbie had known him.

Then he placed his hand on the small of her back and directed her toward Justin's room. "That should be obvious."

"Well, it's not. You're a cop. You should be out trying to find our son, not hanging around here."

His exasperation evident, he asked, "And what if he calls and you can't find me? Or what if he's in trouble and I can't get in touch with you?"

"Oh."

"We should be able to stand each other's company, at least until he's home safe."

She bristled. "I wasn't implying that that was an issue," she said. She wasn't being entirely truthful, she knew, for when Burke was around, it was difficult to keep her feelings about him under control.

"Good. This isn't the time for ex-wife and ex-husband problems. Justin is the issue."

"Absolutely."

For several moments she stared up at him, too aware of the weary lines around his mouth, too aware of his strong body—and too conscious of a sudden and equally foolish need to have him hold her in his arms again.

But she didn't move. She had all kinds of explanations and excuses for her feelings for him, but all of them were moot. Their relationship finished the day they signed their divorce papers, she reminded herself sternly. The only reason they had any contact at all was their son.

Yet this crisis about Justin had caused a change. For one, Burke was here and he wasn't leaving. They had talked more in the past twenty minutes than they had in the past twenty months. Crisis did bring families together, and perhaps that was all this was. When the nightmare was over and Justin was home again... Yes, it had to turn out that way. Justin would soon be home and safe; she had to believe that or lose her mind.

IN JUSTIN'S BEDROOM the walls were covered with posters of rock stars and pennants from both the Boston Red Sox and the Celtics. A collage of photos of Burke alone and Burke with Justin had been pinned on a cork board over his desk. Magazines and comic books spilled from a bookcase, and the bed had been made in its usual haphazard manner.

Abbie squeezed her eyes closed, swallowing once.

Burke's gaze swung around the room, then came back to Abbie. "What's the matter? Did you remember something?"

"It's nothing. Just an impression."

"Abbie, you live with the boy so your intuitive sense about him and his actions should be pretty sharp. Tell me what you're thinking. It could be helpful."

She folded her arms to hide the shudder she felt. "Well, he made his bed the way he always does. When I found the note, it didn't occur to me, but do you think he'd been planning to run away all along and didn't want to do anything to make me suspicious?"

''In other words, if you'd simply glanced into his room this afternoon, nothing would've looked different?''

She nodded.

''Then why did he leave a note? That seems like a dumb move if he wanted to gain time or distance. I'm no shrink, but my guess is that Justin wanted you to know that this wasn't spur-of-the-moment, that he'd given it a lot of thought. His teachers not suspecting anything, you finding nothing unusual about him this morning, the note left where you'd find it...''

Abbie shivered. ''I don't know if I should be less worried or more worried.''

She wanted Burke to reassure her that what Justin had done wasn't out of the ordinary. But he made no move to touch her, and again she damned her instinctive need for him. After all, life without Burke was what she wanted, wasn't it? She was happy. She was successful in her own fashion-consulting business. She'd raised a model son.

But a model son doesn't run away from home, an unpleasant inner voice reminded her.

''Abbie,'' Burke said softly, ''you're blaming yourself. Don't.''

''But I feel responsible,'' she said, her voice bleak. ''Mothers are supposed to know what their kids are doing.''

''Justin is no longer a little kid. He may be only sixteen, but he's old enough to take responsibility for his actions. So let's leave the guilt and blame for another time, okay?''

He walked to the window and swept aside the plaid curtains. Unlocking the sash, he pushed the window up and leaned out. He looked at the yard area below for a long time, then finally closed the window and crossed to the bed. He reached down and lifted up the mattress.

"What are you doing?" Abbie asked.

"Looking to see if Justin hid the same things under his mattress that I did at his age." He pulled out three glossy girlie magazines. "Bingo."

Abbie closed her eyes. Was she so out-of-sync with her son that he could have this garbage and she'd never suspected? Yet Burke had known instantly where to look.

He thumbed through them as if they were harmless comic books. "Did you and Justin argue about anything? Girls, school, sex, anything?"

"We certainly would've discussed his reading habits if I'd known about these."

"Which is why they're under the mattress," Burke said with typical male logic. "All boys read girlie magazines. Part of growing up."

Male logic or not, Abbie didn't like his nonchalant attitude. She wasn't shocked, but she was definitely dismayed.

"Part of growing up? Really. Like having sex and drinking beer?"

"That, too."

"Well, Justin doesn't."

"Doesn't what?"

"Have sex and drink beer."

"Don't be naive, Abbie."

"You're telling me he does?"

"I'm saying he's probably done both. He's sixteen. Let's try to be realistic." He tossed the magazines onto the bed. "I'll ask you again. Did you two argue about anything?"

But Abbie wasn't listening. "I don't believe you can calmly stand here and accept that Justin is reading that junk, having sex and drinking beer."

"I didn't say I accepted it as a father, but I do accept it as a probable fact. Now, let me try once more—did you argue about anything?"

"Ever the cop, aren't you, Burke?"

"Am I supposed to feel pangs of guilt for doing my job?"

"And Justin is that, isn't he? Just your job."

"You know better than that," he said darkly.

She did know better, and she instantly felt contrite. "I'm sorry. I know you love Justin."

"More than anything."

The three words were obviously heartfelt. Abbie took a breath and said, "You asked if we'd argued. No, not this morning."

He'd walked over to examine the papers strewn across Justin's desk. "How about yesterday? Last week? Last month?"

Abbie pressed her lips together, and Burke turned and looked at her.

Then in a voice that made her nerves tingle, he said, "Sweetheart, c'mon, I've already told you—no one's blaming you for anything."

Sweetheart. It had been ages since he'd called her that, and the sensation that rushed down her spine made her shiver.

"It's common for parents to develop blind spots where their kids are concerned," Burke went on. "I'm just trying to get you to open your eyes."

Taking a breath, she said, "There was one thing."

"Tell me."

"It was a couple of months ago. I caught him climbing in that window late one afternoon."

"And?"

"I asked him what he was doing and where he'd been. He got all huffy and refused to tell me."

"So he'd been someplace he shouldn't have been and didn't want to admit it to you when you caught him."

"But he hadn't been drinking, Burke. And I'm sure he doesn't do drugs."

He nodded. "I would tend to agree with you on the drugs. Justin and I talked about that trap when I took him on the tour of the morgue that time. The grimness kinda strips away the glamour and sexiness of drugs. Justin was pretty shaken when we left, which was the purpose of the visit."

"Yeah, sort of the way he was when he was arrested on Halloween," she said. "He told me about the morgue. His exact words were, 'Guess what. Dad took me to see some drug stiffs.' He wanted to show how cool he was about the whole thing, but I knew it had made an impression."

"Which was my intention. He even asked me to arrange to take a couple of his friends who'd been toying with drugs—mostly marijuana, but that could change to harder stuff." He paused for a few seconds, then added, "That was the afternoon last spring when we got back late and—"

"Don't say it. I chewed you out."

"It's okay, Abbie. I should've called you. I guess it just bothers me that I have to watch a clock when I'm with my own son."

She sighed. Burke had a point. She could see how a closely watched clock would seem unfair to him. After all, despite their personal differences, she knew he wasn't going to snatch Justin and disappear. If her intent truly was to be the best parent for Justin, then she wouldn't be stingy or difficult about how much time Burke could spend with him.

And in the area of drugs, Burke was definitely the expert. She was grateful he cared enough to educate not only Justin, but his friends, as well.

She was about to tell him that in the future he could have all the time he wanted with their son when he raised an eyebrow.

She lifted her chin, her defenses rising. "Stop looking as if you can read my thoughts. I was just going to say—"

"That you'll give me unlimited visits from now on?"

"You make it sound as if I'm feeling guilty."

"No, you're bargaining."

"I don't know what you mean."

"Very common in a crisis. Some people try to bargain with God. Some with whoever has control. The doctor, the cop and, in this case, your ex-husband."

"That's ridiculous, Burke. Besides, bargaining with you wouldn't get me anything."

The corners of his mouth tipped up in a grin that just as quickly disappeared. "Bargaining with me would get us both trouble—trouble we sure don't want."

He stepped away from her as if needing to physically put more distance between them.

"Let's get back to his sneaking in," Burke went on. "I noticed sneaker prints outside the window. The ground is soft this time of year, so it's pretty evident he's been using the window as an exit. That day you caught him, did he give you any idea where he'd been or why he wasn't using the back door?"

"He said something about practicing the distance from the ground to the window as a measure of how fast he could climb the ropes in gym."

Burke chuckled. "You didn't buy that, I hope."

"Of course not, but since I didn't notice any odd behavior changes or catch him again, I didn't give it a lot of thought."

"What about a girlfriend?" Burke asked. "Is he still seeing the Peterson girl? Patti, isn't it?"

"Patti, right. No, they broke off about two months ago. There was another girl, but he never talked much about her."

"He tell you her name?"

Abbie shook her head.

"Why didn't you ask?"

"I don't know. It wasn't as if he was on the phone with her all the time or bringing her here. Mostly all he's talked about for weeks is baseball and working on his batting average."

Burke crossed to the desk again and rifled through the papers. He picked up a small flattened box. "I would say this proves his springtime interests go beyond his batting average."

It was an empty condom box. The color drained from Abbie's face. Maybe Burke was right. Perhaps she *had* created deliberate blind spots when it came to Justin. Burke appeared unaffected.

Abbie wasn't. "How can you be so calm and indifferent, Burke? He's hiding dirty magazines, you're assuring me he's probably drinking beer, and now this."

Burke tossed the box onto the desk. "You think because I'm not hysterical that I approve? I don't, but right now finding him safe and alive is a hell of a lot more important than his reading material, a few beers and who he has sex with. At least he's practicing safe sex, and the chances of getting some girl pregnant are reduced."

"A baby? Justin? My God, he's a child himself." But it was possible. All she had to do was watch the evening news to know about the increasing number of teenage pregnancies. Still, seeing her own son in that situation was inconceivable to her.

Abbie swallowed hard. Much of her reaction was maternal, knee-jerk and more than a little denial of what she didn't want to hear.

My God, Burke had always accused her of being too idealistic, wearing rose-colored glasses when confronted by issues she didn't want to face. Justin's growing up, for example. Foolishly, she realized now, she'd viewed him as a boy with only schoolwork and baseball on his mind. As a result, she'd probably missed important signals that had led to his running away.

Whatever his reason, whatever her excuse, her son had felt he couldn't come to her.

The telephone rang just then and Burke left the room to answer it. Abbie took one more look around, then decided there was plenty of time to blame herself later. And she would, regardless of Burke's admonitions.

She went into the kitchen, where Burke was hunched over the counter making some notes, the phone secured between his shoulder and chin. He didn't glance up when she entered.

In a swift sense of déjà vu she was plunged back to the days of their marriage when Burke would huddle with the phone gripped in his hand while she nervously waited to hear that he would have to leave on some dangerous mission.

She shook away the feeling. No more. They were no longer married; she no longer had to worry and fret over him.

Finding Justin and getting him home was all that mattered.

And that only involved Burke as a father.

CHAPTER TWO

"OKAY, LET'S HAVE the names in the area," Burke said into the receiver. "The Missing Children's Association. Runaways. The Shelter. Yeah, got 'em. Thanks. With any luck one'll be able to help. Anything else?" His caller filled him in on another missing teenager. "Could be too much of a coincidence," he said, "but let me have the name." He scribbled on a new page, then tossed the pencil back into Abbie's junk drawer. "Yeah, I'll check it out. Thanks for getting on this. I'll be in touch."

He hooked the receiver onto its cradle and studied what he'd written. Candy Kaufman, 420 Roosevelt Circle. Scowling, he hoped the suspicions gathering in his head were just the result of his cop mentality or the parental reaction of putting the worst spin on information.

There were a number of reasons two kids might run away: hotheadedness over some problem at home, causing the kids to take off in a rebellious huff; one kid's immature belief that running away is easier than facing a difficult decision. If Justin was with this girl, it could be her who was in trouble, the one with a problem at home she couldn't deal with. Burke shuddered. Then came the scariest reason: just for the hell of it.

Burke recognized rebellion because of his own experience as a teen, but in his case he'd run away to get attention from his old man, a bad cop who'd cared more about the next crooked deal than he ever had about his son. Burke never forgot the feeling he'd had in those days that he was no more important than yesterday's newspaper. When his own son was born, he vowed the child would never experience the isolation of living with a disinterested father.

His divorce from Abbie hadn't changed his attitude. Justin had remained important and was never used as a pawn in the breakup. Abbie had been a caring mother and she'd set a good example; her astonishment that Justin would run away was no act. Burke, on the other hand, couldn't shake his own eerie sense of "like father, like son" when he'd been notified.

Burke lived by a self-imposed standard of right and wrong, success and failure. He'd allowed little room for gray areas. Perhaps Justin had been caught up in some nebulous place where the right decision wasn't as clearcut and running away seemed like the only answer.

He glanced over at Abbie, who stood at the sink fitfully rinsing a few dishes. She wore jogging clothes, and Burke remembered that she usually went running in the late afternoon.

She had a slender build, her breasts small and her hips trim but with a little more padding than he knew she liked; hence the running regimen. Her dark blond hair was a tangle of curls, a style that made her look both sexy and endearing, and was perfectly appropriate for Abbie.

In some ways she was incredibly idealistic, a trait he'd sometimes found enviable. How nice to see life as it should be rather than as it really was. Shortly after they were married, he'd come home with a stitched-up knife slash on his arm. A ten-year-old boy had caught him by surprise with a switchblade. Abbie had been horrified that a child that age would even *carry* a knife, let alone attack a police officer with it. Burke had wondered if he was losing his edge; hell, he shouldn't have wasted five seconds trusting the kid. It had shown him clearly that if Abbie's idealism rubbed off on him, he'd wind up dead.

There'd been other similar incidents when her idealism collided with his cynicism, and he'd begun to regret his own selfishness in marrying her. Yes, he'd wanted her with a hunger that wouldn't quit. He'd even married her in the belief that he could easily keep separate his life with Abbie and his life as a cop. Not just any cop, but the *best* cop, driven by his determination to prove he wasn't like his old man. His goal compartmentalized his life—his family in one compartment, his job in another.

When their marriage began to crumble and he faced a choice between Abbie and being a cop, Burke had made the only choice he could—his career. Yet despite their divorce, Abbie's presence in his life remained as a compartment of hope. She was like a burst of sunlight in his own often dark, cynical view of the world. But he acknowledged that her idealism, her willingness to always assume the best about people, also made him angry.

Jogging at dusk when God knows *who* was milling around on the streets. Not being diligent about locking her car doors when she was driving. Assuming honesty in those she met. Even now with Justin running away, he'd witnessed her denial both in trying to explain to the police and in those minutes when they searched Justin's room.

Now as he watched her fill the coffeepot and plug it in, he was determined to ignore the familiar and dangerous gut kick of desire for her.

"Who was on the phone?" she asked, turning just enough so that he could see her profile. Short straight nose, full cheeks, high forehead. Right now those cheeks were slightly flushed, and her lips were a little red from where she'd bitten them. Quarter-size silver hoops hung from her ears—reminding him of the first time he'd made love to her.

He'd never forget it. It was at his apartment. She'd sat astride him on his bed, her hair wilder than usual, and removed her earrings, first one, then the other, the slow simple movements more erotic than anything he'd ever seen . . .

Burke shook his head to clear it. *Don't go down this path, Wheeler, or you'll have more hell to deal with than even you can handle.*

"One of the detectives," he said, still trying to clear his mind of memories.

She turned fully now, tipping her head to the side. "So what did he say?"

He stared at her, fighting his inner reaction. Her eyes were wide and questioning, a swirl of blues. Dark and churning when she was angry, cornflower blue when she was aroused. Always changing, so that Burke felt as if he was forever discovering new things about her. The sweep of lashes gave her a sensual mystery that Burke could have spent endless hours unfolding. He glanced away, determined that she wouldn't pull him into some dizzying spell.

She'd done that once two years after their divorce, and he'd made up his mind that it wouldn't happen again. The world was filled with women with gorgeous eyes, yet none of them could tear him up, make him angry, frustrate him and—

"Burke? When you get all silent and closed down, I know something's going on." Her eyes searched his fearfully. "Oh God, it's not Justin, is it?"

Damn her for being able to pick up on his mood so easily. "No, I just got names of some missing-kids organizations. They've been alerted about Justin."

"And?"

"They'll let us know when they learn something."

"That's it?"

"So far."

He walked into the living room and picked up his leather jacket. Returning to the kitchen, he shrugged into it and said, "I've got to go out for a while. Stay close to the phone." He glanced at his watch. "I'll be back within the hour."

He picked up the notepad and tore off the sheet with Candy Kaufman's name, folded it and shoved it into his pocket. Then, on second thought, he tore off the next two sheets. Knowing Abbie, she'd manage to decipher the pencil's imprint.

"Lock the door behind me."

She grabbed his arm as he started out the door. "Wait a minute. Where are you going?"

"I'll fill you in when I get back."

"No. If this is about Justin, I want to know."

"It may be nothing."

"Don't try to do this by yourself. He's my son, too."

"I'm well aware of that." He tried to loosen her fingers.

"But you want me to just stay here and cool my heels until you come back before you let me know what's going on?"

He heard the edge of anger in her voice, but he didn't want to argue. Not now.

Calmly he said, "I hope to have some answers when I get back."

"You're hiding something, aren't you?"

"Oh, for God's sake!" he said in exasperation.

"I'm not a hysterical mother, Burke. Don't insult me by treating me like one."

He raised an eyebrow. "Aren't you the same mother who gasped over a few girlie magazines and a crushed condom box?"

"I did not gasp! I was simply taken by surprise."

"Exactly. I don't want you to be surprised this time."

"Burke, you're scaring me. Have they found Justin? My God, is he hurt or . . ."

Her voice broke, and Burke, damning his automatic reaction, took her into his arms. She clung to him, and for a crazy instant he thought, This is what I miss. Holding her, feeling her body pressed to mine . . .

Just familiarity, he told himself. No man could live and sleep and have sex with a woman for more than ten years and not have a few nostalgic moments when he touched her.

His hands spanned her middle back, but he didn't move them or pat her or take any liberties that could be misconstrued.

"Abbie, I'm going to check out another possible runaway. I'll be back within the hour," he said softly, his breath stirring her hair. The sudden need to touch his mouth to her ear swamped him. He moved enough so as to not act on the temptation. "Why don't you fix us something to eat? This could be a long night."

He couldn't tell from her body language what she was thinking, but he brushed his lips across her forehead, telling himself it was a natural gesture, given the circumstances, and then set her away from him.

"Lock the door," he reminded her once again, and then quickly left.

He drove his unmarked police car through the downtown section of Walcott and then took the right turn that led into the wealthier part of the city. No modest bungalows or apartment complexes here. It was all manicured lawns and landscaped gardens showcasing the sprawling residences of retired CEOs and successful entrepreneurs.

Pretentious, he decided, looking at the Kaufman house. Lots of windows and angles with brass lights to show it off. Another unmarked police car was in the drive, and Burke recognized Will Gagne, one of the detectives who'd been at Abbie's house. Burke had worked with him until being assigned to an undercover unit working out of Providence, which was fifteen miles east of Walcott. Gagne was talking to a man who looked as if he'd been interrupted from a tennis match.

And sure enough, when Burke climbed out of his car, he noticed a court at one side of the house.

He glanced down at his jeans, glad that Will had gotten there ahead of him. Burke wore street-dealing clothes, which no doubt made him look like the dregs he encountered on a regular basis.

Gagne glanced up as he approached. Always tidy and efficient when working, the detective looked worn and tired, probably, Burke thought, more than ready to seriously consider turning in his gun and retiring where it was warm and boring. He was in his late forties and looked ten years older.

Burke joined him, and Gagne introduced the man as Harvey Kaufman. Gagne turned to Kaufman and told him that Burke was also a cop and that his son had run away, too. "We think there might be a connection to your daughter's disappearance," he added.

Then to Burke, he said, "Mr. Kaufman has a keen interest in police work and detecting."

Burke caught the sarcasm, but nodded sagely.

Kaufman looked at Burke curiously. "Really? You don't look like a cop." Then his eyes widened. "Oh, I bet I know. You're one of those undercover cops, aren't you?"

"Some of the time," Burke said vaguely, keeping his expression bland. He couldn't help but notice the low-road part in Kaufman's hair and the long strands that stubbornly refused to cooperate in his desperate attempt to cover his baldness.

"Let's get back to your daughter," Gagne said.

"Candy didn't run away with Mr. Wheeler's son," Kaufman said firmly. "She's been kidnapped. I know it."

"From what you've told us, that seems unlikely," Gagne said. "There've been no phone calls, no ransom request."

"Well, there will be," the man said, nervously running his hand over his hair to get it back into place. "My daughter has no reason to run away. Look around you. She has everything she wants here."

"I'm sure she's very fortunate," Gagne said, "but according to her teachers and her friends, she wasn't in school today. You said she was driven there by your driver, so she's been gone more than eight hours. A kidnapper generally works quickly—before the victim's family gets smart and calls the police. Now, from the report I received, you didn't call the police until just an hour ago. Why?"

Kaufman looked unsettled by the logic and the direct question. "I wanted to call, but my wife kept insisting Candy would be home." He rocked back on his heels, peering at Burke. "You guys want my take on this whole thing?"

Burke and Gagne glanced at each other. Gagne nodded.

"Well," said Kaufman, "here's how I see it. I read a lot of detective stories and watch those cop shows on TV. This situation looked like a kidnapping to me right from the get-go. Pretty rich girl kidnapped from school and being held for ransom. There was a similar situation over in Newport a few years ago."

"With all due respect, Mr. Kaufman, in that case the family got a phone call about ransom within an hour."

"Well, yes, I know, but I'm very sure Candy wouldn't run away..." His words trailed off. "Ginger—that's my wife—is very upset, so I decided the best thing was to call you guys."

Burke rolled his eyes. Just what they needed—a guy playing detective. "Mr. Kaufman, my son attends the same school as Candy. Did you ever hear your daughter mention a Justin Wheeler?"

The look he cast Burke was disdainful. "Candy is very particular about whom she dates. No riffraff."

Burke muttered to Gagne, "Obviously his awe of cops doesn't extend to their kids." Then more loudly he said, "Kids don't always do the things their parents expect them to do. I have no idea if Justin and Candy are together or even if they know each other.

But it's too coincidental that they would both disappear on the same day. Walcott isn't Boston or even Providence. Justin left a note. Have you looked around to see if Candy did?''

Kaufman blinked and for a few seconds looked startled. "A note?"

"A note saying she was running away."

"I'm telling you, it's a kidnapping. We're wasting time standing here discussing her running away."

Burke had had enough game playing. "Good God, man, this isn't some TV show or detective novel."

He ignored Gagne's warning look and put himself nose to nose with Kaufman. "My son is missing and your daughter might be with him. I don't want to hear your half-baked theories. If these two kids are on the streets..."

Burke didn't even want to think about those dangers. He'd been about to add that Kaufman had better hope his daughter was with Justin and not some pervert, but he kept that last comment to himself. Cops were supposed to be reassuring, and he'd already said enough.

Kaufman paled, his former hauteur dissolving into a tremble. Gagne, too, stared at Burke as if, despite the years they'd known each other, this was a side he'd never seen.

Burke jammed his hands into his pockets and reminded himself that Kaufman was probably terrified, but dammit, so was he. Maybe because he knew the street dangers too intimately, and the idea that Justin was out there somewhere—

From behind them, a car door slammed.

He turned around to see Abbie walking toward them. He narrowed his eyes and swore.

How in hell did she know where he'd gone? He reached into his jacket pocket and curled his fingers around the notepad pages to reassure himself he still had them. He did.

She'd changed her clothes and now wore a blue skirt and a fine-knit long cardigan over a cream-colored silk blouse. Her hair was brushed up and clipped so that the curls seemed to fall in a sort of artful profusion. The skirt was short, and her legs, in beige stockings and low-heeled pumps, were too sensational to ignore.

"I'll be right back," he muttered to Gagne.

Burke halted Abbie's steps a few yards from the two men. "I thought I told you to stay at the house in case the phone rang."

"No, I believe I was supposed to stay home and fix food and wait for you like a worried but dutiful wife." She didn't try to hide her annoyance.

"You know I didn't mean it to sound that way."

"Good. Because I'm no longer your wife."

She glared at him, and her blue eyes and stubborn expression made him think about kissing her instead of shaking her. But despite her brusqueness, Burke knew she was deeply worried about Justin.

"Just in case you forgot," she added.

"Forgot we're divorced? Hell, no, I thank my lucky stars every day," he said bluntly, a little surprised at his words but not about to refute them. She wanted to play hardball, then fine. Besides, distance and anger were a lot easier to deal with than kissing and understanding.

"So do I, Burke," she countered. "So do I."

He shoved a hand through his hair, then cursed. She definitely gave no quarter. "How did you know to come here?"

"Since you didn't write hard enough to go through three layers of paper, I called Larry Thompson and asked him. He was very cooperative. Even the *ex*-wife of Walcott's Cop of the Year for four consecutive years has a lot of clout. I intend to remember that if I get stopped for speeding," she said breezily.

"God."

"And since you seem to think it's all right to leave me out of what progress is being made to find Justin, then I may just call Larry again."

"Abbie, this isn't a contest."

"Don't you dare lecture me, Burke," she said, her voice trembling. "If you had your way, I wouldn't know anything. If you think for one minute I'm going to bite my nails by the phone and whimper with relief when you decide to throw a morsel of information my way, you can just think again."

He lowered his head and shook it slowly. He didn't blame her. He'd just proved his own emotional involvement by that crack to Kaufman. In fact he *was* impressed with her stamina and her gutsiness. No wilting flower here; she saw this situation for what it was and didn't intend to be shoved aside as if she couldn't handle herself.

And face it, Wheeler. You're just not accustomed to your kid and your ex-wife being involved with your work.

"All right," he said at last.

For just a second she seemed taken aback by his agreement, but then she nodded. "Thank you."

She started around him, but he stopped her. "Where are you going?"

"To talk to Ginger Kaufman."

"That's Gagne's and my job."

"We're both mothers. I may learn something you wouldn't."

"Is that why you're all dressed up?"

"These are my working clothes. You know that. Have I asked you why you're in your working clothes?"

"Abbie, just because you're a fashion consultant to a lot of wealthy women..." He shook his head as he realized exactly what that meant, and once more he was impressed. This was certainly the day of amazing twists and turns. "Let me guess. Candy's old lady is one of your clients."

"For more than a year," she said as if she'd found a major piece of a puzzle. "See how much grief you would've saved yourself if you'd just told me you were coming to the Kaufmans'? Now, if you'll excuse me..." She walked ahead of him and he thought about stopping her, but didn't.

He grinned and then immediately suppressed it. Dammit, he didn't want to be delighted, fascinated or enchanted by his ex-wife. He didn't want to note her maturity or her confidence; he didn't want to admit that when he'd expected to be the comforter, he was finding comfort in *her* strength. It was all an aberration, he told himself. Chalk it up as a plus and a way to get information. Nothing else.

Burke stayed a few feet behind her as she stopped to speak to Candy's father. Her openness and graciousness were not an act. "Mr. Kaufman, I'm Abigail Marshall, Justin's mother," she said, extending her hand in greeting.

Kaufman gaped, his gaze jumping from her to Burke and back again as if putting Abbie with Burke was like mixing dark and light. Then he took her hand. "You're the one who dresses my wife."

"Advises her on color and style selection, yes," she said pleasantly.

Kaufman gestured at Burke. "But he said he was Justin's father."

"I use my maiden name for business purposes."

Once again Kaufman looked from the sleek and expensively dressed Abbie to the grungy-jeaned and leather-jacketed Burke. He shook his head in disbelief.

"You just seem so, well, different." He cleared his throat as if unable to think of anything more to say. He took Abbie's arm. "Please come in and talk to Ginger. She's overwrought about Candy."

"Abbie?"

She turned to glance at Burke and then said to Kaufman, "Please. Go ahead. I'll be right in."

Gagne followed Kaufman toward the house. Burke didn't move, but waited until she walked back to where he stood. When she was close enough, he reached up and pulled the clip that held her hair in place. Her dark blond curls tumbled down.

"What are you doing?" She tried to grab his arm to stop him, but it was too late.

"Making you look like my wife instead of a fashion layout."

"Is there supposed to be some point in that comment?"

"Yeah. I can't help wondering just what in hell is going on. Why didn't you tell the man we were divorced?"

"Because it's none of his business."

Burke shook his head and took hold of her arm. "No sale. Why?"

"Burke, let me go."

"When you answer my question."

She lowered her gaze and fiddled with the buttons on her cardigan. "For Justin's sake. I saw the way Harvey Kaufman looked at us. If I said we were divorced, he could've assumed we have a dysfunctional family and Justin had problems. Since Candy could be with him, I didn't want Kaufman to think Justin is a messed-up teenager."

Burke just stared at her, seeing in an entirely new way just how determined she was to be a part of finding Justin. He cupped her chin and tipped up her head. The curls he'd loosened caught the dying sunlight. Before he had a chance to think too hard or come up with fifty reasons why playing with dynamite was insane, he lowered his head and kissed her.

Burke had never been good at denying himself the pleasure of deep kisses with Abbie, and this time was no exception. She stiffened initially and then he felt her relax. He moved his mouth and tongue over hers with an instant kind of intimacy he recognized as dangerous.

Show some restraint, he warned himself, trying to ignore the soft pliancy of her lips, which needed little coaxing, the heady taste of her and the scent of something expensive and coolly alluring. He slipped his hand around the back of her neck, his fingers wandering up and into the tumble of curls and holding her head firmly. At last he pulled his mouth away from hers but didn't release her.

In the softest of voices, she asked, "Is this for the benefit of Harvey Kaufman?"

His eyes darkened, and for a moment he wanted to say no, this is just for us. But he didn't. Going down this road with his ex-wife was painfully delusionary. Once Justin was home, they would again go their separate ways; neither needed awkward memories of intimacy.

Finally he dropped his arms and shrugged. "Yeah, since he's standing at the door over there watching us."

She tried to put the clip back into her hair, struggling with the curls that refused to cooperate.

"I like it better loose," he muttered, knowing he was playing in an inferno.

She went still, and her next words eased out as if she was testing them. "I know you do."

"Loose on my pillow."

"Yes."

Their eyes met for too long a moment, Burke's a dark and erotically decadent green, Abbie's a rich and ravishing blue.

The time-halting, soul-sweeping, provocatively deep stare evoked possibilities both knew they should never consider.

Finally they looked away. Words weren't necessary, nor was any explanation for the tension that snapped like a live wire between them. Both knew that, despite myriad reasons why they shouldn't, making love would be immensely satisfying.

Side by side and without speaking, they headed toward the house and joined Gagne at the door. Kaufman had gone inside.

"You two all right?" he asked.

"I'll be a helluva lot better when this is finished and Justin is home," Burke said, worry about his son once more crushing down on him. He jammed his hands into his pockets so he wouldn't touch Abbie again.

"And Candy," Abbie said.

"Yeah," Gagne said. "Let's see what Mrs. Kaufman can add to this."

THEY WERE GREETED by a maid who led the way into the living room. Draperies in a butter yellow polished fabric hung from the long windows. The furniture was French provincial, the carpets Oriental, and vases of fresh flowers were generously placed throughout. Abbie stepped ahead of Burke and Will Gagne and crossed quickly to Ginger Kaufman, who stood in the middle of the room wringing her hands.

The woman who usually prided herself on her elegant appearance looked pale and unkempt in a gray gown splashed with a giant repeat print of cranberry-colored cabbage roses. Abbie also noticed her frayed fingernails. With Candy missing, the manicure had disappeared with the elegance.

Ginger blinked, then frowned. "Abbie? Oh, my God, did I have an appointment with you today?"

Abbie gently took Ginger's arm in a gesture of support. "No. I'm here because of Candy and—"

"You've seen her? Oh, Abbie, I knew there was an explanation. Harvey insisted she was kidnapped, but that's too horrible to contemplate. Seeing you clears it all up, and if Harvey hadn't had me so rattled... Now I know what happened. Candy went to your shop for that silk blouse I ordered, didn't she? I'd forgotten I'd asked her to pick it up for me after school."

She turned an eager gaze toward the front doorway as if Candy was about to make an entrance. "I'm right, aren't I? This has all been a misunderstanding. Candy is here and . . ."

Abbie and Burke exchanged glances while Gagne just shook his head at Ginger's desperate attempt to justify her daughter's disappearance. "Ginger, I wish she *was* with me," Abbie said softly. "I want all of this to be just a bad dream, but it's not. I'm here because our son, Justin, has run away, too. It's very possible Candy is with him."

The woman backed up a few steps, as if distance would make Abbie's words go away. "No, I don't want to hear any of this. Candy will be home. She's just late."

Burke said, "Mrs. Kaufman, none of us wants to hear it, but we can't discount any possibilities."

Ginger looked right through Burke as if he didn't exist. She smoothed her hands down the folds of her gray gown. Her face softened and her eyes misted. "Candy bought this dress for me for Mother's Day when she was ten years old. At a yard sale. The gown was in its original box and still had the sales tags on it. She knew I loved roses. She was so proud of herself I didn't have the heart to say I didn't like it."

Abbie glanced at Burke again, her eyes begging him not to make any comments. She knew he was impatient for information, and some anecdote about an ugly dress that had nothing to do with why the kids had run away was a waste of time. Abbie guessed that Ginger had put on the gown because it related to a happy innocent time with her daughter. In a bizarre way, Ginger was wrapping herself in the past because it was easier than dealing with the present.

Ginger gave Abbie a sort of one-mother-to-another look of pleading, which Abbie immediately understood.

In what she hoped was a comforting voice, Abbie said, "Justin and Candy are all right. I know they are. In fact, one of the police officers I talked to earlier assured me that most runaways return home within a few hours."

Abbie knew she was raising expectations, giving out a false hope, but in a very real way, like Ginger, Abbie needed to believe that their kids would walk in the door before the day was over.

Will Gagne said, "This is all very interesting, but the issue is two missing kids. Where they went and why are questions that need to be answered."

Abbie and Ginger sat down on a white love seat. Burke stood with his hands in his pockets staring out the window. Gagne made some notes. Harvey Kaufman walked to an expensively stocked bar.

"Anybody want a drink?" No one did, and Kaufman said, "Well, I need one." He poured a generous splash of amber liquid from a crystal decanter into a tumbler. Despite his silence during the exchange with his wife, it was obvious he was having second thoughts about his kidnapping theory.

Gagne addressed Ginger. "We're not absolutely sure the kids are together, but do you recall if Candy ever mentioned Justin as a boyfriend or just a friend?"

"Candy has a lot of friends," Ginger said, tracing one of the roses on her gown.

"I'm sure she does."

"She's an honor student and plays piano. What with practice, recitals and all her homework, she has no time for boys."

"Yeah, right," Burke muttered under his breath.

Ginger was truly refusing to face reality, Abbie thought. Gently she asked, "How about just as a friend? You know, maybe Candy and Justin hung out a bit together at school..."

When Ginger remained silent, Kaufman said, "Now see here. Candy never mentioned—what's his name?"

"Justin."

"I've had enough," Burke said. He crossed to Abbie, reached out a hand to assist her to her feet, then urged her toward the front door. "Come on. We're wasting time here."

Abbie balked, desperation swamping her. To both Kaufmans she said, "Justin is tall with dark hair like his father. He has a scar on his lower lip from when he fell against the television when he was learning to walk. He also wears an ID bracelet like Burke does." Like father, like son, she thought. Symbolic ties. Burke's had been a gift from a now deceased colleague Burke had greatly respected, Justin's a gift from Burke. The boy, who wanted to be like his dad, wore it proudly.

Ginger's eyes widened as if she'd just put two and two together. "He's your husband? But he looks, well, dangerous."

Abbie's patience snapped and she jumped to Burke's defense. "Of course he looks dangerous. He's supposed to. He's one of the best undercover police officers in the state. He's also a terrific father and he's as worried as I am about our son and your daughter. If anyone can find Justin and Candy, he can."

Ginger blinked, her mouth a silent O of astonishment. Kaufman didn't look as convinced.

To Gagne, Burke muttered, "We're gonna split."

The older officer nodded.

Burke steered Abbie into the foyer and back outside. He'd put the Kaufmans into the category he reserved for most wealthy people: self-centered and not living in the real world.

THEY WERE BACK in Abbie's house, and Burke was in a rage. "What is it about rich people? How can they be so stupid? So incredibly unaware? That Ginger... My God, piano lessons, recitals and homework leaving the girl no time for boys? That sounds like something out of the last century!"

"Ginger's been very sheltered."

"Maybe, but what's Kaufman's excuse? Kidnapping, for God's sake. Why the hell doesn't he open his eyes?"

Abbie lifted her mug of coffee and took a sip. They'd left the Kaufmans', leaving Will Gagne to get the other necessary information. Since they'd come in separate cars, Burke had followed her to her house. He repeated his intention to stay there until they had some clue about Justin's whereabouts.

Abbie didn't argue. No question her attitude had changed in the past couple of hours. No doubt it had taken a little while for the full impact of Justin's running away to hit her, and now it finally had. Then there was the realization that working with Burke would be more productive than disagreeing with him at every turn. This wasn't a time for arguing. She'd made it clear that she intended to be involved in the search for their son when she'd gone to the Kaufmans'.

There was a more practical side, too. She didn't want to be alone while her son was missing, and besides, if she was with Burke, she stood a much better chance of being up-to-date with any information about Justin. Otherwise, knowing her ex-husband's penchant for doing things and telling her about them later, he'd have a message passed on to her *after* he'd gone off to search. And that she wasn't going to allow. She intended to go with him. Although he would balk and argue and emphasize all the dangers and how he couldn't do his job with her along, she intended to stand firm. She would not sit home and worry.

Burke pushed aside the report and notes that Larry Thompson had dropped off just after they returned from the Kaufmans'. There was nothing new here, nor had Burke even come up with any new possibilities. As Burke had predicted, Justin's friends had not supplied the police with anything useful.

Now he stood, stretched and then reached for the phone when it rang.

Abbie stood, also, her heart pounding.

"Yeah, what've you got?"

He listened, nodded.

"What?" Abbie whispered.

He shook his head, indicating she should wait. "That's it? Okay, yeah, it's better than nothing." He placed the receiver back on the cradle.

"What? Tell me, Burke."

He put his arm around her and led her to the chair. "Abbie, it's not much. In fact, it's damn flimsy."

"I don't care. Tell me."

"Someone *thinks* he saw Justin getting on a bus headed toward Boston."

"Boston! But he doesn't know anyone in Boston." She hesitated. "Does he? You take him to see the ball games."

"What about your friend Celada? She lives just outside Boston." He scowled. "Hell, I hope he hasn't gone to her. She got arrested for prostitution—"

"She was *not* a prostitute," Abbie interrupted. "She was working for an escort service. She was having financial problems and took the dates to make some extra money. She used to work for an escort service when we were roommates in college, too. And nothing ever happened. I mean, just dinner and maybe a show with these guys, that's all."

"Then she was lucky, or it was a legit service," Burke said skeptically.

"Well, she's doing fine now in fashion design. We talked a month or so ago, and she was all excited about a new relationship." Abbie paused and then added, "You, however, took Justin to see the Red Sox just last weekend."

"Abbie, the likelihood of Justin going to see Celada is a lot greater than his visiting Fenway Park on a night when a game isn't scheduled."

He rifled around in the drawer beneath the phone and finally located Abbie's address book. Quickly he turned the pages.

"Her last name still Owen?" he asked flipping to the *O*'s.

"Of course it's still Owen," she snapped, tugging the phone out of his hand. "And I'll do the calling." She punched out the long-distance number. To Burke she said crisply. "She always thought you were far too sexy."

"Yeah, I know."

Abbie blinked. "You know? She told you?"

"Yeah. In that smoky husky tone she uses when she wants something."

Disbelief filled Abbie's face. "She tried to seduce you?"

"Let's say she wanted to reward me for getting her out of a sticky situation."

"While we were still married?"

"Does it matter?"

"Yes, dammit, it matters! I'm furious at her if she did. She and I always agreed that a woman who tried to steal another woman's man was a sneaky low-down coward who had some drive for sexual power. Why didn't you ever tell me?"

Burke met her gaze, then turned away.

Abbie hung up the phone and grabbed his arm. "Burke? Why didn't you ever tell me?"

"Abbie, let's just forget it."

Her face paled. "You went to bed with her, didn't you?"

"For God's sake, no!"

"Then what?"

"Hell, I wish I'd never brought her up." And why in hell had he? Was he looking for a way to tell Abbie the truth? Some backhanded way to make up for his own terror that night he was supposed to meet with her and why he blew it off?

He couldn't deal with this, not tonight. Watching Abbie, he knew she was sick with worry about Justin, so perhaps his comment about knowing Celada found him sexy had been subconsciously motivated. It had certainly distracted her.

She turned away then, frost lacing her voice. "I'm sorry. I really shouldn't have asked. We've been divorced for a long time. What you do and who you do it with is not my concern."

He chuckled.

She swung around, her eyes blazing. "This is not funny! And if there was never anything between you two, why did you look so guilty? Why did you seem so...hesitant with your answers? We might be divorced, but I know you very well. You're too damn sure of yourself to have let something that important slip unless you had a reason."

He leaned against the counter, saying nothing.

She paced, she scowled and she pointed her finger at him, all the while listing everything that had gone wrong between them. Many complaints Burke had already heard and a few he hadn't.

"Listening to you, I wonder why our marriage lasted a week," he said.

"Don't try to change the subject."

He watched the range of emotions on her face. Her friend Celada was now a successful clothing designer, her one brush with the law hardly more than a case of poor judgment on her part. And yet for Burke, his involvement with it had carried endless ripples of significance.

Finally, knowing he had to tell Abbie something, he said, "I made a couple of phone calls the night Celada was arrested."

"You mean you fixed it so she wouldn't go to jail?"

"Yeah."

"But you never do that sort of thing. Why?"

"Because she was going to call you."

She scowled, obviously confused. "I don't understand."

Burke shoved a hand through his hair and tried to ignore the clammy dampness across his neck. "You didn't need Celada's problems. We were having our own. It was the night we were going to discuss getting a divorce."

CHAPTER THREE

WAIT. ALL THEY COULD DO was wait. Burke had gotten that advice from the missing-children centers. Justin could come home or he might call, so it was crucial that tonight they be there.

Hours had passed, but with no progress. Abbie had called Celada; not only was she not home, but her answering machine was off. Abbie had changed into jeans and a T-shirt and now sat curled in a corner of the couch, wrapped in her grandmother's down-filled quilt watching the hands on the mantel clock. Another minute passed.

It was after midnight and they'd heard nothing.

The phone rang off and on all evening, but it had only been concerned neighbors, the Kaufmans—who wanted to know why more hadn't been done—or one of Burke's contacts at the police department.

No word from or about Justin.

Abbie kept reassuring herself he was all right. She was still trying to find answers for her own deep and frustrating questions. Where would he go and what had caused him to run away?

Questions, too, about her mothering abilities, the effect of the divorce on Justin, and wondering if the marital breakup had been more traumatic for their son than either of them had realized.

She sighed, glad that Burke was again busy on the phone. He would be aghast to learn that simmering among all these thoughts were unanticipated feelings about him. Impressions and sensations she hadn't expected and didn't trust.

In the past, they had tried to cover up, ignore or pretend they weren't having problems by doing the one thing they did right—making love.

Of course, that wouldn't happen now, but the power of the kiss they shared in front of Kaufman had taken her aback.

Then there was the tension between them over the business with Celada. Abbie had been appalled at her own instinctive jealousy—fierce and raw and totally ridiculous. And Burke's admission that he hadn't shown up to discuss the divorce because he'd been busy getting Celada out of a jam so she wouldn't call Abbie had left her speechless. At the time, she'd assumed he was too tied up at work, or delayed, or had any number of other excuses. Whatever the reason, it boiled down to one thing: discussing their divorce had been way down on his list of priorities.

Burke hadn't attempted to broaden his explanation beyond the bare facts, and tonight, she'd let his excuse stand. Self-protection, she supposed, or an acknowledgment that it was five years too late.

So they'd turned away from each other, which showed Abbie, at least, that the barren gap where reason, discussion and explanations should be, remained void.

This wasn't the time to stir dead ashes. Or to be so foolish as to believe a flare of sexual attraction to hold the magic to revive a marriage long over.

She tucked the quilt more snugly around her as if to prove to herself that she needed no warmth from Burke. He'd always been adamant about not making decisions at crucial or emotional moments; perhaps that was why she was so uneasy with these yearnings. She wanted to believe her reactions weren't because of him, but because of the situation. Their son was missing. There was no question about their love for him. Therefore it was only natural they'd be drawn together until Justin was home safe.

But what if Justin didn't come home?

What if he wasn't safe?

What if he'd been hurt?

Stop it, she told herself firmly, tightening her fingers on the quilt until her knuckles turned white.

Justin was a smart teenager; she and Burke had made sure he knew the danger of trusting strangers and of hanging around crime-ridden areas.

Yet he'd willfully and deliberately run away from home.

Abbie couldn't get that from her mind, nor could she imagine her son's reason.

Burke had checked the route of the bus that Justin might have boarded, but the driver recalled little, even at the mention of Candy Kaufman. The driver said he got a lot of kids and didn't pay much attention. Burke had gotten the list of the stops and was now in the arduous process of following them up via police departments along the route.

For the past few hours conversation between them had been at a minimum, Abbie on the couch and Burke on the phone. When he wasn't, he was staring out the front window. She knew he was worried, perhaps more worried than she was, because he knew the danger of the streets. The longer the night went on, the shorter his temper became and the less talkative he got.

Abbie guessed he was piecing together what little information they had in an attempt to find something that didn't quite fit the pattern, some clue that Justin had unconsciously left behind or dropped along the way.

Her thoughts wandered back to the conversation about Celada. Now, in the midst of an unrelated crisis about Justin, she was caught in a time warp of guilt and shame over her anger at Burke because he hadn't shown up to discuss their divorce. When he had appeared the following day, instead of acting with cool maturity, she'd given a brilliant imitation of the wife from hell.

She'd glared at him, her chest tight from holding back tears. And in a brittle voice, she'd snapped, "You'll be pleased to know that while you were out busy making the streets safe I started to uncomplicate your life by getting out of it. I've contacted an attorney about a divorce."

Burke had said nothing, but his eyes had darkened and his mouth had been set in a grim line. He'd been disheveled, his hair long and shaggy and an earring in his left ear—the garb needed for some undercover work he'd been doing in Pawtucket.

Now Abbie pressed the quilt to her eyes and let the tears come. She wasn't even sure what they were for. For Justin, or her own regret, or for Burke and the terrible way she'd treated him so long ago.

Maybe all three.

The phone rang, and Abbie rubbed at her eyes as she heard Burke pick it up. She glanced up to see him swing around and motion to her.

In a gruff voice rife with emotion, he said, "Justin! Where are you?"

Abbie bolted off the couch, almost tripping in the tangle of the quilt.

She rushed over to Burke, who put his arm around her and let her listen. With his other hand he adjusted a small recorder he had hooked into the telephone line.

"Justin, sweetheart..." She gripped the phone as if it was a lifeline to her son.

"Mom..." He gulped. "I'm okay."

Burke said, "Where are you?"

Abbie added, "Sweetheart, we'll come and get you. No questions asked."

Another gulp and a pause. "Don't worry about me."

"Your mother is scared to death, Justin. Where in hell are you?"

A long pause, then, "I gotta go."

"No!" Abbie screamed, her terror so raw it made her voice raspy. "Justin!"

But he'd hung up and the dial tone droned in her ear.

Burke quickly punched out the call-trace code number the phone company had provided. It turned out that Justin had called from a pay phone in the south part of Boston, an area called Sade Court. Abbie's heart soared with hope, then just as quickly plummeted. The pay phone didn't take incoming calls. Burke phoned the nearest Boston precinct and gave them the info he had plus Justin's description. He was assured a patrol car would be sent but warned not to expect a miracle.

Abbie buried her face in her hands. Burke tried to take her in his arms, but the moment he touched her, she shoved him away.

"Why did you yell at him?" she accused.

"I didn't yell at him."

"You did! You yelled and swore at him."

He stiffened, but his voice stayed calm. "Because he's not only done something stupid, he's got you scared out of your mind."

"Maybe it's not stupid. Maybe he has a reason." She knew she was grasping for something, anything, her voice riding the edge of hysteria.

"Of course he has a reason, but he sure as hell hasn't bothered to let anyone know what it is."

"Well, now he probably thinks you're angry at him."

"Guess what. He's right."

Abbie glared at him. "Well, that's just wonderful, Burke. He's God knows where and, instead of being reassured that we're concerned, he now believes his father, who's supposed to love him, is furious at him."

"Supposed to love him? Goddammit, if I didn't love him, I wouldn't be furious. Runaways tend to forget that the ones left at home are just as frantic as the kid was when he ran off in the first place. Whatever his reason—good or dumb—running off just complicates it. It doesn't solve the problem."

Abbie shivered, all her fight and anger dissolving along with her strength, so that she had to lean against the counter for support. "I ... I can't deal with this." She took a deep, shaky breath. "Burke, I'm so afraid for him."

He drew her into his arms and this time she didn't resist. "I know, sweetheart, I know. I'm afraid for him, too."

She glanced up, and in that instant she saw the naked fear in his eyes. A fear she'd seen only once before. She frowned, but she couldn't focus; her mind was awash with concern about Justin. She slipped her arms around Burke's waist and rested her cheek against his heart.

In a softened voice, she murmured, "I'm sorry."

"Shh, it's all right. Call it stress and anxiety. Pretty normal for both of us."

He brushed his lips across her forehead before he tucked her tightly against him. He was like a bulwark of support, she thought as she buried her face in his neck.

For a time he held her, his hands rubbing up and down her back, her fingers curled into the warmth of his shirt. No words were spoken, and the only sounds were the ticking of the mantel clock and the steady pounding of their hearts.

After a few minutes he eased her away from him and glanced down at the recorder, which he'd turned off.

"All isn't lost. I got the number and we know for sure he called from Sade Court."

Abbie felt numb. "Then he *was* on that bus."

"Looks like it. Anyway, I've got the call on tape. Lot of background noise while Justin talked. We might be able to pin something down more precisely."

He played the tape back and Abbie listened with growing interest.

Burke replayed the tape several times, asking Abbie what she heard. He made a list and put names to the sounds. Burke isolated each one until her ear was as attuned as if she'd been using her eyes. She was amazed that when she concentrated, she could identify individual sounds in the cacophony of background sound.

The hollow sound of an outside pay phone.

Traffic, horns, screeching brakes, car stereos.

A shriek.

Strip music.

Merry-go-round music.

Abbie stared at Burke. "I can't believe the tape picked all that up."

"Surrounding noises are often better clues than the obvious one—in this case Justin's voice. You were listening to him. Can you tell me what you heard in his voice?"

Abbie tried to recall the emotions she'd heard. "Fear. Indecision. Concern about us."

"Terror?"

"No."

"Resolve?"

She hesitated, then nodded. "Yes."

"Yeah, I caught that, too. Which means he isn't on his way home."

Though she realized Burke was probably right, she hadn't allowed herself to think that way until now. "Oh God."

"Look, I'm going to do some checking and see what I can find."

His statement, Abbie guessed, involved more than the obvious. She also sensed he wanted her to trust him.

"I'll call you as soon as I have something," he said, stepping away from her.

She knew she should nod and say yes, but she couldn't. Already her mind was racing in all the wrong directions. She would become a basket case just sitting here.

"I can't stay here while you go and look."

He frowned, his mind obviously getting in gear for what he intended to do.

"You're not going with me," he said flatly and then turned back to the phone. He punched out a number.

"This is Wheeler. I got some background noise on Justin's call. Listen." Burke flipped a couple of switches and punched another button. The noise played into the phone. He rewound and replayed the short conversation at least a dozen times. Finally he said, "Yeah, that's what I thought. Thanks. Tell Gagne I'm gonna check this out."

He hung up the phone, unplugged the recorder and started to leave the kitchen.

"Burke?"

"You heard what I said, Abbie. You're not going with me."

"I most certainly am."

Patiently but firmly he said, "No. Sade Court's a rough part of town. I don't want to have to worry about you."

"He's my son, too, Burke!"

He sighed. "Why don't you let me do my job and bring him home?"

"Because if you and I had done our job in the first place he wouldn't have run away."

"This isn't the time to hash out our mistakes. Besides, you've been a spectacular mother."

"Don't patronize me, Burke."

"Is that what you think I'm doing?"

"Yes, I do. You're tossing me a big compliment hoping to pacify me. Then maybe I won't be so annoyed about your refusal to let me go with you."

He sighed. "I'm sorry if it annoys you, but you're not going with me. Period."

She stepped closer, her expression firm with resolve. "Yes, I am."

"Goddammit, Abbie—"

"And don't swear at me, Burke. I'm not Thompson or some rookie cop who asks no questions. My son is out there in the middle of the night, in a rough and dangerous area, a place where there are strip joints and—" she shuddered involuntarily and then whispered "—heaven knows what else." With a gritty determination that came from her soul, she said, "I'm not staying here."

For a long moment neither said anything further. Abbie straightened her shoulders, lifted her chin and glared at him. He glared back with one of his intimidating looks.

Finally he shoved a hand through his hair and cursed. "Okay. Get ready to go. I want to be on the road right away."

Inwardly she sagged with relief. "Then you know exactly where in this Sade Court he called from."

"Yeah."

"Where?"

"Remember that merry-go-round music? There's a bar there that plays it. He must have been in the place."

A clawing fear gripped her. "Sounds creepy. Just how rough is this Sade Court?"

"Pretty rough. The Court caters to the wants and cravings of teenagers. Everything they need to know to die young."

BURKE SPRAWLED in a chair in the living room to wait while she grabbed a sweatshirt and put on shoes and socks. It was close to two in the morning, and he had passed exhaustion hours ago.

No time to be tired.

No time to show the strain.

No time to think about how terrified he was for Justin.

He closed his eyes as a film strip of the last time he'd been in Sade Court rolled through his mind. It had been two years ago when he'd been asked by one of the Massachusetts police departments to assist in an undercover operation. They'd needed an unknown face who knew the drug and porn markets well enough to slip in unnoticed. Burke had spent a month there and come out thanking God his own kid was too smart to get mixed up in that scene.

So much for thankfulness and Justin's good sense, he decided now as he listened to the distant sounds of Abbie moving around her room.

Sade Court was a hellhole of recklessness and godlessness. Drugs of every kind and price were sold with the ease of penny candy. Hookers so young they couldn't vote or buy a beer, yet they would do fantasy sex for a few bucks.

Loneliness and despair. Flash and noise and empty lives. Nightmares and heartache. Blows and back doors and street juice. Pimps swathed in chains of gold, driving expensive cars and looking for kids like Candy and Justin.

He muttered a long string of curses. Hell, if Justin and Candy got sucked into the Court, any innocence either of them had would only be a memory.

And Burke wondered about the Kaufman girl. Thinking through those few seconds of Justin's call, Burke remembered that Justin had hesitated a couple of times as if he was turning from the phone and whispering to someone.

Burke didn't believe Abbie had caught the slight hesitations. Until he was sure, he'd decided not to say anything. For the thought of Justin's taking care of himself in the Court was unnerving enough; the thought of his having a girl with him was terrifying. Some pimp could decide he wanted Candy, and Justin would be history. As for Candy, he thought grimly, she'd never be the same again.

Burke heaved himself from the chair. He wanted to get moving before Kaufman paid them a visit. He knew the man had been calling the station every hour for news, and once he was told Burke was going to find Justin he'd no doubt want to come along.

Abbie, he could handle, but not Kaufman.

"I'm ready."

Burke glanced up. She'd brushed her dark blond curls back and secured the mass with barrettes. In her sneakers, jeans and a black sweatshirt she looked like a child herself. The contrast to the fashionably dressed woman she'd been at the Kaufmans' made Burke smile. And also like a child, she was vulnerable and innocently unaware of what she would experience in the next few hours. Ignorance might not be bliss, he thought ruefully, but it was definitely optimistic.

He gripped her arm and hustled her out the door and into the car. There was no time to waste.

Neither spoke for the first few miles, but after they'd pulled onto the interstate heading north, Abbie glanced at him and said, "You smiled when I came out of the bedroom just before we left. What was that about?"

He glanced at her. "Oh, just something about how you look."

"Why? How do I look?"

"Like hell."

He caught the small smile that curved her mouth now and guessed he'd said exactly what she wanted to hear.

"I didn't want to look out of place," she said. "Like I didn't belong to you."

Burke's pulse took a racing leap at the offhand comment. Perspective and focus, he reminded himself. He and Abbie were not here to deal with each other; Justin was the issue.

Besides, Abbie had a habit of speaking first and regretting later. He knew better than to take her comments at face value. Nevertheless, he couldn't resist picking up on her last one.

"Abbie, no one ever believed you belonged to me. You're too classy to have fallen for a cop."

She tipped her head to the side. "But I did fall for you. Even my mother, who'd always wanted me to marry a doctor or lawyer, was enchanted by you."

The timing of her little burst of nostalgia made him realize they were both avoiding the uncertain present in favor of the already settled past.

"'Enchanted' isn't exactly what I would've called her feelings when she met me. Overprotective and nervous is more like it."

"She wasn't overly protective as much as worried I was marrying someone I couldn't handle. In a way she and I are alike in that we see life the way we want to rather than the way it really is. After my father died, she kind of pulled herself into a shell and concentrated on me instead of her own life."

"You were just a kid when he died, weren't you?"

She nodded. "Twelve. Heart disease killed my grandfather, too, so Mom always pushed Dad to get regular physicals, but he never wanted to take the time. He was a salesman and traveled a lot, but I think that was an excuse. Personally I think he didn't like doctors—some sort of guy thing, this not admitting feeling sick. I think Mom always felt if only she'd pushed him and nagged him..."

"Doesn't work, Abbie. People have to take responsibility for themselves."

"Yeah," she said, then changed the subject. "I talked to Mom a few days before Justin ran away. She sounded happy and settled." Abbie glanced at Burke, realizing he probably had no idea what she was talking about. Until six months ago her mother had lived in Walcott. "Did Justin tell you she'd moved to California?"

"Yeah, he did. Sun and fun and surf, huh?"

"Not the surf, but she loves the warm weather. She was fortunate to get a job with one of those guided-tours-to-the-stars outfits. A friend of hers who lives out there helped her get settled. If I didn't call her once a month, I think she'd forget she had a daughter."

Abbie, like Justin, was an only child, but Abbie couldn't imagine not keeping up with her son's life even long after he was married and on his own. Yet at the same time, she was pleased her mother had made herself a life apart from hers. Their relationship had changed from parent and child to something new. Surely there was a lesson to be heeded about the changing roles within a family.

"Well, I'm glad she's happy. It's to her credit that she's living life for herself and not trying to smother you and Justin. I presume you haven't let her know he's run away."

Abbie shook her head. "There's not anything she can do but worry. I'll call her when he's home safe and tell her about it." And he would be home safe. They would find him and bring him home. She believed that with all her heart. She had to.

She glanced at Burke, thinking back over the years when happiness seemed so simple. Marry the man you love and have his children. She couldn't help but wonder if her mother's initial worry that Abbie couldn't handle Burke had been a vital key.

Relaxed by the gentle motion of the car and drum of the engine, she liked that they were talking and getting along instead of arguing or struggling with the tension that was always between them.

Abbie said, "You were very different, Burke, from the boys I dated in college. They were all nerdy and serious. You were a little wild and unsettled, but Mom said you had a good future ahead of you. That had really been her thing—to see me married and nicely ensconced in a two-story house with a porch, a vegetable garden and babies that arrived long enough after the wedding so that the neighbors wouldn't be counting the months on their fingers and gossiping. We did good with Justin. It was a whole year before he arrived."

Burke snorted. "Not because we were all that careful. When I think of all those times when neither of us was thinking beyond the next sexual high, it's a wonder I didn't knock you up a few weeks after we met."

He kept his eyes on the road ahead. There were few cars at this hour, but the speed at which he was driving took considerable concentration. He could feel her gaze on him, though.

"We were..." She paused as if searching for a respectable word.

"Hot for each other," he said bluntly.

"We were, weren't we?"

"Always."

I still am, he thought painfully. And at times he knew she was, too. Except now wasn't way back then. Now they were reeling under all the misunderstandings, hurtful words, things done in anger, a divorce and a hundred gaps between them it was too late to fill.

"I was going to be the perfect wife and we were going to have the perfect marriage," she said wistfully.

"So much for perfection."

"It could've worked."

Burke was amazed to hear her say that. "Sure. If all it involved was making love. But out of bed we had a lot of problems."

"The main one being what you did."

"What I still do."

They fell silent for a few minutes, neither, it seemed, having anything further to say on the question of what had happened to love and trust and devotion and forever after.

At last, though, Abbie broke the silence.

"Burke, why did you marry me?"

"Seventeen years and a helluva lot of arguments later and you're asking me that?"

"Yes. Since we were already sleeping together, it wasn't because of sex. You know I would've lived with you if you'd asked."

Burke couldn't believe they were having this conversation. She was treating the relationship between the two of them as if it was as much in the balance as finding Justin.

"You weren't the live-in-without-a-license type, Abbie. I knew that the minute I met you. You had marriage and a white picket fence in your eyes."

"I guess I was like a lot of girls who saw marriage to a handsome man as the beginning of a happy future. I know," she said quickly, "too much of a rosy scenario, but what's wrong with being idealistic? With wanting a relationship that's happy and works?"

He gripped the wheel harder. "Nothing's wrong with it. Making it happen is the tough part."

"You told me the first time we discussed it that the only thing you wanted in life was to be a good cop—the best."

"Probably a little too much fierce enthusiasm, but yeah, that was and still is important."

Or *was* it? Burke found himself a little stunned that he would even question what had always been his life and his single-minded goal.

He shrugged and said, "Coming out of a family that leaned more toward the illegal than the legal pretty much set the pattern."

They both fell silent again, and Burke began thinking back, rolling around in his mind his personal goals. He'd set a pattern for himself to achieve them, and now for the first time he realized he'd never taken that next decisive step of declaring the pattern broken.

What was his benchmark? Five years of distinguished service? Ten years? Plaques and commendations? The respect of the men who worked with him, under him and over him? When did he sit back and say, it's finished? When would he allow himself to be satisfied that he'd proved a Wheeler could be honest, that his blood wasn't bad?

Yet here he was at thirty-seven, close to twenty years with the department and he was still driven, still looking over his shoulder as if he could get caught unawares by some in-born trait that proved he was a fraud.

He'd devoted his entire adult life to the achievement of one objective—be the best damn cop there was. The problem, ironically, was that he hadn't a clue how he'd know when it was okay to acknowledge that he'd accomplished his goal, done his duty and become the best.

Yet all the while he was being Supercop, the rest of his life was decidedly *un*super. In fact it was little more than a gaping, empty compartment with false walls and a weak foundation. He'd never even been able to open up enough to reassure Abbie, because he was so unsure himself.

He'd been responsible for the failure of their marriage. And even after a five-year-old divorce, one thing had remained consistent. He still desired her.

But Burke knew that desire and pleasure and sexual satisfaction often had little to do with love. He couldn't say he loved her; the emotion behind the word, the power it had to hurt and destroy, had been ingrained in him by a father who claimed he loved him but never showed it.

Grimly Burke realized he'd repeated with Justin what he'd always loathed in his own father: not spending time. Like most kids, Burke had wanted attention, but he'd had to settle for material things instead. Among them had been a flashy red convertible when he was sixteen. Burke had come racing in to tell his father all about how he'd made the senior all-star baseball team, but his father had waved off his excited chatter. He'd been busy poring over the papers he'd brought home from work, and so he'd handed Burke a set of keys, told him they were for the new car parked in the drive and said, "She's all yours. Take her for a drive. I got some business to take care of."

Burke had stared at the keys, his eyes blurred with tears. Once more when all he'd wanted was a couple of minutes to share some news, his father had given him a *thing,* rather than listen to him. Burke couldn't help making a comparison. Oh, he and Justin talked, but there'd been times when Burke had cut him off or told him he had to get back to work. Had Justin, too, believed his father wasn't interested enough in his own kid to listen? Maybe.

If he'd listened more carefully, if he'd been more available, if he'd been a better father, Justin might be asleep in his bedroom tonight, not hiding in Sade Court.

He shook his head to clear it. He might be able to relish the satisfaction of a successful career, but his personal life was in shreds. And now he was on his way to try to salvage at least a part of it.

He stole a quick glance at Abbie. He hadn't been with her for such a long stretch of time in years, and he found himself wanting to talk, knowing that for her it would ease the strain of too much worry about Justin's safety. Yet so far, every conversation had taken too personal a turn. Now as he drove he listened to the silence, to her soft breathing, to the tiny voice inside him that urged him to lighten the mood, to ease her unease or at least be a concerned ex-husband.

Suddenly she spoke. "Burke?"

"Yeah?"

"Do you really think I look like hell?"

He stole another glance, grinned, then reached out his hand and ruffled her hair. "Definitely."

She sniffed in pretended offense. "So do you."

He chuckled. "I'm glad we agree on at least one thing. We should be able to walk through Sade Court without turning a head."

"Maybe by this time tomorrow night..." she began hopefully.

"Let's take this one step at a time, Abbie."

"You don't want me to hope or expect anything, do you?"

"Of course I want you to hope. If I didn't have hope going into an investigation, there wouldn't be any reason to bother."

"You just seem so...so cynical. So objective."

Objective, he thought wryly. If there was one thing he wasn't about Justin's running away, it was objective.

But he said, "It has to be that way. Otherwise I would've burned out years ago."

"Like you burned out on our marriage?"

He decided not to dodge her jab. No matter how much he wanted to ignore it, he knew she wanted the bald truth.

"I didn't know what being married to you would mean," he said in a low voice, "and when I began to realize what it was, it was too late."

"I don't understand."

"It meant letting you into my heart, and when I tried to do that, I found out I didn't have one."

He heard her give a tiny gasp, but he didn't say anything more. For what could he say? He'd told her he lacked the capacity to love her, to be the husband she wanted, and certainly he'd proved that. He'd given her pain and heartbreak and taken years from her that would have been better left for a man worthy to love her.

His mouth set in a grim line. He'd done her a serious injustice. She deserved more. The sooner Justin was found, the better for all of them.

CHAPTER FOUR

INNOCENCE, ABBIE KNEW instantly, could not have survived in Sade Court. Lights, noise and too-young kids trapped in the carnality of unrestraint, no rules and little responsibility. Despite the late-April promise of warmer weather to come, nothing here held any hope of tomorrow.

She shivered, not so much from the night chill, but from the pervasive despair.

"Pretty, isn't it?" Burke said, his disgust apparent. He parked the car in a brightly lit area and turned off the engine.

"Pretty grim, I'd say."

"There's a chance Justin isn't here, Abbie."

It was difficult to tell if he wanted to reassure her or himself.

Through the windshield, a garish strobe light above a raucously loud entrance to a building spun the colors so fast that watching it made her slightly nauseated.

Turning her gaze back to Burke, she said, "I almost hope he is, because if he isn't..." She let her words trail off. She couldn't bear to say them aloud, because if he wasn't, they were at a dead end—and

Justin might be in an even worse place. The possibility was horrific.

In a resigned voice she asked, "How do we know where to start?"

"With Johnny Rebel." Burke opened the driver's door. At her puzzled look, he said, "Come on. If there's a single bright spot in this den of iniquity, it's Johnny."

She opened her door and climbed out. Burke took her arm and they crossed the street.

Two boys Abbie guessed to be no more than thirteen looked her over with a frankly sexual perusal that shocked her. Burke gripped her arm more tightly and led her toward a low building made of clapboard and brick. Unlike most of the other structures, its dull paint was clean and free of graffiti, but the heavy locks and bars on the windows belied any ideas that the place was safe from vandals.

Burke pulled open the door and allowed her to go in ahead of him. The room was ablaze with lights, the walls painted a soothing pale green. A teenage girl with thick amber-colored hair, expressive green eyes and a healed but nasty scar on her cheek glanced up from a table. Abbie wondered if anyone in Sade Court ever slept. It was close to four in the morning, yet this young girl and all those kids outside were wide awake.

When the teenager saw Burke, her face broke into a grin.

"Burke!" she squealed, and pushed her chair back from where she'd been sorting through posters of missing kids. She hurled herself like a whirlwind into Burke's arms.

He caught her and hugged her fiercely. "Pammie, you're looking wonderful. How are you?"

Her eyes gleamed bright and clear. "Clean. One year, eight months, six days and—" she peered at the big clock on the wall "—forty-five minutes."

Burke grinned. "How many seconds?"

She tugged on her bottom lip while she pretended to count. "Eighteen," she said, preening.

"I'm proud of you," he said, and Abbie noticed a slight catch in his voice. "You've put on some weight, too."

Instead of taking offense, the girl smiled even more widely. "Yeah, Johnny tells me I'm getting fat, but better fat than dead, huh?"

"Definitely better," he said.

Abbie hadn't moved, and now Burke turned to her and introduced her as his wife. "Pammie was turning tricks to feed her coke habit and got caught in a raid when I was doing some undercover work up here. The judge was lenient since it was her first offense and put her into a rehabilitation program."

Well, thought Abbie, her gaze still on Pammie, his comment earlier about being incapable of love certainly didn't apply when it came to helping others. In that area, Burke had consistently shone. She knew that kind of love wasn't the same as married love, but it showed that Burke was certainly capable of caring.

Pammie touched her scar, and her expression seemed to say it was a battle won rather than a battle lost. "I got this from my boyfriend when I told him I was going to get clean," she said, apparently having no problem talking about her past. "Burke made me a promise. If I got my life together, got into drug rehab and got clean, he'd send me to college."

She grinned and then turned back to Burke, saying with a pride that made Abbie's eyes smart, "I graduate from high school in June, and guess what?"

"What?"

"I made the honor roll last term!"

"Good for you."

"And I have a college all picked out."

"Terrific."

"Well, it's really a modeling school. But there's good money in modeling, and the booklets they sent me promised travel and lots of new experiences."

Abbie glanced at Burke, but his expression showed only honest interest. No surprise or disbelief, not even a question. Yet surely he must have realized that Pammie couldn't be a model.

The teenager was tall and slender and extraordinarily pretty, true, but the scar would prevent any reputable modeling agency from even giving her a second look. Burke, however, just nodded and listened as Pammie talked on.

Finally he said, "You'll have to show me the stuff they sent you."

"Oh, sure." She glanced at Abbie, then back to Burke. "My God, I didn't even ask you why you're here."

"Our son ran away, and we think he might have come to the Court." Burke said the words so easily they might have been discussing someone else's child. Someone else's problem.

Abbie, to her own astonishment, didn't even wince. Either it was the atmosphere of Sade Court or her emotions were so shredded by worry that she was numb. She knew, however, she'd become far too accustomed to the word *runaway* when it was applied to Justin.

Pammie said, "I'm sorry. Here I am yakking about me when your kid is missing. Johnny's in his office. Let me get him."

"Thanks, Pammie."

The girl opened a nearby door and went inside.

Abbie turned to her ex-husband. "Burke?"

"I know what you're going to say. She can't be a model."

"But she'll be crushed."

"Yes."

"Someone should tell her."

"Probably. But part of maturity is learning that life has consequences. Sure the scar wasn't deserved. The jerk that cut her was a real bastard, but she'd chosen to be with him."

"You're blaming her?"

"No. But like it or not, life doesn't always deal out roses even when we do the right thing. Pammie was messed up. No one lives like that and comes out of it without scars. Some physical—and some emotional."

Abbie glanced at a magazine sitting open on the table. It showed an ad for cosmetics and featured a doe-eyed fashion model with full, pouty lips. The message conveyed to the consumer was that the product enhanced beauty, and of course the model already had smooth satiny skin.

"Burke, why wouldn't she realize? I mean, as much as I hate it, flawlessness is almost a necessity in modeling. Surely she must know that a scar would prevent any hope of a modeling career."

"We can discuss this later," Burke said as the office door opened.

A man of about thirty-five dressed in cowboy boots, Western-cut jeans and a snap-front plaid shirt emerged and sauntered toward them. This had to be Johnny Rebel, Abbie thought. Only the Stetson was missing.

"Burke, man, it's good to see y'all. This pretty little thing has got to be Abbie."

Abbie nodded, his slight Southern drawl sounding odd but charming in New England.

She was, however, somewhat perplexed that he knew immediately who she was. But then, Burke had introduced her to Pammie as his wife. Obviously fewer questions would be asked or speculated on if it was assumed they were married. Still, Abbie was curious about Johnny's comment. It was as if Burke had, at some point in the past, talked favorably about her.

She extended her hand to Johnny, who took it in a firm no-nonsense shake. "No one could miss that you're from the South," she said with a smile.

"Texas. Used to work with runaways down there, but after coming up here to visit my kid sister, Donna Lee, I decided to stay." He grinned with obvious fondness for his sister and his decision. "Our family has shrunk to just her and me and my nephew. Always have liked to be around relatives, so I stayed awhile. Then when a couple of kids in the neighbor-hood ran away, I helped look for them. Discovered this hellhole called Sade Court and decided to open a shelter. Been here about five years."

To Pammie, he said, "Darlin', would you make sure the room upstairs has clean sheets on the bed?" Pammie nodded and scurried off.

Then he whispered out of the side of his mouth, "You know, Burke, if it was anyone but you, she'd tell me she ain't the maid." He shook his head and grinned again. "And when I think that her first day here she cowered like whipped dog. Man, what a change. Her self-confidence and self-esteem have risen faster than my mama's biscuits."

Then, as if sensing the touch of humor was out of place, he sobered and said, "But you're here about your boy, Pammie tells me."

Burke nodded. "I figured you'd be the best place to start, and we needed a place for a base."

Johnny said wryly, "Not up for the local kootie house, huh?"

Burke grimaced. "I'm partial to a bed without bugs or dirty needles."

Johnny led them into his office, a room that threat-ened to sink under the weight of files, missing-children posters, boxes of clothing and plastic bags filled with such necessities as toothbrushes, combs and sham-poos.

"Grab yourselves a couple of chairs," he said, "and we'll see what we can do."

After they were seated and Johnny was back be-hind his cluttered desk, Burke filled Johnny in.

He emphasized the possible inclusion of Candy Kaufman and detailed the brief phone call from Justin.

Johnny leaned back in his chair, propped his foot on an open drawer. He gave Burke a look so serious that Abbie knew, despite his Southern charm and humor, when it came to runaways he was all business.

"He done any drugs?" Johnny asked, his eyes on Burke.

"I don't know," Burke answered honestly. "None we've been aware of." He glanced at Abbie.

"Drinking? Comin' home wasted?" Johnny paused. "Any liquor missing from the house?"

Burke again glanced at Abbie.

"No," she said. "I, uh, I mean, we don't keep much on hand, so if it was gone we'd know."

Burke agreed. He said, "My guess is he's at least drunk beer, but only because it's so common among teenagers."

"Sexually active?"

"Yes."

Abbie pressed her hands into her thighs and just nodded her agreement when Johnny looked at her. She felt as if she was somehow being unfair to Justin for exposing him this way. To Johnny's credit, he made no judgment.

"Girlfriends? Is he promiscuous?" he asked Burke.

"I don't think he's promiscuous," Burke said. "But he's had girlfriends. And we found an empty condom box."

Johnny nodded, leaning forward. "Falling grades?"

Abbie said, "His grades were down last term, but Justin tends to get lazy after the Christmas holidays and then his grades pick up in the spring. I didn't think anything of it."

"Problems with either of you?" Johnny asked. "Outward rebellion? Arrests? Not coming home nights?"

Coming from Johnny, the questions sounded oddly routine. Answer so many in the affirmative and he'd stamp Justin as an official runaway.

Burke stood and walked to the window on one side of the office. The rhythmic flashes of the strobe light swiped away the outside darkness.

Without looking back at Johnny, he said, "Nothing we've been aware of." He turned around, and the frustration in his expression was obvious. "It's like a damn puzzle where the pieces that should fit don't. The patterns, the things that usually send a kid running don't seem to apply."

Johnny didn't agree or disagree. "A few minutes ago you mentioned a girl named Candy Kaufman. Could she be knocked up and they went to get an abortion?"

"My God, no!" Abbie said instantly.

Neither Burke nor Johnny said anything, making the silence instructive. She had the distinct impression both men thought she was in serious denial.

Finally Burke said, "That thought did cross my mind."

Abbie sat forward, startled. "You never told me you thought that was possible."

"Because that's all it is. A possibility."

Johnny added, "Could be that the kids were afraid of your reaction, Abbie. If they ran away and got the abortion and then came home, you'd never be the wiser. To them that may appear to be a better solution than handling your reaction to a pregnancy. Kids tend to believe that what their parents don't know and, I might add, don't *want* to know, doesn't hurt anybody. So shading the truth or just plain lying is an advantage."

Abbie bristled at what she perceived to be a lecture or, worse, a condemnation of her parenting skills. She was already wrestling with some guilt in that area.

Briskly she said, "I know you're an expert on runaways, but you don't know my son. I do. Justin neither shades the truth nor lies."

The silence again spoke volumes. And Burke's silence particularly annoyed her. Why wasn't he agreeing with her or at least being supportive of Justin?

Finally Johnny pushed his chair back and got to his feet. "Look, why don't y'all get some sleep? I'll call around and do some checking. If Justin is here in the Court, someone'll have seen him."

Burke took Abbie's arm to draw her to her feet. "I'll get Abbie settled and go with you."

Johnny shook his head. "Let me take the first looksee by myself. You're a stranger here, an adult stranger furthermore, and despite the excesses of Sade Court, these kids are very suspicious of strangers. Besides, someone might recognize you."

"I doubt that. The last time I was here was quite a while ago and I was pretty scruffy looking."

"True," Johnny said, "but let me get started and set things up for you. It's the least I can do."

Abbie pushed her earlier irritation aside. "We might find Justin sooner if Johnny lays the groundwork," she said to Burke. Although she believed that was true, she also knew she wasn't about to be left in some room cooling her heels and worrying while Burke went off in search of Justin.

"A wise lady, Burke."

Burke nodded. "Yeah. Sometimes too wise."

After Burke got their things from the car, he and Abbie followed Pammie up a narrow staircase to a dimly lit hall. The carpet runner was a dull gold color and worn to the jute backing from years of traffic, but it was clean.

Pammie opened the door to a room with a window that looked out over the spinning strobe light.

"The bathroom's across the hall," she said. "The sheets are fresh and clean towels are there on the dresser. Extra blankets in the closet."

Burke and Abbie both expressed their thanks.

The teenager walked over to the window and lowered it to mute the street sounds, then switched on the small bedside lamp. In a sad voice, she said, "The noise never stops. They're all afraid, you know. If they're silent they have to listen to themselves, but worst of all, they can hear their future crumbling."

"Too much pain and despair under the silence, isn't there?" Burke said in a low voice.

Abbie wondered if he was thinking about himself—his life as a cop, the danger and the pressure. Or maybe he was thinking about all the silences in their marriage. Not the verbal ones, but the emotional ones.

Pammie nodded, looking far too wise and far too savvy for such a young girl. She went out and softly closed the door behind her.

Alone in the small room, Burke and Abbie glanced at each other and then at the double bed with its thick quilt embroidered with baskets of geraniums. The pillows had been plumped and the covers turned back invitingly.

Abbie, however, knew Burke had no intention of sleeping in the same bed with her.

He walked across a green throw rug and moved an old-fashioned upholstered chair nearer to the window Pammie had lowered.

From the inside, the room could have been in an ordinary house in an ordinary neighborhood, but the garish spinning strobe light quickly put paid to that notion. Abbie sighed and picked up the bags he'd dropped near the door and moved them aside. "Burke?"

"Better get a few hours' sleep," he muttered without looking at her.

"Why did you let Johnny and Pammie all think we're still married?"

In a monotone, as if his mind was elsewhere and her question was quite pointless, he said, "Because space is a problem here and Johnny would've wanted to make sure you got a separate room if I'd told him we were divorced."

"Oh."

Her heart plummeted. She immediately chastised herself. Why was she reacting this way to him? What had she expected him to say? That he wanted her in his life and in his bed?

When he said nothing more, she crossed to where he'd sprawled in the heavy chair. His legs were stretched out and propped on the small radiator beneath the window.

His position emphasized the snugness of his jeans, the flat, almost concave, stomach, the broad shoulders and the strong defined jaw. In his dark green eyes, she saw wariness, felt a sense of foreboding. What kind of promises was he making to himself? She wasn't sure she wanted to know.

He stared out the window, his attention on the flashing strobe.

Abbie folded her arms to keep from touching him. Suddenly the chill she'd felt in the car when they first arrived returned. But this time it went beyond goose bumps at the thought of Justin, and maybe Candy, in this godforsaken place. The iciness had more to do with herself, with her feelings about Burke and some foolish hope that he might still care for her. A hope she resented for its futility.

In a conversational tone, she said, "I thought the main reason for not revealing that we're divorced was to avoid questions."

Slowly he swung his gaze toward her, but his eyes were shuttered, as if he'd been contemplating private things and had suddenly realized she was with him.

"What are you talking about?"

His question typified his ability to close himself off
from her. Abbie had seen it dozens of times during
their marriage.

Talking to him and then realizing he hadn't heard
her.

Arguing with him and realizing he wasn't listening.

And here now, even though he'd reluctantly brought
her along, he was closing her out as he'd always done.
Drawing a line between who he was and who she was,
what he did and what she wanted.

She knew then that taking a room together had no
significance at all. He'd already forgotten or dismissed the topic. If she had any brains, she'd step
away, find the bathroom and get ready for bed.

Let him sit here alone with his mental puzzles, she
decided. He didn't need her now any more than he
ever had. For sure he didn't want her here, but since
he was stuck with her, he'd simply do the next best
thing. Close her out.

Damn you, Burke. Nothing ever changes, does it?

Abbie could feel her temper rising. An almost nostalgic handicap of those days when she and Burke argued; rather, *she* argued and he let her rail and rant
and then either took her to bed or walked out the door.

In as controlled a voice as she could manage, she
said, "We were talking about sharing this room. I
thought you just wanted to avoid questions about our
relationship."

"Questions? Why would they ask questions?
Johnny's divorced and so is his sister. I doubt ours
would shock him."

"I meant," she said tightly, "because of Justin running away."

"Oh. And Johnny might think our divorce was a contributing factor?"

"Yes."

"It took a long time for it to contribute," he said with a tinge of sarcasm.

"But certainly those factors have occurred to you. At least the broken family."

He sighed and scrubbed his hands down his face as if to wipe away his weariness. "Yeah, I've thought about it."

"Do you think it has something to do with why he ran away?"

Burke fixed his gaze on her as if wanting to make sure she heard exactly what he said. "Want me to be blunt?"

She braced herself. Suddenly she knew why he hadn't told her he'd considered that Justin and Candy may have indeed run away because she was pregnant.

Burke knew her too well. He knew she embraced an idealistic view of their son, and so Burke had instinctively sheltered her when Justin didn't live up to that ideal. It was the same reason he hadn't wanted to bring her with him to Sade Court: he'd wanted to protect her from this seamy side of life.

She rubbed her eyes with her fingers, almost wishing she could get rid of those rose-colored lenses Burke so often accused her of wearing.

"Yes, I want you to be blunt."

"Then, no. I don't think his home life was the reason he ran away."

He paused, then continued. "I do think, though, that he could lay a helluva guilt trip on you, which I suspect is already happening."

She lowered her head, and Burke reached up and took a handful of her baggy black sweatshirt, winding the cloth tightly around his fingers.

Abbie watched his fingers mesh with the cloth. "Maybe it's easier to find something concrete from the past to blame rather than try and figure out what the problem is." She curled one hand around his wrist, needing suddenly to touch him. "Maybe we shouldn't have gotten divorced."

"Stay together for the sake of the kid," he said slowly, as if examining the idea from every angle and looking for its merit.

"Just until he was out of school and on his own."

"And what kind of home would he have had with two people arguing and fighting constantly?"

"Our differences weren't *that* bad," she said softly.

"No rosy revisionist history, Abbie. It was hell and you know it. You wanted me out of police work and I told you that wasn't going to happen. We argued about that at least twice a week. Pretty clear-cut differences if you ask me."

She couldn't refute that. Perhaps she *had* closed her mind to some of the major quarrels they'd had. Why had she ever thought that loving him, wanting his children and being what she'd thought he wanted would be enough? Especially when he'd never said he loved her, never trusted her enough to share his work?

And yet she'd chosen to believe that what they had was gold, that mere words didn't matter. She loved enough for both of them. How foolish, how naive she'd been.

"Maybe we should've compromised more."

"Abbie, we had major differences. All my life I wanted to be a cop. Going into our marriage, you knew that. You knew how important it was to me to prove that at least one Wheeler wasn't going to end up in prison."

"But you *have* proved it. Over and over again. I can't imagine any situation where you would do anything even close to illegal." She scowled suddenly, recalling what he'd done for Celada. Technically he'd done something illegal when he fixed it so Celada wouldn't go to jail. And he claimed that his sole reason was to prevent her from calling.

My God, was doing something illegal preferable to meeting her to discuss the divorce?

Before she could reason it through, he said, "But from somewhere you got the idea I would change or decide that being married was more important."

Abbie stared at him, a sick feeling in the pit of her stomach. "You're saying that our marriage and me, maybe even Justin, were second place and would never have been anything more?"

She wanted him to deny it. She wanted him to call her comment a damn ridiculous assumption. But he'd told her he had no heart, hadn't he? Oh God, oh God, please...

For the longest time he didn't say anything. She swung away, more hurt than she believed she still could be.

His hold on the sweatshirt stopped her. Her eyes were swimming with tears she didn't want. She tried to wriggle her shirt free of his hand, but to no avail. "Dammit, let me go."

"No."

"Your silence answered my question."

He gripped the sweatshirt even tighter. "I'm saying that I had different parts to my life. As long as being married and being a cop stayed separate, we were fine. You insisted on blending them. I didn't want that."

"But—"

"Cop work is dirty stuff. I worked hard to leave all that behind when I came home. You just wouldn't let it alone."

"But our marriage wasn't all arguing and being nasty to each other."

He shrugged.

"You don't want to talk about this, do you?"

"The bigger question is, why do you want to? You want me to tell you I still have the hots for you? You want me to say that in the sack we never missed? We just never clicked the rest of the time?"

He shoved a hand through his hair and let go of her sweatshirt. "Why don't you go lie down on the bed and get some sleep."

She didn't move. "You don't want to talk about any of this, do you? Just like when I tried to bring it up when we were married."

"It's over. It's all in the past. Dredging it up and discussing it now is pointless."

"But don't you see? If we had talked about it and tried to work it out, we might have saved our marriage."

"We might have? We? *You're* the one who wanted me to quit the department. *You're* the one who accused me of marrying you just because we had good sex. *You're* the one who told me at top volume that I wanted the divorce to uncomplicate my life. That, as I recall, was followed by about six weeks of total silence from you. None of those things have much to do with working it out."

"There were extenuating circumstances."

"Yeah, like a realization that what we had wasn't enough."

"Of course it wasn't enough! You never said you loved me or trusted me or wanted a life with me except in bed!"

Instantly she was appalled at her outburst. She'd sworn to herself she would never debate this with him, for surely she would lose. Now here she was blurting it out like a frustrated child. But it was too late to stop.

Burke looked away, his face blank, his body perfectly still.

In a halting voice she said, "Maybe...maybe I've taken off the rose-colored glasses. During our marriage I saw things as I wanted to see them. I thought I could deal with your being a cop and I found out I couldn't. Now I find out—oh God—that not only was I a lousy wife, b-but a lousy mother."

"Abbie—"

"You know it's true."

"It's not true!"

"Then where is he?" she asked desperately. "Why didn't he come to me or to you if he's in trouble? Why did he run off to somewhere like this place? And if Candy's with him, why didn't we even know he was seeing her? Why would he keep it a secret?"

Burke got to his feet and lifted her up in his arms.

"What are you doing?"

"Putting you to bed."

"No."

"With me."

"You're going to sleep with me?"

"Abbie, we're here in the same room and there's only one bed. Surely you didn't expect me to sleep in the chair."

"But we can't."

"We can. Our son is missing and tonight I need to be close to his mother."

Words failed her while he set her down on her feet beside the bed and deftly pulled off her sweatshirt. Her bra was black, but it might as well have been a training bra for all the attention he gave it. He steadied her and went to work on her jeans, tugging those down, revealing a scrap of black panties. He then reached behind her and pulled the covers back.

"Sit down," he said, keeping his eyes averted. When she did, he unlaced her sneakers and pulled them off, then her socks. "Okay, get into bed."

She did as he said, pulling the covers up to her chin and feeling ridiculously like a virgin.

Burke took his own clothes off and she unabashedly watched him. Too many years had passed since she'd seen him naked, yet the familiar spiral of sensation that came at the sight of all that muscled leanness reminded her that a part of her would always care deeply for Burke. Perhaps even love him. But she reminded herself to keep those feelings and emotions under tight rein.

He turned off the light and slipped in beside her. Without asking, he pulled her into his arms and settled her beside him.

"Burke?"

"Go to sleep, Abbie," he muttered.

She curled into him, tucking her hands against his belly and absorbing his warmth. "Can I at least say thank you?"

"For what?"

"For being honest with me. I know sometimes I'm not very nice or easy to understand."

He slid his hand down her back and she felt his chin against her hair. "Neither am I, so let's just call this a new step for us."

She blinked. For us? Had he realized what he'd said?

She snuggled closer. Maybe he hadn't, she mused, feeling more than pleased. Maybe Burke had more heart than he realized.

CHAPTER FIVE

"JUSTIN!"

Abbie sat bolt upright in bed, the covers pooling in her lap. Blinking, she stared through glazed eyes, her heart hammering. Sunshine drifted into the bedroom and splotched over the heavy upholstered chair where Burke had sprawled just hours ago. Sunbeams flowed across the throw rug, the mussed quilt and her.

No sign of Justin.

No sign of Burke.

She'd only been dreaming that Justin was standing beside the bed, asking her where his black jeans were, his hair waving over his forehead, his grin infectious, the earring glittering in his left ear. She'd objected to the earring and they'd argued, but then she'd finally relented. The issue wasn't important enough to wreck their relationship.

God, she thought dismally, what she wouldn't give now for an argument with him. The deep fear of the past twenty-four hours reemerged.

Taking a deep breath, she slowly stretched, pushed the covers back and climbed out of bed. She was still wearing her bra and panties, and she recalled those moments with Burke.

Our son is missing and tonight I need to be close to his mother. How wonderful that had sounded. Sighing wistfully, she knew she would feel ridiculous this morning if she'd broken that unspoken rule of no intimacy. She knew Burke was aware of the rule, too.

The very fact that he'd told her to go to sleep clarified his intent. They were together because of Justin, but for no other reason.

Wasn't there some pearl of wisdom about a crisis bringing people closer? Making them cling more to each other? And couldn't that clinging and closeness too easily spill into other areas such as sexual intimacy?

She quickly made the bed.

Well, she decided as she fluffed the pillow that still held the indentation of Burke's head, whoever had come up with that bit of wisdom hadn't met her ex-husband. Between their conversation and their chaste hours in bed, Abbie had no reason to assume they would ever have anything more than they had right now—a sharing of Justin. And if he wasn't found...
She shuddered at the possibility, but then shook off the negative thought. Of course he would be found!

Yet this morning she felt empty and oddly restless. What puzzled her most was why Justin's running away and her wanting to be close to Burke had any connection at all.

She'd had Burke once. The three of them had been a family. Maybe she wanted that again, but beyond the passage of time, little had changed. He was still a cop and she still wanted him to quit being a cop. Maybe...

You're on a dangerous path, she warned herself. *You're beginning to look through those rose-colored glasses again. Show some objectivity and keep those leftover feelings for Burke in perspective.* Once Justin was found, she and Burke would simply be parents again. Divorced parents. Nothing more.

Sighing, she gathered up her clothes, a towel and her toiletries and headed for the bathroom.

Twenty minutes later she returned to their room and found Burke standing by the window, holding the curtain aside. He was dressed in jeans and a dark shirt, and his service revolver and shoulder holster were slung over the chair. She'd known he brought it; its blatant visibility only emphasized what he thought of Sade Court.

He was holding a mug of coffee, and he'd set one down on the dresser for her. She lifted the hot mug and sipped carefully, then asked, her voice still a little husky, "Have you learned anything new?"

Instead of answering her, he said, "I thought we'd go and take a look around. Sade Court is marginally safer in daylight. I called Gagne. He said there's nothing now from the missing-children agencies. He's begun to widen the search to outside New England."

She lowered the mug and gripped it, glad for its warmth on her suddenly chilled hands. "You don't believe Justin has run that far, do you?"

Burke shrugged. "Depends on why he ran away and what he has in mind. I had a case a month or so back where the kid hitched all the way to Oregon."

"Hitchhiked!" Hot coffee sloshed from the cup onto her trembling hand, but she barely noticed the scalding drops. "Oh God!"

He turned toward her and for the first time she saw deep worry lines. She knew he'd slept little, if any, and she guessed that his thoughts had already jumped to all the worst scenarios. "Look, I doubt he's left New England. The phone call was only last night and it wasn't the action of a kid determined not to be found."

"That makes sense." She put the mug down, but needing something to do besides stare at him, she picked up her hairbrush. "What about Johnny? Did he find out anything?"

"Maybe."

"Maybe? What does 'maybe' mean?" Her pulse began to race.

Burke watched her hands as they pinned and arranged her hair. His face was so carefully blank it scared her.

"Johnny asked around and found someone who said he thought he saw Justin late yesterday."

Her hands fell to her side, her eyes wide. "Found someone? Who?"

"A local drugstore owner."

Abbie felt a surge of relief. A store owner would be a pretty reliable source. At least it wasn't some hooker or drug dealer. To her chagrin, she realized that while she desperately wanted to find her son, she also wanted to keep her image of Justin as a good clean-living boy intact. It was difficult enough dealing with his running away; the other things were too dreadful to consider.

"You think he might've called us from this store?"

"No. Remember what I said last night about the bar? The merry-go-round music we heard on the tape? It's from a bar and dance hangout called the Merry-Go-Round. That's where he called from."

"Oh, yeah. I said the place sounded creepy."

"It's worse than that."

"Oh." She steeled herself. "You've been there."

"Yeah, when I was doing undercover work here. It's the core of Sade Court. Dealing, hooking, you name it, it's been done or tried at the Merry-Go-Round."

Abbie sat down on the bed, her knees a little shaky. The thought of her son in a place like that—my God, there was no end to the terrifying possibilities.

"What did you do there?" she asked.

"Worked the bar mostly. It's a grim, amoral place, Abbie. If hell has a sewer, the Merry-Go-Round's the prototype."

Their eyes met in the spill of morning light. Their mutual concern for Justin connected them even more tightly than before. Without words, both knew if they didn't find Justin through the store owner, they would have to go to the Merry-Go-Round.

Abbie whispered, "Do you think Justin has been hanging out there?"

"God, I hope not." He added, "But let's take it one step at a time. First we'll talk to this store owner."

She finished with her hair and drank her coffee.

Burke pulled on the shoulder holster and then shrugged on his leather jacket. "We're just going to be parents looking for their kid, okay?" he said.

"You don't want anyone to know you're a cop."

"Exactly. Nervous we don't need, and in Sade Court cops have a way of making people very nervous—and apt to lose their memories." He glanced at her. "Ready?"

"Yes," she said, energized by a sweep of sudden and unexpected euphoria. Finally they had a direction. It felt like they were making progress.

Outside, Burke took her arm. "Stay close."

She certainly had no intention of arguing with him. The streets were deserted, as if an all-night party had finally worn everyone down. Two men slept on the sidewalk, one holding a brown bottle, the other snoring so loudly a stray dog sniffed and started to lift his leg but then moved on. Abbie noticed that the strobe light still flashed its garish colors, but in the daylight it looked faded and weary.

For the thousandth time she wondered why Justin would run away to come here. Was he in some dark corner trying to keep warm and safe? Was he hurt and bleeding and needing help? She shivered. Sade Court didn't look like a place that had a lot of good samaritans.

Burke gave her arm a squeeze. "Don't feed your worst fears, Abbie."

She glanced up at him. "But you're scared, too, aren't you?"

"In a hundred ways."

She slipped her arm around his waist. "Thank you."

"For being scared?"

"For telling me. You're usually so sure of yourself, so in control of everything, that sometimes I feel guilty for not being more objective."

Abbie knew Burke had always emphasized the necessity of objectivity in his work. Otherwise he would have been an emotional basket case years ago. But what she found more enlightening was that her fear he'd been anesthetized to the brutalities of the streets simply wasn't true. He'd kept his emotions tightly in check, but she'd also seen the toll Justin's running away had taken.

They crossed the street to the drugstore. Burke knocked. Three quick raps, a few seconds of silence and then three more. A Closed sign hung in the barred window, yet within a few minutes the door was pulled open as far as the pair of inside chain locks would allow—maybe two inches. Not enough to really see the person behind it.

"Johnny Rebel sent us," Burke said.

"Got any proof?" a male voice rasped.

Burke reached into his pocket and pulled out a black-and-white photograph. He showed it to Abbie, and her mouth fell open in shock. It was a photo of Justin standing in the aisle of a store. She'd never seen it before.

"Where did that come from?" she asked.

"The in-store surveillance camera here picked it up."

Abbie studied it, wanting to deny the obvious. "It . . . it looks as if Justin is stealing something."

"Yeah, that's what it looks like." He passed the picture to the man on the other side of the door.

While Abbie's mind absorbed this new twist—her son a thief—the man behind the door studied the photo. It seemed to take him forever. Then, apparently satisfied, he worked the locks and opened the door.

He was a small, stooped man with a permanent scowl and smelled faintly of camphor oil. Once they were inside, he quickly closed the door and secured the locks.

"My security man don't come in till noon, so I don't open till then." He led the way into the darkened store, walking toward the back. Burke and Abbie followed.

"Name's Gus. I'm the owner." He led the way down an aisle stocked with cold medicine.

Burke said nothing.

Gus glanced around as if expecting something or someone to leap out of the shadows. Finally, at the back of the store near a small prescription counter, he stopped.

"Johnny says your kid's missing?"

"Yeah."

"And this here's a picture of him?"

"Yes!" Abbie exclaimed, unable to keep silent.

The stooped man grinned, revealing even white teeth. Dentures, Abbie thought. "You must be the mama," he said.

"Yes."

"Johnny said the photo was taken yesterday afternoon," Burke said tersely, and Abbie could tell he wasn't interested in anything except the picture.

"Yep. Right over there in aisle three."

Abbie asked, "If it was taken in your store and you gave it to Johnny, then why did it take you so long to look at it? It was as if you'd never seen the photo before."

"I was lookin' to make sure it was taken in my store. All the businesses around here use the same security outfit."

Abbie nodded. "What's in aisle three?"

"Female stuff mostly."

Female stuff? Abbie was having a hard enough time imagining her son as a shoplifter, but his taking something from the aisle with sanitary napkins was too ludicrous to consider.

"And do you know what he took?" Abbie asked as they made their way toward aisle three.

"Yep. Very careful of inventory control. Around here a man'd be out of business in a week if he didn't do his inventory. Can't tell what he snitched from the picture, though, just that the little bastard is shoving it in his jacket."

Abbie's defenses geared up, but Burke gave her a "don't react" look.

"Didn't catch him, neither. He zigzagged out down the side aisle." Gus pointed toward the camera. "This is how I see it. He looked up, spotted the camera and got scared. Good thing, too. This here picture came out real nice." A telephone rang and the man turned and hurried toward the prescription counter to answer it.

Abbie whispered, "Burke, there has to be an explanation. Justin is not a shoplifter."

"Probably not," he said, his tone vague and unconvincing. He was staring at the surveillance camera.

"What are you thinking?"

"That our kid is smarter than we've been giving him credit for."

"That doesn't sound like the compliment it should be."

He glanced at her, his eyes hard, his voice rough. "Don't forget the Wheelers have a long illegal history."

Aghast, she said, "Burke, surely you don't think that Justin inherited a penchant to steal!"

"It's pretty hard to dismiss what's in this picture."

"But if he has a good reason..."

"Abbie, most thieves have a good reason. The problem with Justin's reason is that he had other options and chose not to use them. Options like calling us and saying he's in trouble or doing something really weird like coming home."

"Oh. So now you're being sarcastic. That'll help."

"Look, I'm wondering what kind of trouble he's in that he has to steal."

The store owner returned.

"This way. I'll show you what he took." He came to a stop and pointed to a shelf that was about shoulder height. "There, one of those."

Abbie stared, her heart tumbling. Burke's and Johnny's suspicions were right. "Those are pregnancy-test kits."

"Yep, that's what they are. Had a girl come in here the other day who was no more than twelve buying one. Thought it was for her mama, but nope. It was for her."

Burke took a package from the shelf and then glanced once again at the photo. "You're positive this is what he took?"

Gus shifted a little, pressed his hand on his lower back, then winced with obvious pain. "Hey, look, I know what I got in my store. I know what I sell and what these little punks try to steal. Your kid took one of those. Now, you gonna pay me for it or am I gonna report him to the cops?"

Abbie shook her head in disgust. "Our son is missing and all you care about is a few dollars."

"Lady, in this part of town dollars are easier to find than runaways. I'm sorry for your troubles, but my business don't work on feeling sorry for parents who can't keep tabs on their kids."

Abbie stiffened, wanting Burke to jump to their defense, but he appeared to be deep in thought.

Unable to let the store owner's words stand, she snapped, "How dare you accuse us of being bad parents! You don't know any of the circumstances."

Gus peered at her shrewdly. "I know your kid stole a pregnancy-test kit, so that means he's got some girl knocked up and neither one of you knew what was going on. Hey, parents are pretty smart about buying the right clothes and feedin' and schoolin' their kids, but when it comes to stuff that really matters—like sex and drugs—most of 'em don't have a clue what their kid's doin'."

Burke glanced at the price on the kit, took out his wallet and paid the man.

"We appreciate your help," he said, taking Abbie's arm. "If he shows up again, would you call me at Johnny's?"

"Maybe. Should call the cops. Thievin' little punks."

Burke pulled out two twenty-dollar bills, folded them into thirds and tucked them into Gus's pocket.

"Call me," Burke repeated.

"Sure thing," Gus said, smiling and patting his pocket.

NOT UNTIL THEY WERE back outside did Abbie say anything. Burke had put his sunglasses on and was glancing up and down the street as if she wasn't even with him.

"You paid him for information," she said, honestly surprised. Burke, who always made a point of doing everything legally, had actually *bribed* someone.

"Yeah."

"That's all you can say? 'Yeah'?"

"What do you want to hear?"

"I want to hear *why* you bribed him."

"I think that's obvious. I want to find Justin, and if forty bucks will buy another pair of eyes, then I'm going to spend it." Again he glanced down the street.

"If you were a runaway with a pregnant girlfriend, where would you go?"

Abbie scowled, still unsettled by seeing Burke pay the drugstore owner bribe money. Nevertheless she said, "If he came to this drugstore, wouldn't it follow that they'd be in this area?"

"Yeah, unless he chose this one because it was a long way from where he really is." Burke paused for a moment, his brow wrinkled in thought. "The girl. Why wouldn't she have gone for the kit?"

Abbie blinked. "Maybe she was scared."

"Or she didn't know how to shoplift, which is the more obvious answer."

"And Justin does?" Abbie felt her heart sink even farther than it already had. How little, it seemed, she knew her son.

"It would seem so. Maybe they didn't want to spend the money for one. Going to a clinic, even a free one, would mean filling out a lot of forms. Justin probably didn't want to chance that. So he did what seemed to be simplest."

Abbie said, "You and Johnny talked about Candy being pregnant. If that was the reason they ran away, why would he shoplift a pregnancy kit?"

"Good question. Maybe they weren't sure. They're just kids, after all. Maybe Candy *thought* she was pregnant, they got scared and ran and now for some reason they aren't sure."

"But that's good," Abbie said, hope rising. "If she's not pregnant, they'll come home."

"Or Justin wants her to make sure before they make the next move."

"Like terminate the pregnancy," Abbie said, wishing with all her heart Justin had come to her. "Oh, Burke, that's a huge decision for two kids to make alone."

"So is the one to run even farther."

"What do you mean?"

"I mean, if Candy is pregnant we can't eliminate their running farther as a possible result."

"Keep the baby and hide forever? My God!"

"Look, I'm just throwing out possibilities. He snatched the kit and is nowhere to be found. Obviously cash is a problem, so it stands to reason he's going to have to get some help, steal again or do something else to get money."

Abbie shivered. "I thought I was scared before. Now I'm terrified."

He glanced in the direction of the Merry-Go-Round. "Yeah, it scares me, too. Because the most lucrative money-maker around here is dealing drugs or pimping..."

JOHNNY AND PAMMIE greeted them when they returned. Pammie had learned earlier from Burke that Abbie was a fashion consultant, and now she stood in front of her, grinning and holding a stack of fashion magazines.

"Abbie, can I ask you some questions?"

Abbie smiled, glad for something to take her mind off the distressing thoughts about Justin. "Of course. Did you find some things you like?"

"Well, sort of. But I wanted to ask you about color and what you think will be good for my portfolio."

Burke and Johnny had gone into the office.

Abbie took a deep breath. She couldn't do anything for Justin at the moment; maybe she could help Pammie.

She knew she had to bring up the scar. If Pammie was warned of how it would be seen by a modeling agency, then at least the young woman would be prepared.

"Let's go look at those magazines. I wanted to talk to you about a few things, too."

"I know I need new clothes and some polish, but you can give me some advice on those, can't you?"

Abbie nodded and followed Pammie into a small room off the main area.

IN JOHNNY'S OFFICE, Burke paced from one end of the room to the other.

Johnny took the chair behind his desk. "From the scowl on your face, I assume Gus had some news."

"I wish to God he'd had Justin." Burke quickly filled Johnny in, all the while considering the possibility of his son dealing drugs to survive. After all the talks he and Justin had had on that subject, Burke was more than angry at his son; he was severely disappointed. "I need some names, Johnny."

"Burke, let me give you some advice. I think it would be better if we got someone else on this case. Your objectivity is shot to hell."

"I don't need advice. Just names."

"And what about Abbie?"

"She'll be okay here."

"And what if you don't come back or, worse, come back in pieces?"

"I've left everything to her and Justin. She knows who my lawyer is."

"Burke, for God's sake, let me call the cops. They could send in someone who—"

Burke's eyes darkened. "I *am* a cop, remember? And this is my son. No way in hell am I gonna step back because my objectivity might be clouded. He's run away, and if I'm partially responsible for that, the least I can do is make sure I'm there when he's found."

Finally Johnny sighed. "Okay, but go in there with your antennae up. I don't want to have to comfort the widow." He lowered his voice and gave Burke three names.

Burke nodded. "Thanks. Tonight can't come soon enough."

For the rest of the afternoon, Burke made himself stay busy with phone calls to various teenage hangouts and shelters in the area, anywhere that Justin could be. But no luck.

As the day lumbered on, the sky darkened with clouds. Rain was forecast and the possibility of thunderstorms.

Burke had gone up to their room to do some planning for later that night. God, how he wished he'd insisted on Abbie staying home. He didn't relish her questioning him about what the next step was. The truth was, he was restless and wanted to dig into the corners of Sade Court. Doing that without Abbie's knowledge wasn't going to be easy.

Deciding to break up the hours until he planned to make his move, he took her to an Italian restaurant a couple of blocks away. It was a small place with excellent food that he remembered from his previous work in the area.

After they finished their dinner and were enjoying the last of the chianti, Abbie leaned back in the chair and asked, "So what did Johnny say?"

"He gave me some names. I'm going to check them out."

Turning his glass, Burke considered the direction of his thoughts. He wished she'd stayed home and yet he found he needed her—for reasons that had nothing to do with logic or good sense. Justin's actions, their being forced to deal with the unknown, with unrelenting worry, were driving them together in a way that would never have happened otherwise. They were finding out things about their son they didn't know.

And they were finding out things about themselves.

Burke knew one thing for sure. He wanted to be with Abbie, completely and intimately. The why of it troubled him, because his gut told him that his desire went way beyond the superficial satisfaction of sex.

He said casually, "I'm in the mood to make love, Abbie. What do you say?"

She looked stunned by his straightforwardness. "You want to make love?"

"Mmm. I don't suppose you're protected from getting pregnant..."

She narrowed her eyes, and it was obvious to Burke she thought he was trying to distract her from the worry about Justin. "What if I said yes?"

"I'd say great. I don't have to use a condom."

She tipped her head to the side, pausing a few seconds, then said, "If I was using birth control, then—" She cut her words off and gave him a direct look. "You aren't at all curious about who I'm sleeping with?"

"I don't have a right to be curious." His mind mentally clicked through all the men she might know. Picturing her in bed with any man, never mind one he knew, sharply annoyed him. Jealousy seemed ludicrous, but it coiled inside him regardless, with all the subtlety of a cobra. He just barely reined it in.

She sagged back in her chair, looking decidedly disappointed. "And here I was hoping for raging jealousy."

He glanced at the way her breasts rose and fell, recalling them encased in the black bra, remembering his determination the previous night to keep his hands off her.

In an even voice he said, "How about I make you forget him?"

She took a sip of wine, her words coming carefully. "You're serious, aren't you?"

"About us making love? Yeah."

"Why?"

His eyes darkened, and he knew that this intensity, this need for Abbie, wasn't about Justin or being forced together by a crisis; it wasn't even about having sex; this was about him and Abbie, of their joining in an intimate way so that he could draw warmth and strength and hope from her. So that she could make him feel less lonely, not so scared. But he couldn't tell her all that; he couldn't allow himself to open up his heart, for when this was over—

"Burke?"

"I want you," he said in a low voice. "I want to feel you come."

He saw her eyes widen at his admission and then just as quickly narrow in suspicion again.

Abruptly she pushed her chair back, her face flushed with anger. She tossed her napkin onto the table. "I don't like this, Burke. We've always been sexually attracted to each other, but we've also been careful not to allow anything to happen since the divorce."

"Except once."

"And that was totally unplanned. It just happened."

"In my car."

"And we didn't discuss it beforehand as if we were planning a dinner party."

"Yeah, we did. We discussed doing it in the car or going to a motel."

"You know what I mean," she said. "It was spontaneous and natural."

Her tone was so exasperated he had to grin. She was right, he knew. Eagerness and excitement had never been a problem for either of them.

"And hot."

She sighed wearily as if unable to deny his words. "Yes. But this way, the way you're suggesting it now, is so... so clinical. That's what makes me suspicious. We never had that kind of choreographed lovemaking even at the worst times of our marriage."

"I would hardly call the circumstances now the best environment for choreographed lovemaking."

"I wouldn't, either, which makes this doubly suspicious."

"What if I told you I wanted you because I was lonely and scared? What if I said I wanted to wear you out so you'd go to sleep? So I could go out by myself and check out the contacts Johnny gave me?"

"The first I wouldn't believe. The second... well, yeah, given that long talk you had with Johnny and knowing you don't like my being here and your worry about Justin... then yes, that I can believe."

Relieved he didn't have to open up and elaborate on his loneliness and fear, he said, "Good choice."

He drank the rest of his wine, and pulled out of his wallet more than enough cash to cover the tab. Then he got to his feet, helped Abbie to hers and, taking her arm, led her to the restaurant door.

Once outside, he cupped the back of her neck and lowered his head, his mouth meeting hers in a lingering kiss. He drank in the taste of wine and willingness, for he knew she wanted him just as much as he wanted her. He knew it too damn well, and as their time together lengthened he knew he wasn't going to be able to keep his hands off her much longer. He lifted his mouth, deliberately ignoring the provocative wetness on her slightly opened lips.

Sighing, he said, "I planned to satisfy you, and then after you were asleep, I was going out to look around. There's just one minor problem."

"What's that?"

"It's going to make it tougher than hell to walk away from you when all this is over."

In their room a few minutes later, Burke watched her from where he'd sprawled on the bed. Admitting his weakness for her made him feel less like a cop and more like her husband. The hell of it was he liked having her here with him. He liked watching her, absorbing that elusive scent that always surrounded her, contemplating the satisfaction he knew he'd find making love to her. Crisis or not, his longings had to do with what they'd once had together.

He clasped his hands behind his head, her motions drawing his gaze. She'd changed into a short nightie. He could see the lace edging of the matching panties and couldn't help but smile. The top dipped low between her breasts, and her cleavage was tantalizingly visible.

He liked her brashness, her bold sureness of her effect on him. He extended a hand toward her, but she swept out of his reach and said primly, "I've concluded you're right. Making love would make our relationship very difficult once Justin is back home."

She moved toward the chair, which was still sitting by the window. "So you needn't worry," she added. "I'm sleeping here. You take the bed. I'll be quite comfortable."

"How about a compromise?"

She gave him a wary look. "What?"

"We'll both sleep in the chair and you can be on top. That way we'll have plenty of room."

Her look turned to a glare. "Very funny. But I know you, and all this silly sexual innuendo is just a ploy. If you really wanted me, you wouldn't be lying there watching me."

He pushed himself up and leaned against the headboard. "You think I don't want you?"

"I think you're up to something."

He lifted an eyebrow. "Well put. Come over here."

A flash of lightning scored the black sky followed by a crash of thunder. Abbie jumped.

"Abbie, come on, sweetheart."

"If I didn't know better, I'd think you arranged this."

"The lightning and thunder? Hardly." He extended his hand. "You know you hate it. Come here."

More lightning was followed by a close slam of thunder that sent her running to the side of the bed. But she didn't drop into his arms the way she'd done in the past. She just stood there, shivering, wrapping her arms around herself.

She ducked her head, her hair spilling over her face so that Burke couldn't see her eyes. He touched her hip, then her waist, coaxing her closer and finally drawing her down till she was sitting on the bed.

"Abbie—"

"No." She twisted out of his hold. "I'm not going to curl up in your arms because of a convenient thunderstorm."

"Convenient! It's damn *in*convenient. I planned to do some work tonight. This kind of weather will have everyone in some hole waiting for it to end."

"I know what you're doing. You're deliberately presenting me with what went wrong when we were married. You're methodically and carefully pointing out my suspicions of your motives. You want me to know that's why we can never be anything more to each other than Justin's parents."

Burke absorbed her words. Had he been doing that? At some deeper level was he trying to convince himself and her that too many things kept them apart? Or that what had brought them together—their missing son—was only a temporary joining, not the seeds of a new relationship?

He rolled to the other side of the bed and climbed out. He walked around the foot and moved to the window, where the rain lashed against the glass. He leaned one hand against the sill and considered his deep desire for her, his sudden realization of how damn lonely he was and if he simply admitted that, there would be a lot more honesty between them.

But he couldn't; he couldn't because he wasn't sure if what he felt was real or all tangled up in their shared worry about Justin. He feared it was more bonding in crisis than bonding a relationship.

He shoved his free hand through his hair in frustration. Only with Abbie could making love be so complicated.

CHAPTER SIX

ABBIE SHUDDERED.

Not at his long silence, but at the despair she sensed in him. She doubted he was even aware of it. Yet if she'd had to explain why she felt it was true, she'd have been hard-pressed for words. Instinct, she decided.

She wanted to cross the room and wind her arms around him. How much simpler that would be. She, too, realized that the physical side of their relationship was much simpler to deal with. Coming together in an intimate needful way was easily explained.

The deeper relationship, the one of trust and substance, was complicated. A different kind of commitment. It was more changeable, while at the same time its basis depended on solid trust. That foundation was what had been missing in their marriage.

Burke didn't turn around. A few raindrops splattered onto the sill. His stance was somewhat guarded, and he rubbed his hand across the back of his neck. He muttered something about not knowing his own mind or his own son, but she didn't catch it all.

"What?" she asked.

"Just thinking out loud."

He cursed then, but she knew it was directed at himself.

Finally, still leaning against the sill, he said, "The last five or six times I've been with Justin were some of the best times we've ever had. It hasn't been a lot of deep, serious stuff, just time together. I never had that with my old man. He either had an excuse or he was rushing off somewhere." Burke paused a few seconds, then continued, "After we were divorced, I vowed I'd never be too busy for Justin." He paused again, and now he looked at her. "As hard as this is to say, I have to admit I was skeptical about him running away. It just didn't sound like something Justin would do."

Confused, she asked, "But at the house when we were in his bedroom, you made it sound as if there might be a good reason. You didn't seem all that surprised."

"Abbie, you were worried and scared . . ."

"And you weren't?"

"Yeah, but I was also puzzled."

"You were trying to keep me from getting hysterical, weren't you? You knew that if I saw you all flustered and unsure, I wouldn't have been able to deal with it."

"Don't try to read my motives," he said, suddenly looking uncomfortable.

"Why not? You do it to me. You've always made me feel as if you know me better than I know myself."

Abbie took a blanket and wrapped it around her chilled body. She got up and began to pace. Her temper suddenly teetered on the edge and she wasn't certain why.

"It's true, Burke. Even before we were married you told me that it was a bad idea and that I wasn't going to be able to deal with your being a cop."

"That's not what I said. I said you had some idealistic vision that being married and having kids would make me give up the force and find a safe, less stressful job."

"Maybe I did," she said softly, knowing the real reason. She'd loved him and she'd wanted to make sure she didn't lose him.

She'd set her career aside for the first few years simply because being Burke's wife and Justin's mother were more important, and she'd felt completely fulfilled.

Burke had never laid out a list of rules as if he were king and she some servant. She'd loved his partnership attitude. But now she wondered if subconsciously, or perhaps even deliberately, she'd created her own rules, which she'd expected him to follow. His comment certainly indicated he believed she had.

Taking a calming breath, she said, "So what did you do all those years we were married, Burke? Weigh my words and wishes and then deliberately set about to do things differently?"

"This is a conversation and a situation I shouldn't have gotten into," he said irritably.

"Well, it's certainly a discussion you've always avoided."

Often she'd accused him of dodging any talk that involved his work or what he felt and thought deep inside. More of his compartment mentality, she supposed. Yet being with him now made it impossible for her to stop thinking about the gaps in their marriage. The gaps in trust when it came to his talking about his work, coming home frustrated and brooding in silence, closing her out when she tried to comfort him. She'd yearned to be there for him the same way other wives were for their husbands, but he'd never allowed it.

"Because I knew it would go where this one is going." Burke shook his head wearily. "An argument with no resolution and we'd just wind up in bed." In a low voice he said, "And right now that might solve one problem, but it would create a helluva lot of others."

They watched each other, their eyes locked in silent combat. Her breathing was rapid and she clutched the blanket more tightly and protectively around her.

Burke leaned his back against the window frame. He was still facing her, his eyes calculating, yet she saw something more. Her instinct again, perhaps, but she was sure some other emotion was there. Regret? Remorse?

She rubbed her eyes. What was the point in pursuing this? Burke wouldn't admit to regret or remorse for the mistakes of the past; no doubt he assumed she would then ask him a hundred more questions.

She felt rueful. He was right; she always had too many questions and not enough answers.

She decided to get back to the topic of Justin's running away. It was safer somehow. She felt more in control.

She asked, "What did you think when you heard Justin had run away?"

He seemed surprised at her sudden shift, but not sorry. "Honestly?"

She nodded.

"I was embarrassed as hell," he said. "Here I am a cop who's supposed to be on top of this kind of stuff, and I'm taken completely by surprise when my own kid takes off."

Slowly Abbie moved over to where he stood. "Come away from there," she urged, taking his arm. "I don't want you to get struck by lightning."

"You're not going to chew me out?"

"For being honest? No."

Without pulling the blanket away, he stepped toward her and drew her into his arms. He slid his fingers into her hair, tipped her head back and brushed his thumbs across her cheeks. "Before, you would have, you know."

"Would have what?"

"Chewed me out. Called me insensitive."

"Oh. You mean when we were still married." At his nod, she continued, "But then you wouldn't have been honest. You would've scowled and muttered something about statistics on runaways and that Justin didn't fit the profile."

"You know me too damn well."

"I was married to you."

He steadied her against him, her body fluid and warm. Abbie was aware that the crackling wire of tension between them in the past hours was dangerously close to snapping. Yet halting this easy and much-needed succor also felt wrong. Being in his arms felt simply too damn good, and she wasn't going to deny herself. She'd once been deeply in love with Burke, and at this particular moment those old feelings tugged at her again.

Lowering his mouth, he coaxed hers open and brushed her tongue with his. At her whimper, he did it again, then lowered one hand to her hip, drawing her closer. She released her hold on the blanket and he kicked it away before nestling her into the cove of his thighs.

They'd always had this mutual passion, and just as in the past, she let herself fall into that familiar abyss of sensation and pleasure. It felt right to let go. She wanted this. She knew she'd never stopped wanting Burke.

Her mouth close to his, she asked in a whisper, "Are you going to kiss me again?"

He grinned, softly blowing a wisp of her hair from her cheek. "I'm trying to keep some semblance of control."

"Why?" His heart beat hard against her breasts; the soft satin of her nightie that separated her from him soon became more of a nuisance than any sensual abrasion. "Are you afraid I'll read too much into it if we allow ourselves any intimacy?"

As if to defy her question, he tucked her even closer. She felt the length of him. Hard and warm. Steel heat and an erotic burning. She wanted to melt into him.

He murmured, "I'm afraid it would be too easy to make love and then believe we could take the next step of rebuilding our relationship after Justin is found."

He was right. Perhaps that was what she really wanted. To try again with Burke.

"Abbie, I don't want to pretend that making love now means I'm saying we could have a relationship later."

"I understand that," she said quickly. She knew that was what he wanted to hear. She *was* too vulnerable with Justin missing. Did making love mean she wanted to rekindle their relationship? It didn't have to.

"Being together now doesn't have to be complicated," she murmured.

He chuckled. "Not complicated? Just *kissing* you is complicated." Then to prove his point, he kissed her. Not lightly, not mouths brushing and tongues tasting, but with a consuming hunger that burst forth with scorching force. He explored her mouth with his tongue, moving and sliding with the kind of ease and sumptuousness he had always shown. Her hands gripped his waist at the same time as he cupped her bottom and rocked her pelvis against his in an erotic motion as old as time.

Abbie wanted him, desired him, needed him, and only her pride kept her from begging. Heated shimmers scurried down her spine, along with the sense of rightness, and yes, even the recklessness she'd always felt with Burke.

Perhaps it was the dangerous sexiness that rolled off him as if he'd owned the trait, perhaps that instinctive sensuality that was as much a part of him as his walk, his husky voice, his penetrating green eyes.

Burke lifted his mouth and drew in a long, deep breath. "Kissing you is powerful stuff," he said in a low, intense voice. "And when you're in this skimpy nightie..."

He backed away and looked at her. Not with a slow perusal, but with a covetous longing. He cupped her breasts, rubbing his thumbs over the hardened nipples, making her gasp. Then he slid his hands lower, over her stomach, lower still until his fingers feathered along the hem of her nightie.

Finally, while Abbie tried to control her rush of breathlessness, he moved his hand to the satin panel of her panties. She tried to draw back, to tamp down her arousal.

"Easy, easy..." Burke said.

"Don't. Please..."

"You're not afraid. Not you."

She shook her head, but the motion was a lie. She *was* afraid—afraid he wouldn't touch her. But she couldn't tell him that.

Then he cupped her. Abbie melted. Her body reached for his touch and pressed into it with a spiral of intensity that lifted her higher and higher. Her climax rushed through her, proving the power of his touch and the raw need within her that just a stroke of his palm could create. Her breath returned with a shudder as she sagged against him.

Burke simply held her. "Ah, Abbie..."

She was thankful for the darkness of the room. Rarely did she blush, but her cheeks flamed hotly.

"I didn't mean for that to happen. I mean, I didn't know it would. You must wonder—"

"Shh, don't. You don't need to explain desire." He didn't move his hand away, but gently held her.

Nerves jangling, thoughts scrambling, she said, "Please don't think I planned this."

"I don't."

"It's just that when you kiss me, I tend to..."

"Respond passionately."

But she didn't hear the soft understanding in his tone. My God, what kind of mother was she, anyway? Her son was missing and she was busy making love with her ex-husband!

Pulling out of Burke's arms, she picked up the blanket and put it on the bed. She pulled on her robe, belting it tightly around her.

"We've admitted we aren't going to attempt another relationship, and yet here we are..." Words failed her.

Burke folded his arms and eyed her with some amusement. "Here we are wanting each other."

"Yes."

"And you feel guilty about that?"

"Don't you?"

"Did it ever occur to you that this might be another way to deal with what's happened?"

"By having sex?"

"Why does that have to be any different from holding each other as we did last night?"

"Because it just is," she stated flatly, hating it when he got all reasonable and logical. She wished she could sail out of the room and pretend none of this had happened.

Burke shook his head. "Abbie, let me see if I have this straight. You think that if we don't make love, then Justin will turn up safe. If we do make love, then we don't deserve to find him because we took pleasure when we shouldn't have.''

She fiddled with the belt of the robe. He was right. She couldn't justify avoiding lovemaking because they should be spending their time worrying about Justin and Candy. Shouldn't she be so distracted by the events of the past twenty-four hours that sex would be the last thing on her mind? Was this flare-up of desire because this was Burke and there was a part of her that was eternally connected to him?

Or was it simply that deep inside she still loved him?

He continued, ''Making love isn't just for sex. Sometimes it's companionship. Sometimes it's to ease loneliness.''

''Maybe.''

''Now, having said that...'' Burke stepped back from her and turned once again to look out the window.

In those few tense seconds, Abbie knew there would be no further lovemaking between them that night. She told herself that was best and certainly smart and wouldn't cause complications later.

She sighed. ''I suppose I should say thank you.''

''Abbie, wanting each other and using that closeness to deal with the uncertainty of Justin is okay, but actually following through and making love is going to cause a helluva mess later.''

''Yes, of course, you're right.''

He shoved a hand through his hair, and for the first time Abbie saw his frustration.

''Look,'' he said. ''I take full responsibility for this. I started it in the restaurant.''

Did that mean he hadn't been serious about wanting her? Had the past hour been for the sole purpose of diverting their thoughts from Justin?

"No, it's fine, really." She turned so that he couldn't see the disappointment in her eyes. "I agree with you. Once Justin is found we'll be going back to our regular lives. If we were to start some kind of sexual relationship, it'd be very difficult to just put it aside."

He didn't say anything, and she wished she had the courage to swing around and look at him directly.

Finally he suggested, "Why don't you try and get some sleep? I'm going downstairs to see if Johnny has learned anything new."

Having said that, he pulled on his shirt and boots and left the room without waiting for her to argue or comment.

When the door was closed and she was sure she was safely alone, she covered her eyes with her hands and cried. Cried for the love she'd lost and for the love she'd never have again.

When Burke returned to the room, it was about ten o'clock, and she was curled in a ball in the middle of the bed. He went to the bed and pulled the quilt up around her shoulders. Then, moving quickly and quietly, he changed his clothes into snug jeans and a T-shirt displaying the logo of a heavy metal rock group.

He glanced at Abbie. She was still fast asleep. He crossed to her suitcase and rummaged through her things until he found her earrings. He slid the small hoop into his left ear, wincing a little. It had been weeks since he'd had an earring on, and the hole had closed somewhat. He removed his ID bracelet and dropped it on the dresser. He hadn't shaved since that morning, so his beard stubble gave him the unsavory look he wanted. Lastly he pulled on his leather jacket and tucked a small metal box into a pocket.

He uncapped the bottle of whiskey Johnny had given him and tipped the bottle to his mouth. The liquor burned, and he bared his teeth while the alcohol made its way down his throat. He took another sip, this one not so biting. After a final swig he recapped the bottle. His purpose was to smell like booze, but also not to wince if he had to pour down a straight shot.

He walked back to the bed and stared down at Abbie. Slowly he leaned over and lifted her hair so that he could kiss her neck. She stirred.

"Easy, Abbie..."

"Burke...don't go..."

She rolled to her back, her hand sliding up his thigh. He grabbed her wrist, stopping the motion before she reached her intended target.

"You're a dangerous distraction, Abbie Wheeler."

"Please don't get hurt."

"You can reward me when I get back." With that, he bent low, turned her palm up and pressed his mouth into the center. He curled her fingers in and then tucked her hand beneath the quilt.

"I wish you wouldn't go," she whispered with a huskiness that made him exert all his control not to pull her up into his arms and run his hands down her body, luxuriating in the smoothness of her skin, memorizing every curve.

Arousing thoughts about her were as dangerous as playing with explosives. Already he dreaded walking away when their search for Justin was over, when their son was home safe. Or maybe he dreaded that he couldn't ever put her out of his life. Justin was and always would be a factor, but Abbie was just as much a factor.

He bent his head and brushed her lips with his.

"You've been drinking."

"Trying to get rid of the taste of you," he murmured, and kissed her once again. "It doesn't work."

"I'm in your blood, Burke Wheeler."

"Yeah, that's the trouble."

He stood and for a moment drank in the sleepy eyes, the mussed hair, the slightly swollen lips. He slowly pulled on his leather gloves. Then he reached down, slipped the covers back and cupped first one breast, then the other. At last, reluctantly, he straightened. "Sleep tight."

"Be careful."

"Always."

THE NIGHT IS its own master.

That had been a saying Burke had heard during his rookie days on the streets. Step into the dark alley, the unlit corner, the shadow of a building, and greet the grizzly and the nasty. There was something about the dark, the shadows, the lack of light, that brought out the demons.

Here in the coolness of the April night, Sade Court rocked and rolled with a bald ruckus that made him very aware of his back and made his thoughts churn with terror for his son.

He pushed open the door to Raffles, a corner bar where Johnny said "business" was conducted in Sade Court. Despite the blue, smoky air and the topless dancer on a slowly turning wooden riser, the bar didn't look quite as seedy as he'd expected.

The music ground out from a cheap sound system, and the young woman gyrating could have been no more than twenty, but with moves and, Burke guessed, knowledge that went far beyond her years.

He made his way to the bar. He signaled the bartender; the man looked more like a prize fighter who should have quit while he was ahead.

"Yeah? What's it gonna be?"

Burke met his gaze directly. "Jack Daniel's. Stogie said to ask for the stuff you didn't water."

Stogie Snyder had been a dealer Burke had helped send to prison during the time he'd worked Sade Court a few years ago. He was still serving time, but Johnny had said that Stogie continued to command great respect among the small- and big-timers in Sade Court.

The bartender studied Burke, his eyes sharp and suspicious. Burke knew the cautionary stare. He guessed the questions in the bartender's mind: Was this guy with the liquor-control board or was he really a pal of Stogie's?

Apparently deciding to test it, the bartender reached for another bottle. Burke shook his head. "The fourth one from the left."

The bartender gave him a hard look but took the fourth bottle. "How you want it?"

"Three fingers, no ice."

He poured, then pushed the glass at Burke.

Burke took a sip. It hadn't been watered. "Stogie said I could find Jeep here."

Again the bartender hesitated, glancing down the bar. Gesturing with just a nod, he said, "Third stool from the wall."

Burke picked up his bourbon and moved in the direction the bartender had indicated. Two men stood talking to Jeep. One wore a lot of gold chains and the other wore a hat with enough feather plumes to cover the topless dancer.

God, he thought, nothing like being obvious. It was a side of the underworld Burke had never fully understood. Men who wanted to be unknown, invisible and out of sight dressed so that every eye was drawn to them.

Jeep was not one of those, however. He looked so ordinary he would never be the one described if a cop asked a passerby who he'd seen. Burke knew immediately that Jeep was also the most dangerous.

Jeep bounced and swayed to the raucous music. Burke set his drink on the bar and slid onto the stool next to Jeep. For a moment he watched the dancer, who was finishing up her number. He felt Jeep's eyes on him before he spoke.

"Saw you come in. You new around here?"

"Yeah, came to see you. Stogie says you're the guy in charge."

He gave Burke a long look before turning aside. "I'm busy."

Burke shrugged and reached for his drink. Jeep said something to the two other men. They laughed, but a few seconds later walked away.

Jeep leaned closer to Burke. "Okay, man, talk. Who are you and what do you want?"

"Heard you're the man with eyes under the street."

Jeep sat back as if contemplating the stranger and what kind of trouble he might cause. "Who the hell are you?"

Burke shrugged, watching the dancer step down from the wooden riser. "I was told names get you wasted in Sade Court."

Jeep snapped his fingers, and a man who outweighed Burke by thirty pounds lumbered over.

"Yeah, Jeep," the flunky mumbled. "Saw him come in. Moves like a cat. Empty eyes."

"Check him for a wire and a piece."

Burke stood while the big man patted him down. He stopped when he came to Burke's pocket.

He dipped his fingers in and pulled out the tiny metal box. "What's this?"

"Don't shake it."

"What is it?"

"High-tech ammo."

"Nitro?"

"More powerful. It explodes if exposed to uneven temperatures. Like now, you holding it in your hand so that one side is warm and the other side is cool."

The flunky paled as if suddenly presented with a live cobra. "Careful, it can be unstable, too."

Jeep frowned, glancing from the tiny box to Burke. "You're bluffing."

"Could be. You'll know for sure if you open it."

No one moved.

"So how come you can carry it around and it don't hurt you?"

"I invented it."

Jeep and the goon looked at each other.

Jeep said, "Give it back to him. Carefully."

"But, Jeep—"

"Do it!"

Burke took the metal box from the flunky and very slowly eased it back into his pocket.

"Clear out," Jeep said to the bigger man. He backed away, mumbling about the old days when bombs were big enough to see.

Once again alone with Burke, Jeep said, "So how come I ain't seen you around?" It was more an observation than a question.

"Did some federal time."

"What'd they get you for?"

Again he shrugged.

"Dealin', huh?"

"Mostly settin' up the squid, but I got suckered by a fed. One stupid mistake and it was all over."

Jeep peered at him. "Gotta learn how to spot the cops. They think they're so goddamned smart, but most are dummies." He glanced up and motioned toward the door. "Like that stupid bastard over there.

Probably some guy who wants to be a hero in his department. Figures he'll come down here, shake down some of the riffraff and then claim a big bust for the TV cameras.''

Burke turned and looked in the direction Jeep pointed. The dim lighting and the heavy haze of smoke made visibility tough, but Burke saw a man in a suit and tie working his way to the bar. Whoever he was, Burke knew he wasn't a cop. The clothes weren't the giveaway, but the walk, the careless manner and the obvious out-of-his-element attitude were.

Jeep said, "So you got snagged."

"Big time."

"Got any names besides Stogie's?"

Burke thought quickly, then remembered Muggy Greene, a Boston hood who'd moved his operation into New Jersey. "Muggy said you were the man to see in the Court."

Jeep lit up as if someone had just told him he'd won the lottery. "No kiddin'?"

"He said you can be a smart-ass, but you own the street."

"Muggy said that about me?" He preened, and Burke had to use all his willpower not to smile. These guys were all the same. Tell them one of their nasty acquaintances had given them a compliment, and they acted as if they'd been awarded a medal of honor.

Burke had witnessed the same reaction in his old man. The names Burke heard dropped were never the honest, hardworking guys, but the shills and overage

punks who got lucky and rich and too damn powerful.

"Hey, Muggy don't mess with dummies," Jeep responded, relaxing a little. "So what you want from
me?"

"Any new squid on the line?"

"Like in fresh-faced and eager?"

"You got it."

Jeep described one kid who could give him contacts. "He hangs out at the Merry-Go-Round. Check
about seven tomorrow night. On the carousel by the
outside horses. Goes by the name of Glassy. You'll see
him."

Burke nodded.

Jeep warned. "Forget the squidettes. Tail does good
working the mattresses, doin' the johns, but they're
lousy on the street."

Burke shuddered but managed to show the expression Jeep expected.

Jeep grinned. "Women today gettin' too much
power. We gotta keep 'em where they belong. In the
sack and happy to comply."

Just in the way stray thoughts can snag and bind,
Burke thought of Abbie, but not in any docile way.
She might be in the sack and on more than one occa-
sion happy to comply, but when it came to indepen-
dence and handling herself, Burke knew she'd leave
most men in the dust. Nor could he honestly eliminate himself as one who was awed and enchanted by
her.

Burke and Jeep exchanged some departing words, and Burke tossed a few bills onto the bar.

Jeep pushed them back to him. "For Muggy's friend, it's taken care of." Burke nodded and moved toward the door.

"Wheeler! I've been looking for you." It was the man in the suit and tie.

Burke swung around. For a minute he thought he was seeing things, but he wasn't. Unfortunately.

The man in the suit was Harvey Kaufman.

CHAPTER SEVEN

BURKE'S INSTINCT kicked in.

Desperation born of necessity and the need to protect the setup he'd just painstakingly erected made his decision. What in hell Kaufman thought he was going to do in Sade Court was a question for later.

Harvey's face reddened and he sputtered, "Damn you, Wheeler, you should've—"

But before he could finish, Burke slugged him.

A punch to the gut, then when Harvey grabbed his stomach and tried to straighten, Burke landed a smooth uppercut that crumpled him to the floor. The bar area around them cleared of customers as Burke stood spread-legged over Kaufman. He didn't relish the heat he'd take later for this, but he knew he'd had no choice. If Kaufman had identified him, the two of them would be dead meat before the hour was over.

Jeep's flunky lumbered to Burke's side as if action such as he'd just witnessed wasn't worth getting into a sweat over. Others milled around. Finally Jeep appeared, his fingers working to adjust the knot on his tie, a smile playing on his mouth.

He glanced at Kaufman's crumpled body. "Couldn't resist, huh?"

"The son of a bitch insulted me," Burke said, knowing that in this kind of crowd an insult was as good an excuse as any to take a guy out.

Jeep shrugged. "As I said, some cops are dumb." He signaled to his minion. "Take care of him."

Burke shook his head. "Let me handle him."

"Gonna blow him up?"

"I'm gonna make sure he doesn't bother me again."

Jeep's eyes gleamed. "I could use a guy like you. When you get done doin' whatever you have to do, we'll talk."

"Sure. Sounds good."

Again Jeep snapped his fingers at the flunky. "Help the man get the garbage out of here. Use the back door. Never know if the cops are cruisin' the neighborhood. He don't need to run into 'em."

The burly man came over, but Burke already had Kaufman up. His head wobbled back and his eyes were glazed. How long it would take for him to fully regain consciousness, Burke didn't know. All he knew was he had to move and move now.

At the back door, the flunky said, "You sure you don't need no help? I hate cops, and icin' one would be a real pleasure."

"No thanks. This one's all mine."

Outside, Burke walked, gripping and dragging the stumbling Kaufman past a Dumpster and into an alley. He hauled him into the shadows and leaned him against the side of a building. Burke took a few deep breaths and decided that for a guy who played so much tennis Kaufman should've been more limber. He started to sag and Burke grabbed him.

"Kaufman, wake up."

The man mumbled something incoherent.

Burke considered taking him back to Johnny's, but immediately dropped that idea. For one thing he didn't want Kaufman to know where he and Abbie were staying, and for another he didn't know what in hell he'd do with him once he had him there.

Burke stared at him, his eyes narrowing as he considered possibilities. First of all he'd better find out what Harvey had expected to accomplish by parading around in this hellhole. He'd looked as much out of place as Burke had looked standing in their gold-inlaid living room.

Burke smacked him on the cheeks. "Come on, Kaufman. Time to join the living."

Harvey's head lolled to the side and Burke saw the blood around his mouth. His eyes rolled and then tried to focus. "What happened?" He gulped, swaying and then clutched his stomach. "I think I'm gonna be sick."

Burke stepped back while Harvey parted company with his last meal. Afterward he wheezed and shuddered, steadying himself against the building.

Burke reached into Harvey's pocket and pulled out a handkerchief. "Here. Wipe your mouth."

Harvey did as he was told, wincing as he rubbed at his cut mouth. Finally he raised his head and looked at Burke uncomprehendingly. Then he stared at the smear of blood on the white cloth in his hand, and at last his head jerked up, his eyes reminding Burke of swollen bugs.

Weakly he stammered, "You . . . you hit me."

Burke glared at him, his voice low and sharp. "What in God's name are you doing here?"

Harvey blinked, touched the cloth to the corner of his mouth once more and then worked his jaw gingerly. After making sure none of his teeth were loose, he scowled as if finally getting events back into focus.

"I'm looking for my daughter. Why didn't you call me and let me know you were coming here? I waited to hear something, and when I didn't, I called the police. I certainly can't thank you for giving me any information."

"That's because I don't have any. I don't even have any about Justin."

Harvey stared in obvious disbelief, then tried to push Burke out of the way. "Maybe you want to hang around places like that bar and talk to all your sleazy friends, but I plan to find out where my daughter is."

Burke didn't budge. "Kaufman, get real. Do you think you can just walk up to some kid or some bartender, show them a picture of Candy and they'll give you directions to find her? No one in Sade Court wants to help you. They couldn't care less if Candy is here, bleeding to death in some alley or playing the whore."

Even in the darkness, Burke saw the color drain from his face.

"You bastard!" Harvey sputtered. "How dare you talk that way about my daughter!"

"I'm not talking about your daughter. I'm talking about what goes on here, how totally soulless the place is. This isn't TV with all the bad words cleaned out."

A horn honked near the front entrance of Raffles, and Burke frowned. It was three quick honks—like a signal.

He was about to step out of the alley when Harvey said, "That's Ginger." He drew himself up. "I told her to wait in the car. She's probably worried."

"You brought your wife up here?" Burke asked incredulously.

Harvey sniffed and then neatly folded his handkerchief. "Ginger is very good at sensing places Candy has been."

Burke lowered his head and shook it slowly. "Shit."

Harvey finally pulled himself away from the wall of the building.

He shook a warning fist at Burke. "You just wait, Wheeler. I think I have a very good case for police brutality."

"Kaufman?"

"What?"

"If I hadn't hit you, you'd be occupying a Dumpster right now, so shut the hell up."

Harvey opened and closed his mouth, reminding Burke of a fish, then managed to get out, "You can't talk to me like—"

Burke clamped his hand over Harvey's mouth, ignoring his bulging and furious eyes. "Let's go and find your old lady before someone hijacks her and her car."

He moved out of the alley with Harvey in tow. Burke prayed that Jeep or one of his flunkies didn't decide to appear in the doorway of Raffles.

Harvey's wife and his Mercedes were parked under a streetlight. Still astonished at their total ignorance of the dangers, Burke decided she must have read the manual about parking in a well-lit area.

He gripped the still-wobbly Harvey, and when they got to the car, Ginger Kaufman gasped. "Oh, my poor darling, what have you done to him?" Then she looked fully at Burke, recognition coming slowly. She frowned and then shuddered. "My God—"

"Unlock the back door."

She quickly did as she was told.

Burke shoved her husband inside and moved around to the driver's side. He slid behind the wheel, jammed the car into gear and with a squeal of tires did a U-turn in the middle of the street.

He didn't turn on the headlights and ignored Ginger's shriek when a car pulled out in front of him. He jerked the wheel, missing the other vehicle by mere inches. He drove a few blocks until he came to an all-night convenience store.

"Stay here," he ordered, getting out and slamming the door before either could argue with him. He went to the outside pay phone and punched in Johnny's number.

"Burke, thank God. I was getting worried. Everything okay?"

"If you call almost getting wasted because of a couple of dumb civilians, yeah, I'm okay." He filled Johnny in on the details. "Do me a favor. Wake up Abbie and tell her I need to talk to her."

"Hang on."

Burke glanced at the car and the two figures huddled inside.

Poor fools, he thought. Maybe he'd been too hard on them, but why in hell they thought they'd find Candy with the ease of asking directions to the airport just blew his mind.

"Burke?" He could hear the anxiety in her voice. "Where are you? You're not hurt, are you?"

"Sweetheart, I think I just might have been safer in bed with you."

"This is not the time for jokes. What happened?"

"The Kaufmans are here."

"Candy's parents? Where? How?"

Quickly he filled her in on what Harvey had told him.

"I have a feeling that when they learned you were with me, they thought Sade Court was like the movies instead of real life."

"Are they okay?"

"No. They're in the way, and I need them out of here so they don't get hurt." Burke paused a moment. "Abbie, I want you to take them back home. I don't trust them to go on their own and there isn't anyone else."

A few seconds went by before she asked, "Where are you?"

He gave her the directions to the convenience store. "My keys are on the dresser," he told her.

"I need to get some clothes on, then I'll be right there."

"Thanks, sweetheart."

He hung up the receiver and stared at the phone as though waiting for her to call back and give him an argument. She hadn't argued, she hadn't asked any questions. She'd simply agreed. He shook his head, amazed and pleased and impressed.

He walked back to the car and climbed into the front. Ginger had moved to the back seat, where her husband slumped into the brown leather cushions, moaning. She cradled him as she would a baby, murmuring soothing and encouraging words.

Burke said, "Abbie is going to drive you back home."

As if suddenly realizing how wimpy he looked curled up in his wife's arms, Harvey pushed away from her. "Don't hover, Ginger."

She looked hurt.

Harvey ignored her. "Listen, Wheeler, I don't appreciate you riding roughshod over me. I came here to find my daughter."

Burke reminded himself that Harvey's actions, while stupid, were also what any parent in his situation might have done. Burke just didn't want to be too understanding, otherwise Harvey might get the idea he should stay.

"I know you and your wife are worried, but your being here is a problem. Guys in that bar thought you were a cop." Burke left out the word "dumb," chalking his reasoning up to the guilt he felt for blasting the guy because he'd acted exactly as what he was—a worried father looking for his lost child.

Harvey straightened. Burke swore he saw a slight preening.

With a sense of wonderment, Harvey asked, "They thought I was a cop?"

"Yeah, and they wanted to take you out."

He frowned. "Take me out? What—"

"Kill. It means kill."

Ginger gasped and her eyes grew big as saucers.

"You mean like in those contracts where they hire some goon to come in and do away with you? That's what they wanted to do with me?" he asked as if he'd been chosen for some honor.

Ginger clutched him. "Harvey, darling!"

Burke smiled to himself. Good old Harvey. He actually had a fantasy about being a cop and doing dangerous stuff.

"Right," Burke said, "and you sure don't want that to happen." His tone was grave. "I know Ginger agrees that the best place for you both is back home. I promise you I'll call when I have something. In fact, I'll have Abbie keep in touch just so you know what kind of progress we're making."

"Okay," Harvey said. He touched his lip. "I guess I've had about enough action."

Headlights flashed across the parking lot and Burke recognized his car. He got out when Abbie stopped a few spaces away. Seconds later he slid into the passenger seat and before he got the door closed she was in his arms.

As he held her, he decided this was definitely one of the things he'd really missed about being married to her. As much as they'd fought over his work, she'd always rushed into his arms the moment he came in the door.

"Abbie, I'm okay," he murmured, drinking in her warmth and scent and the realization that the longer it took to find Justin, the harder walking away from her was going to be.

If tonight had shown him anything, it was that his worry about Harvey getting hurt was minuscule compared to the fear of Abbie getting hurt. His decision to leave her behind this evening had been dead-on.

He acknowledged that she was probably safe at Johnny's, but the new tip about this guy Glassy and his own exposure to Jeep had changed the circumstances. Even as Burke held her, he realized how little control he had over her actions. He didn't want her where she was in danger, but at the same time she filled the hole in his own life.

In the past few hours, his resolve to keep her out of his thoughts and heart had substantially unraveled. His desire for her had caused him to be distracted and unfocused. That wasn't her fault, but his, and now, with Kaufman here, he faced potential chaos.

He should've left orders that Kaufman not be told where they were. Stupid error, he decided grimly. The kind made when a cop wasn't totally focused on what he was doing.

Then again, he thought darkly, this near disaster had cleared his thoughts with remarkable swiftness.

Sliding his hands into Abbie's hair, he held her head against him, relishing the warm, sweet feel of her. He thought about her staying with him.

Should Jeep see her with him, he'd jump to the obvious conclusion that she was his girlfriend. If she was a policewoman, that would be an advantage, for she'd know how to protect herself while she assisted in the search for Justin. But she wasn't. She was a civilian like Harvey Kaufman, and look how *he'd* screwed up. Burke wasn't going to let her put herself in that kind of danger, even though he recognized she was a lot smarter than old Harvey.

So clearly, Abbie, too, was better off at home. Maybe this incident with the Kaufmans would convince her of that. After all, since she was willing to take them home, she might be able to be talked into staying there, too.

She drew slightly away from him, her eyes luminous in the dim light. "Johnny said you sounded furious."

She ran her hands over him as if checking for wounds. He gripped her wrists and stopped her. "Abbie, this is going to get risky." He told her what he'd had to do to Harvey.

"You punched him!"

"Yeah. Things are heating up, and I don't want you to get caught up in anything."

She looked at him, her thoughts revealed in her expression. Burke knew then that, at best, her compliance on the phone had been temporary. Perhaps a willingness to give him the benefit of the doubt until she could learn exactly what he had in mind.

She pulled sharply away from him. "You don't just want me to take them home. You want me to stay there, don't you?"

"I don't want you to get hurt. I don't know what in hell is gonna happen now that I've made some contacts, but more important, I haven't the vaguest idea if any of this will help us find Justin.''

"Burke, I know you too well. If this was a waste of time, you wouldn't be doing it.''

"You're wrong. A lot of what I do can't be measured by the time it takes. It's a painstaking process of choice and elimination. I could be up here for months.''

"And you think I can just go back home, go to work and wait for your phone calls?'' She regarded him with a look that dared him to argue. It was clear she believed he didn't understand the way she felt.

A raw tenseness bristled between them.

"Why does that sound familiar, Burke? I'm supposed to stay home and not worry, as if you made doughnuts for a living or something.''

He closed his eyes and sank back in the seat. "I don't want to argue with you, Abbie.''

"I know you don't. You want me to do just what you expect Harvey to do. Obey you and not hassle you with questions you don't want to answer.'' She took a huge breath. "But there's a major difference between this time and all the other times I stayed home and fretted. Not only is Justin involved, which is reason enough for me to want to be here, but *I'm no longer your wife.* I don't have to do what you tell me.''

You didn't always do what I told you when we were married, Burke thought ruefully, but he kept the thought to himself. No sense in throwing gasoline on the fire.

He did, however, damn himself for allowing her to talk him into bringing her here in the first place. Civilians in police situations were always loose cannons. And then there was all that sexual byplay and the total stupidity he'd shown by admitting his desire for her. How much simpler if his feelings for her were as clear as his cold logic.

He shuddered to think of where he'd be and what they'd be doing if Harvey hadn't shown up. He *knew*. And his body did, too, proving it by reacting in an entirely too-predictable way. All the more reason she shouldn't be here.

"I'm not telling you, Abbie, I'm pleading with you."

"For my own good?"

"Of course for your own good. What other reason would I have?"

"That you know something and you don't want to tell me."

Her eyes bored into him in seconds of expanding silence.

"There *is* something, isn't there?" she persisted. "Maybe whatever you're not telling me is the same reason you want the Kaufmans out of here. Is it?"

She gripped his shirt as if suddenly her worst nightmare had come true and he'd been responsible. Like watching the evolution of horror, Burke saw her face turn ashen. He was about to deny the direction he knew her thoughts had taken, but it was too late.

"My God, they're dead!" she gasped. "Justin and Candy are dead, aren't they?"

"No!"

But she didn't seem to hear him. Her voice rose into hysteria. *"Justin is dead!"*

Burke wrapped his hands around her upper arms and shook her. "No! Justin isn't dead."

But he might as well have saved his breath. "How do you know?" she said. "You don't know. You're just saying that because it's what I want to hear. I hate you. I hate you. This is all your fault!"

Her scatter-shot emotions had him trying to fill in the blanks. "Abbie, stop it!"

She pushed at him, her fists pummeling his chest. "You were never there for us. Not emotionally. We were never more important than your damn job. You never shared with me. Even when I wanted to have a baby, you never acted as if you wanted one. You always kept yourself encased in that separate compartment away from us. Now God knows what's happened to Justin, and now, damn you, you're doing it again. Trying to send me away, ignoring my right to know about my own son. You think you have the right to control everything. Well, you don't! Damn you, you don't!"

Burke stared at her, the outburst drenching him like a bucket of cold water. Her words poured through him and summarized in a bizarre way the deep divisions between them.

"Damn you, damn you..." Her arms worked frantically against his grip on her arms. "I hate you, Burke Wheeler," she cried. "I hate you—"

Burke slapped her, the sound sharp and explosive in the close interior of the car. She went totally still, her eyes so wide the white seemed to drown the blue. Then she raised her hands and covered her face, her body losing its rigidity as if all her fight had suddenly leaked out.

He pulled her into his arms and rubbed his hands up and down her back. She shivered and curled close against him. "Please tell me the truth, *please,*" she begged in a resigned hollow monotone.

Burke tipped her face to the light and whispered, "Do you honestly think I would be sitting here calmly if I thought Justin was dead?"

She took a shuddering breath. "I—I don't know."

"You don't know?" Astonishment made him tighten his jaw.

"How would I? You were never that enthusiastic about having Justin in the first place. Even when I told you I was pregnant, you just stood and stared at me for a long time as if you wished it hadn't happened."

"Not because I didn't want him. It was me, Abbie. I wasn't sure if I was capable of being a good father—God knows I sure didn't have much of an example to follow. I was having a helluva time being a husband, and a kid just seemed like a massive hurdle I wasn't sure I could manage."

"I was afraid our marriage was headed for trouble, and I thought a baby—"

"Saving a marriage with a kid?"

"Desperation doesn't always see the cool logic in things. Sometimes desperation makes for desperate decisions."

"Yeah, well, great as Justin is, he couldn't save our marriage. We never should've gotten married in the first place. You know that and I know that."

She shrank back as if he'd spit on her.

"Abbie, look, I'm sorry. God, how in hell did we get into this argument?"

She shook her head, obviously not wanting to accept his apology. "You let me think you wanted me to come here to drive the Kaufmans home when the real truth is that they were the perfect excuse to get rid of me, too." She sagged in the seat and lowered her head.

"And because I don't want any of you hurt," Burke protested. "Because worrying about civilians is distracting and can louse up even the most careful investigation... Oh hell." A dark sense of despair and frustration slid through his thoughts, but he shoved it away. This wasn't the time. Getting Abbie and the Kaufmans back to the safety of their homes was what mattered at the moment.

Abbie shifted away from him, picked up her purse and reached for the door handle.

In a cool, detached voice, she said, "I appreciate your concern for my safety, but I'm not staying home. I'll be back sometime tomorrow. As long as I'm home I'm going to check on a few things. Do you need anything?"

She might as well have been talking to a stranger.

"Yeah, I need you to not come back here."

"That wasn't one of the choices."

"I was afraid of that."

She opened the door and the dome light came on. Burke wished he hadn't looked at her. Her eyes were clear and direct, her body language closed to any suggestion he might make.

In a resigned voice, he said, "Will Gagne is off duty, but call the station. The desk sergeant will arrange for someone to bring you back here."

"I'm perfectly capable of driving myself."

"We don't need two cars up here."

The moment he said it, he realized how irrelevant the comment was. His frustration, his fear for Justin and this seesaw relationship with Abbie had him talking without thinking. Abbie clearly had no intention of paying his words any heed.

"Good night, Burke," she said, and with that, she got out of the car and walked to the Kaufmans' Mercedes. She opened the driver's-side door and climbed in.

Burke watched her turn and say a few words to the distraught couple, then she started the engine.

If she'd just driven away, that would've been one thing. Or if she'd given him a haughty look, he could've at least assumed she felt something, even if it was anger.

But she looked right through him as if he wasn't there. As if he was just a guy sitting in a nearby car.

Burke watched until the taillights disappeared, then moved over to the driver's seat and turned on the ignition. He glanced at the clock. *You're a fool, Wheeler. And more than that you'll be setting yourself up for a helluva fight.*

Yet it would be almost eighteen hours before he could make the contact at the Merry-Go-Round. Maybe once Abbie had driven the Kaufmans home, she'd have had time to cool down and listen to reason.

Burke followed the signs to the interstate.

On one level he told himself he needed to explain the misunderstandings between them.

On another level he wanted to clear the air once and for all.

On an even deeper level he wanted to take her to bed.

This time, however, the force of that knowledge hit in places other than his gut. It seared his heart and soul.

He grimaced. He should stop now before it was too late. Take the next turn and go back to Johnny's. But he didn't. All those layers of thought narrowed down to one issue.

Abbie. His relationship with Abbie. And with that realization he knew he was in enormous emotional trouble.

CHAPTER EIGHT

"OH, ABBIE, I just can't help wondering if going home is the right thing to do," Ginger said anxiously.

Abbie glanced sympathetically into the rearview mirror at the woman's worried face. Despite the events of the past hour, Ginger looked better than she had when Abbie had talked to her in the Kaufmans' living room the other day. At some point she'd obviously faced the reality that Candy had indeed run away.

"I know how you feel, Ginger. Waiting is really hard."

"We should be *doing* something," Ginger wailed. "Poor Candy. She could be hurt or at the mercy of some terrible people."

Abbie bristled but then realized Ginger wasn't being specific. She was just expressing a mother's natural concern for her daughter. Abbie said, "If Candy is with Justin, I'm sure she's all right."

"You know for certain she's with your boy?" Harvey asked, leaning over the back of the seat.

Yes, Abbie thought, she was ninety percent certain they were together, a conclusion based on Justin's shoplifting the pregnancy-test kit. It didn't mean Candy was pregnant; perhaps she just wanted to be sure she wasn't. Ruefully Abbie realized that Burke would call that overly optimistic. Still, it was possible. And there was also the possibility that the baby wasn't Justin's. That he and Candy were just friends.

She grimaced as she thought of Burke's reaction if she said that. He'd give her one of his raised-eyebrow, get-real looks and say bluntly, "Friends? You know better than that. With few exceptions male and females mate. They don't form platonic relationships."

Gripping the wheel more tightly, she slowed down for the exit ramp off the interstate. Justin as a father was such a foreign concept she'd made up her mind it couldn't be possible. The empty condom box certainly indicated he was no virgin, but it also showed his good sense. My God, was she really rationalizing something that, deep down, worried and scared her?

"Abbie, you're awfully quiet," Ginger said, leaning forward and touching Abbie's shoulder. "You're not falling asleep at the wheel, are you? That happened to our neighbor and he ended up driving into someone's picture window. Remember that, Harvey? Poor Arthur. He wasn't hurt, but he was so embarrassed."

Abbie grimaced. "No, I'm wide awake. In answer to your question, Harvey...since we haven't found them, I can't be totally sure, but as Burke said, two runaways who went to the same school, had some classes together and disappeared at the same time would indicate that they're together."

The Kaufmans asked more questions and then Harvey related in great detail his experience at Raffles. Ginger was properly shocked. Abbie had no doubt Harvey was revising the events a little. She was grateful that the direction of the conversation kept her mind off the way she'd left Burke.

But soon the recollection of his phone call and request for her to drive the Kaufmans back to Rhode Island for their safety focused her thoughts on Burke's other, more personal, reason for his request. Getting her out of Sade Court.

Apart from both of them struggling with their unexpected sexual attraction, she knew Burke didn't like her being there with him. She could accept concern for her safety, but she knew from her experience with Burke in the past that he didn't like to have to account for his whereabouts and what he was doing. He'd had that attitude when they were married. While his police work was often undercover, therefore shrouded in secrecy, there'd always been a darker part of Burke that no one touched. Tonight, when she'd awakened just before he'd left for Raffles, she'd felt that dark presence. Oddly it had excited rather than frightened her. She hadn't yet figured out why. But when he put on his gloves before he touched her, she'd sensed he'd stepped into that dark persona where touching anything clean needed gloves.

After he'd left the room, she'd found herself aroused. Not surprising, given her reawakened feelings for Burke, but she'd been determined to keep those feelings in perspective.

Truthfully, she'd been rather proud of herself and her self-control. Yes, in the past few hours, there'd been a few kisses and some sexual teasing, but considering the grim circumstances that had brought them together, those lighter moments had offered a measure of relief.

But she didn't dare take them seriously. Burke's getting tangled up with her again was preposterous. He'd been very clear about why their marriage hadn't worked. Giving their relationship another try because they'd gotten close during a stressful time would be the height of insanity.

Abbie sighed. How could two people have left so much unresolved? For surely tonight's confrontation proved they had done just that. Arguments, accusations and barbs thrown back and forth—admittedly most by her—had accomplished nothing.

Abbie switched on her turn signal and slowed down. Silence had dominated much of the last few miles. Harvey had fallen asleep and Ginger held him, patting his back.

"Abbie?" she said just as the car swung into a turn.

Abbie glanced in the rearview mirror, and this time saw that Ginger's eyes were glistening with tears.

Before Abbie could ask what was the matter, Ginger gave a sob and said, "I'm so frightened for Candy and Justin."

"I am, too," Abbie admitted. She smiled understandingly at the distressed woman.

"But you seem so strong and...and together. At the house you were completely calm while I was still trying to deny anything had happened. And I know I've let Candy down."

"Let Candy down? I don't understand."

Ginger dabbed at her eyes with a tissue, then shook her head as if whatever was bothering her had become an unbearable burden.

"I have to tell you. I know I should've said something before."

Abbie felt real alarm. "Said something before? What is it, Ginger?"

The woman's mouth trembled, but she lifted her chin as if to say she'd come this far and couldn't back down now.

On a shaky breath, she whispered, "I knew Candy was seeing Justin."

Abbie stared in the mirror a moment too long, so that when she returned her gaze to the road ahead, she had to jam on the brakes when a car pulled out in front of her.

Gathering her wits, she said, "You knew they were dating? But at the house you acted as if you'd never heard of Justin."

"I know."

"It was all an act?"

"No, no, not all of it," Ginger said desperately. "I really didn't believe Candy had run away. I was sure there was some other explanation. When you came in I was honestly surprised to see you. Oh God—" she lowered her head, shaking it back and forth "—it was as if there were two voices inside me. One denied everything I was hearing, and the other simply dismissed what you and Harvey and the police were saying."

Abbie felt a rising frustration and anger. "You should've said something. We might be closer to finding them if you had."

"But if I'd said anything then, there would've been more questions and Harvey would've been furious. He's been pressuring Candy for weeks to accept a date from the son of one of his business partners. He's a nice enough boy, but Candy wasn't interested. I told Harvey we couldn't arrange dates for her, but he was adamant she not end up with . . ."

"Riffraff like Justin," Abbie finished for her. Her stomach was tied in knots.

"Yes."

"But she did." Abbie thought of the pregnancy-test kit. "Do you know how long they'd been seeing each other?"

"I believe the first time she mentioned him was around St. Patrick's Day. She said she was going to the parade with him. She told me that he was in her chemistry class and that he was a hunk and totally wonderful. Those were her exact words."

Abbie couldn't recall any major attitude changes in Justin. And except for climbing in his bedroom window that time, there'd been little change in his behavior. Either that was a good sign or her son was a consummate actor.

"Abbie . . . there's more . . ."

Again Abbie glanced in the mirror. Ginger's eyes met hers in a way that told her she'd better stop the car.

She pulled to the side of the road, shifted into Park and turned around enough in the seat so that she could see Ginger.

"I'll come up there with you," Ginger whispered. "I don't want to chance Harvey hearing this." She held her finger to her lips in a hushing motion, then carefully untangled herself from her sleeping husband. She opened the car door and got out, then climbed into the front seat.

Abbie mentally braced herself.

Harvey began to snore, but still Ginger kept her voice to a whisper. "Candy and Justin were, uh, they were, well, you know, doing it."

Abbie's heart thumped as she digested what she'd known but didn't want to acknowledge. "They were having sex? You know for sure?"

Ginger nodded and Abbie saw the hot color in her cheeks. "I play bridge every Thursday, so I'm not home when Candy comes in from school. It's also the day our maid is off. One afternoon about three weeks ago, I had an upset stomach and came home early. I found them in bed in Candy's room."

Abbie swallowed hard, no longer able to invent reasons or excuses. She wished suddenly that Burke was there. None of this was making sense to her.

These kids hadn't been gripped by a sudden hormone overload in the back seat of a car. No unplanned passion. No groping and petting that suddenly went too far.

This had been planned as if they were two adults engaged in an affair.

She glanced at Ginger, feeling guilty and responsible for Justin's behavior while at the same time knowing, realistically, she wasn't. "I don't know what to say."

"I've shocked you. Believe me, I was shocked, too."

"Do they know you saw them?"

She shook her head. "I didn't go any farther than the door." She smiled, but without pleasure. "Do you know they hadn't even closed it? Broad daylight. Amazing. When Harvey and I were first married, I never wanted the lights on I was so embarrassed. And here's my daughter in the middle of the afternoon..."

Ginger turned and glanced out the window as if somehow the whole issue might just go away if she thought about it differently. "Do you know I tried to find another reason for their being in bed together—other than the obvious one?" She pressed her lips together, then said wistfully, "Why do parents always want to believe their children are angels who would never do what other kids do?"

"Because rose-colored glasses are easier to look through than the other kind," Abbie murmured, knowing why Burke was always making her look beyond her own illusions.

"Now I realize I should've confronted Candy. But I honestly didn't know what to say, nor did I know what it would accomplish. Just seeing them, I knew their relationship had been intimate for a while. Telling her not to have sex with Justin... Oh, Abbie, I think my silence may have helped cause this mess."

Abbie patted her hand. "No, Ginger, don't think that way."

But she couldn't help but wonder if she herself would've handled the running away differently if she'd known. She understood why Ginger hadn't told Harvey, but why had her son kept Candy such a secret from her and Burke?

What little reassurance Burke had given her about being a good mother now teetered on wobbly legs. Had she somehow raised a son who, despite her best efforts to encourage him to share his problems, was in essence exactly like his father?

Did Justin, too, keep his life in separate compartments and choose what to tell and what to keep back?

Ginger sniffled. "I've always allowed Harvey to have the last word when it comes to Candy. I should've taken more control. He's just so adamant about things, and if he knew she was, uh, having sex right under his own roof..." She shuddered. "I don't want to think about what he would do. Then when you walked in..."

"You didn't connect me to Justin?"

"No. I was still in shock over Candy being gone, and it just didn't occur to me she would be with Justin. Those early hours are still a blur. When the realization did hit me, I wanted to take you aside and tell you, but if I'd asked to speak to you alone, Harvey would have wondered what was going on. After you left, he ranted for hours about Burke. He kept saying over and over again that his Candy would never run off with your son. She was too refined. After listening to him go on and on, I had myself convinced they weren't together."

Harvey stirred in the back seat. His voice was muffled as he asked, "We home? How come we're stopped?"

Ginger twisted in her seat to face her husband. "Almost home. I got into the front to give you room to stretch out."

He mumbled something else and fell back to sleep.

Abbie said, "Thanks for telling me, Ginger. I can't say that the information makes me feel better, but at least I know what we're dealing with."

Ginger said, "After seeing some of those kids in Sade Court, I hope they *are* together. At lcast Candy would be with someone she trusts."

IT WAS ALMOST FOUR in the morning by the time the cab Abbie had grabbed at the Kaufmans pullcd up in front of her house. When she paid the driver and climbed out, she was surprised to find she wasn't tired. Too much to think about, she decided as the cab drove off. This whole new slant on her son.

Sex in the afternoon, and in Candy's bedroom to boot. Not some late-Saturday-night necking session in the family car that had gotten out of hand. She shook her head ruefully. It was the planning that got to her. Her curly-haired little boy had planned assignations for sex with this girl and apparently hadn't felt even a shred of guilt....

With her head lowered as she searched her handbag for her house keys, she didn't immediately see the car in the darkened driveway. When she did, she came to a halt on the front steps and stared as if she were seeing things.

Burke's car?

She crossed to it and touched the hood. It was still warm and she could hear the soft relaxing noises of the engine. Narrowing her eyes at the vehicle as if it were somehow at fault, she swung around and marched back to the front door of the house.

She unlocked the door and pushed it open, aware suddenly of a maelstrom of emotions. Fury and curiosity, tingles along the back of her neck and a lump of anticipation low in her stomach. She tried to concentrate on the fury.

Damn the man! No doubt he intended to reinforce his demand that she remain here, and wanted to do it without the Kaufmans waiting a few feet away.

No lights were on in the house, but then Burke didn't have a key. Which meant nothing, she realized with annoyance. No doubt he knew how to climb in and out of windows just like his son.

"Burke?" she called, then flipped on the lights. The room burst into illumination and Abbie blinked.

"You took long enough," he said in a low voice that sounded laced with underlying meaning.

He was sprawled on the couch, his feet propped on the coffee table. He hadn't changed from the clothes he'd worn to Raffles. Her earring still glittered in his ear. His arms were folded across his chest and his gloves had been tossed onto the table. She also noted an empty tumbler from her bar with melting ice cubes.

She shivered despite the warmth in the room, and once she met his eyes for longer than a few seconds, the instinct that told her to turn and run roared to the surface.

It was the fear of the dangerously erotic dance of arousal that had begun in Sade Court and could not be as easily escaped here. Why location made a difference she wasn't sure, but she knew it did.

"Unlike you," she said in her best brisk tone while she struggled to rein in her wildly raging emotions, "I didn't break the sound barrier. Besides, I didn't know there was a rush for me to get back here."

"You're forgiven. Besides, you gave me time to stop at the all-night drugstore."

"Forgiven?" she asked, barely able to control her temper. "I don't recall offering an apology."

Before he could comment on that she zeroed in on his second statement. "And if your shopping was for what I think it was, you're making a lot of assumptions."

He studied her with such intensity she felt exposed.

In an even voice, while his eyes remained locked with hers, he said, "Pammie asked me yesterday if I could get her a copy of that local fashion magazine you're involved with."

Abbie blinked in momentary confusion. He picked up a magazine from the coffee table and showed it to her. It was the latest issue of *Chic*. Abbie regularly contributed fashion advice, and her friend Celada had, as a favor to Abbie, done a spring layout in the latest issue. The two women had often collaborated on fashion projects—something they had done since working together on costumes for a play while they were in college.

Now Abbie looked at the magazine in confusion. While she had discussed fashion design and modeling with Pammie, she'd never said anything about the magazine.

To Burke, she said, "Pammie asked you?"

"Mmm. I told her about the magazine. She'd never heard of it, so when I said you were their fashion guru, she was immediately interested." He watched Abbie with an even expression, almost as if he was holding himself in check.

Abbie's eyes narrowed. She made herself stand perfectly still and kept her voice carefully in control as she said, "I don't believe you just followed me down here in the middle of the night because you had a sudden urge to buy a magazine."

"You're right. What else do you think I stopped to buy?"

She should whirl around and leave him here with his ridiculous question-and-answer games, but dammit, she wasn't going to be intimidated in her own house!

She took a deep breath, gripped with a sudden need to establish her advantage. "Something kinky like satin ropes, or maybe something messy like apricot jam?"

He chuckled. "If my memory serves me right, we never needed props. Just you and I were more than enough." Then from the floor beside him, he picked up a small cardboard box and tossed it to her. She caught it, holding it as if suddenly presented with a grenade. She wasn't sure whether to throw it back and stomp out or open it as if that in itself was some erotic rite.

Abbie felt heat roll down her spine, and she knew that the longer she held the box, stared at it, the more she opened herself up to one undeniable fact.

She wanted him. She wanted the passion that would allow her to forget about Justin for a few moments, feel that sweet flood of release that had been building in her since Burke had walked into the house after Justin ran away. Since that moment he kissed her just a few feet from here.

How she wished it was only making love that drew her to him, for as strongly as she tried to deny it, she knew her feelings went deeper. Her love for Burke had never died; it had lain dormant and buried and hidden, because her heart was safer when she denied her feelings, even to herself.

Now those feelings of love sprang to life, but she didn't welcome them.

She couldn't let him know what she was thinking, what she was feeling.

"Shut the light off," he said in a low growl that revealed emphatically that the primary purpose of his trip was to be with her *in every way possible*.

She tried to shake off the soft demand in his voice, which slid through her like quicksilver. She concentrated on keeping her knees from buckling beneath her.

How could he still have such a devastating effect on her? How could he make her heart pound, her pulse race and her blood run thick and hot? Why had this one man always been a temptation?

Even when she was most furious with him, there was a part of her that responded to him with sensations that flowed beyond the physical and into some eternal place of knowledge where love blossomed pure and true. An inviolate place where love was unfettered by anything mortal like fights, the sting and rawness of divorce, the private compartments of his life.

Burke couldn't deny that he'd come here deliberately. It wasn't confusing why he found her so desirable in the midst of the terrifying circumstances. A crisis had brought them together as parents; a crisis had brought them together as lovers.

He studied her, no doubt guessing that her suspicion, so evident when she'd first walked in the door, was now at war with her needs. That was the kicker; he knew she wanted him, too.

The silence between them only heightened Abbie's desire.

"You shouldn't be here," she whispered a little too desperately, at the same time knowing she would rush to stop him if he tried to leave.

"You shouldn't be way over there," he countered softly.

"Burke, I know what you're doing."

"Crossing a line I swore I'd never cross with you again."

"Then why?"

"I want you," he said baldly.

No fanfare, no ducking the truth, no decorating his desire with pretty words or, worse, words that could be construed as commitment or forever after or a renewal of their past.

"Shut the light off, Abbie," he said again.

Tell him no, she commanded herself. He won't force you. Just tell him no.

But instead she took a deep breath and said, "If we're going to make love—"

"Not if. We're going to."

"Fine, but if we are, I want the lights on."

"The second time."

She gulped and her heart and pulse began to gallop. "Second?"

"Or third. Come over here."

She turned off the light but made no move toward him. She could not let him simply possess her.

She lowered her head, suddenly glad for the room's darkness. Who was she kidding? She wanted him both with her body and her heart. It was easy to admit to the sensuality, but revealing her heart . . . she couldn't do it. He would withdraw from her and remind her of all the reasons love wasn't enough.

Burke, however, was more honest. No attempt to hide that he wanted her. And he knew if he'd tried to wrap that want up in pretty bows of promise and ribbons of love, she wouldn't believe any of it. Her willingness just hours ago in Sade Court made her reluctance now less believable.

The streetlights offered scraps of illumination. When her eyes adjusted, she tossed her handbag onto a chair and marched across the room, coming within inches of his booted feet.

She dropped the box of condoms so that they landed right on the zipper of his fly.

He glanced at the box and then slowly raised his eyes and said, "They work better unwrapped, and they fit better when I have my pants off."

It occurred to Abbie that their positions were exactly the opposite of what they'd been when he arrived after Justin ran away. Then she'd been seated and had felt overwhelmed by him. Now she was standing and he was seated—and she still felt overwhelmed.

She crossed her arms, refusing to smile. "Why exactly are you here? And don't tell me it's to have sex. We could have done that in Sade Court."

"I was trying my damnedest to resist you," he said wryly.

"And you did."

"Now I can't. Not anymore. I need you."

The honesty and simplicity of his words made all her barriers collapse. She could no longer resist him.

He reached up and curled his fingers into the waist of her jeans. Tugging her forward, he said, "Let me spoil and indulge you, Abbie."

"You're not playing fair when you act all sweet and loverlike," she complained, not meaning a single word.

With the deftness of a man on a mission, he had her in his lap, then turned and positioned her expertly so he could roll her beneath him.

His hands pushed into her hair and he settled himself against her with such a sweet, satisfying fit it was as if they did this every night.

"I should be saying no and fighting you," she whispered even as her own hands slid around him and her fingers bathed in the skin and muscles of his back.

"And I should be accusing you of seducing me."

"I never—"

He cut her off with a long, deep and very wet kiss. "Not what you've done, Abbie. Simply what you are."

She drifted into the sensation of his hands whispering down her body, his words spilling like sparkling jewels. Her heart latched onto them as if they had power in themselves.

"Oh, Burke—"

"Shh. Let's see if we can use our mouths for something more interesting than talking."

Without giving her a chance to agree or disagree, he kissed her with a crushing force that not only made her sizzle but gave her a sense of just how badly he wanted her. He undid the buttons of her shirt and pushed the material aside, cupping her breasts through the lace of her bra, bringing his thumbs to their hardened centers.

Abbie groaned, wriggling to get free of the restriction of clothes. He kissed her again and again, his hands touching her, his mouth nipping her ears, her neck.

Her hands pushed at the clothes, but with their bodies so close she made little progress. No doubt realizing this, he rolled off her and got to his feet, standing so that she had to look up the long length of him.

She shivered at the sudden exposure of her skin to the air but made no attempt to cover herself. Without taking his eyes from her, he pulled off his shirt, the mass of dark chest hair making her catch her breath. He removed the earring and dropped it carelessly on the table behind him. He then shoved his hands through his hair before moving them to the snap on his jeans.

Abbie closed her eyes and swallowed hard. Here was her chance to be safe from the pounding of new emotions, the resurgence of feelings for Burke that she'd put aside and at least *tried* to forget.

She should shake her head no, get to her feet and leave the room. He wouldn't stop her, and in some ways she wondered if he would have preferred she do just that. For Burke was giving her that one last opportunity. By separating them to shed his clothes, he was saying, *Leave now if you really don't want this.* But she did want this, she wanted him, and despite a minuscule amount of common sense that nudged at her, told her she would have a thousand second thoughts later, she reached for the snap on her own jeans.

Watching him, she enjoyed his cool precise moves, the deliberate pauses that he knew only made her more eager, more determined to possess him. She shoved off her jeans and dispensed with the shirt completely.

Coming slowly to her feet, she stood in her black lace bra and panties.

She slid her hands around his waist and felt his heat, the roaring beat of his heart against her cheek. With him firmly in her arms, she drew a deep breath and said, "How do you do this? How do you separate yourself so entirely from what you want to what you take? Burke, it's as if you think—" She cut off her words when she felt his hands grip her arms as if to push her away.

Burke stared down at her, at the ease with which she rested against him, the intrinsic trust she had in this part of their relationship. His eyes narrowed, his own clawing desire clamoring for satisfaction.

Why, in all the years, all the times they'd made love, hadn't he realized how bound up his emotions were with her? Why hadn't he known? Why now, tonight, when their son was missing? Why, when they'd both agreed years ago that any attempt to reconcile would be a disaster?

He shook away the realization. No, not now. Now he just wanted to bury himself in her. Later he would deal with his feelings for her. Hell, maybe later his feelings wouldn't even matter. Later he'd have proved that good sex could effectively satisfy them both. Later the line he'd crossed could be justified. He could back away. He could make it all rational and explainable.

She'd always satisfied him, completed him, better than any woman he'd ever known. She'd always had the power to make him wonder about choices, to make him rethink and reconsider.

He was no fool. Not only didn't he trust himself to be totally open with anyone, he especially didn't trust himself to be totally open with Abbie.

Deal with our bodies, he told himself. *Drown your-self in the sweet relief she can offer. Make her forget the nightmare that might still await us in Sade Court. For just these few minutes make her gasp and make her come. That's all this is about. That's all it can ever be about.*

He cupped her chin and lifted it, and saw the shimmer of desire in her eyes.

"Here or in the bedroom?" he asked in a husky whisper.

She swallowed. "You're angry."

"Not at you. Right now, I'm hard and you're hot," he said with no attempt to deny what was and had always been instinctive and immediate between them. "Let's do something about it."

Instead of the words sounding disconnected to her, they pushed her beyond hearing the tiny voice that kept reminding her she was a fool to allow this.

Burke eased her down onto the couch. He quickly dispensed with her bra and panties, and with a smooth execution that always astonished her, he was on top of her. Protection in place, he slid deep into her body.

She arched up, her legs wrapping around his hips as if he might escape.

"God, you feel good," he murmured, kissing her eyes, her cheeks, her mouth.

"You, too. Oh, Burke, it's been so long..."

He pushed deeper into her, then lifted away enough so that he could watch the range of emotions, the flush of color in her cheeks.

Slowly he began the ancient rhythm, pushing deep, pulling out, making her gasp and clutch him closer. He basked in the wonder of the power she had over him— and the power he had over her. He wanted to hold back to see her pleasure pour through her, but he couldn't. His own desire had been too long denied, and in the dizzying moments of heat and passion, Burke lost it.

"Ah, Abbie..." he groaned, burying his face in her neck. He felt her legs tighten, her hands grip his back.

Abbie cried out as her own body, too, found release.

They lay sprawled and spent, their faces hidden in the curves and coves of each other's bodies.

Seconds inched into minutes, and their breathing slowly lost its ragged sound.

Finally Abbie sifted her fingers through his hair. "If only it was always this simple..."

"It is, Abbie. We're the ones who make it complicated."

She propped her head on one hand. "So if I tell you I love you, would that be too complicated?"

He went still. "Don't be ridiculous," he said gruffly. "A few minutes of great sex is just that, great sex."

She steeled herself against showing any emotional reaction to him. Stay cool and upbeat, she reminded herself. "Then it's a good thing I didn't slip and say any words that would make this more complicated, isn't it?"

Burke threw his forearm across his eyes. "Oh God, Abbie..."

"Just making sure, Burke," she said with a breeziness she didn't feel. "I didn't want you to think I was counting on anything to follow."

He rolled away from her. "I care about you, Abbie. You're the mother of my son. You've been incredibly supportive of my relationship with Justin, and you put up with a lot while we were married."

"That sounds like a commendation for a job well done." She got up and quickly scrambled to gather up her clothes. "But you're exactly right. I did put up with a lot. Loneliness, worry that the next phone call meant you were dead, terror that our marriage was falling apart and . . ." *Getting a divorce I didn't want,* she finished silently.

She kept her head down, for she knew if she looked at him, she would do something totally female—like burst into tears.

When she had her clothes, she started to walk past him, but he grabbed her arm and pulled her around to face him.

"And what?"

"Nothing," she said. "It doesn't matter. It was a long time ago. The important thing is *now,* and finding Justin."

He let her go and turned away as if he, too, didn't want to press the subject any further.

She added, "And by the way, I'm going back to Sade Court with you." She automatically braced for an argument.

But to her amazement, he didn't argue or even try to reason with her to make her change her decision. It wasn't until she stood beneath the hot shower, with shampoo dripping down her cheeks, that the expression she'd seen in his eyes clarified the real truth about their relationship.

It was easier for Burke to have her with him in Sade Court than to have her back in his life.

Now she knew why she never should've made love with him. She desperately wanted much more than physical gratification.

She wanted him back in her life.

CHAPTER NINE

ABBIE WOULD'VE WELCOMED a silent aftermath.

As they drove back to Sade Court the following afternoon, they were like two commuters sharing a ride, not a man and a woman who'd just had unbelievable sex. Abbie wanted to grab him and shake him. After all that had happened between them they were talking and acting like virtual strangers.

He asked her questions about her work. Yes, she still enjoyed giving fashion advice and assisting her clients in choosing the best colors, fabrics and styles at the most affordable prices. No, she didn't plan to expand the business until Justin was out on his own. Even as it was now, she felt that the time she had to spend away from home was excessive.

"Do I hear some self-blame in your voice about running a business instead of staying home?" he asked without looking at her.

"Probably," she said wearily. "The thought that if I'd been home this might not have happened has occurred to me."

She stared out into the April sunshine. Truthfully it had more than occurred to her; it had beat relentlessly at her conscience.

"You make yourself sound like a neglectful mother." He paused as if he was about to say more, and Abbie found herself holding her breath. Then he did. "I've seen a few of those, and trust me, you're not one of them."

In one sense she knew she'd never neglected Justin, but then again perhaps it was a matter of opinion or degree.

The Kaufmans, too, couldn't be called neglectful. They had provided well for Candy's needs, they loved her, and Abbie knew for a fact that Ginger was an at-home parent. However, since seeing Justin and Candy in bed, Ginger must have asked herself a million questions about where she'd failed as a parent. Abbie hadn't yet told Burke about this development, but apart from making a strong case for Justin and Candy being together, it added little to where they were now.

Everything between her and Burke had changed. They'd made love, they'd argued, they'd showered and they'd slept together. Routine in a way, but not for them. Not for the past five years. Yet here they were discussing surface things, mundane and unimportant things.

Abbie shook her head at the odd turn of events, but more so at their exchange after those moments of passion.

Had they really debated the issue of love and whether or not she loved him? They'd delved into the powerful sexual attraction that refused to be contained by simple denial of its existence, but maybe their lovemaking was nothing beyond a diversion from worry about a runaway son, a need to close themselves away and temporarily forget the frightening reality.

She glanced at Burke. If he was experiencing any of her worries, he gave no sign of it. But then what had she expected? A confession of love? Of regret for their divorce?

Abbie wasn't selfish; she would have settled for just a crumb, one small indication that he had feelings other than lust for her, but now, with his distance, she decided she might as well have been riding in the car with Harvey Kaufman. It made her angry and it made her sad, but most of all it made her wonder why she still responded so deeply to Burke. It was too easy to say she loved him. Real love wasn't one-sided, but reciprocal.

The miles skimmed by, the silence between them like sharp glass with a "don't touch" warning. She tried to relax, even tried to sleep, but she was too troubled about Justin.

Forty-five minutes later, Burke shifted in the seat beside her and asked softly, "You asleep?"

"No." She rolled her head to the side and studied him.

His face seemed more keenly defined in the shadows, his mouth more grimly set. He wore jeans and a T-shirt, his leather jacket tossed in the back seat. The muscles in his upper arm were as tight as his hand was rigid on the wheel. She desperately wished she had the right to curl up next to him, to seek comfort from his warm body...

Burke said, "I called Johnny this morning while you were still sleeping. There's a possible lead on Justin."

She sat up straight. "Why didn't you tell me?"

"I'm telling you now."

"Dammit, Burke, you know what I mean. You always leave me with the feeling that more is going on than shows on the surface."

"Probably because there is," he said pointedly, and she wondered if they were only talking about Justin.

Shaking out her thoughts, she chastised herself for being ridiculous. That was just rose-colored-glasses thinking and she knew better.

Burke continued, "Besides, I wanted to chew it over in my mind before you bombarded me with questions."

He flipped on his directional signal and took the exit off the interstate.

"You could've chewed it out with *me*." She knew she sounded petulant, but she felt an urgent need to hold on to the one link she had with Burke—Justin.

Instead of picking up on her comment, he said, "Pammie saw a kid who looked liked Justin last night in the Merry-Go-Round. He had on jeans, a Boston Red Sox sweatshirt, curly brown hair and he wore a gold earring."

Abbie said cautiously, "That's what Justin was wearing, but it could also be a lot of other kids."

"So I reminded Pammie. But she saw a girl with him. Long blond hair almost to her hips."

"Candy."

"It would seem so."

"Why didn't Pammie approach them?"

"She tried to get through the crowd, but they left before she could reach them."

"Did she have any idea why he might've been there?"

Burke said nothing for a few moments, and she wondered if he was thinking or debating about what to reveal.

"Burke?"

"Yeah."

For the first time she saw fierce pain in his expression. In that moment she forgot all about her resolve to keep her distance.

She wrapped her fingers around his arm and squeezed. He glanced at her quickly, then swung his gaze back to the road—but not before she saw a flicker of emotion there. She said softly, "There's something you don't want to tell me, isn't there?"

"Only because it's just speculation."

She stared. She knew that the main business in Sade Court was drugs. As hard as it was to ask, she couldn't refuse to face the possibility. She'd done too much idealistic clinging already when it came to her son.

"You think Justin is dealing drugs, don't you?"

"I didn't know I was that transparent."

"I'm too familiar with some of your looks, Burke. Justin doing anything illegal would cause you a lot of pain."

To her surprise, he put his hand on her thigh. "Come closer."

She moved as close as she could get. Suddenly she regretted her negative thoughts about him. No wonder he'd said so little about what he'd learned. No wonder he'd asked her superficial questions about her work and acted so aloof. This new information was eating at him and he was having a tough time dealing with it. The perfect cop, as Burke always tried to be, wanted to set the perfect example, and here his own son was doing something illegal.

"You're blaming yourself, aren't you?"

"Hell, I don't know who I'm blaming. But Justin knows better, and God knows I've tried to make the line between legal and illegal so unmistakably defined he can't miss it. And yet, if what Pammie thinks she saw is correct, he's either dealing drugs or he's a bagman for a dealer. She got close enough to see he had a roll of cash. She called his name, but he stuffed the money in his pocket and he and Candy split."

"Oh, my God. Shoplifting and now this. It has to be because he needs money."

She took a deep breath and told herself not to assume the worst. And if it was, at least he and Candy were alive and unhurt. She needed to keep focused on finding them. She could worry about the other stuff later.

She said firmly, "At least we have something solid to go on. They are here. It's just a matter of time before we find them."

"You never cease to amaze me, Abbie," Burke said, obviously taken aback by her compliance. "When I think you'll freak out, you don't."

"That's because the female mind is very complex," she said staunchly. "You men always assume we're little flowers who'll wilt in the slightest heat."

He chuckled. "And we men want to be protective."

"Protect us or your egos?" she returned.

"Probably both," he said with some reluctance.

Burke turned the corner and brought the car to a stop across the street from Johnny's.

Shutting off the engine, he looked at her as if suddenly about to test her stamina. "You up to doing some slumming tonight?"

"Go to the Merry-Go-Round?"

"Yeah. Think you can hang on me as if you can't wait to get me into bed?"

She wasn't sure if he was serious or teasing. "I don't know, Burke. You can be pretty hard to convince."

He narrowed his eyes, watching her with a new kind of intensity. "Not when it's you."

She met his gaze, trying to read the emotion that had governed his comment. "I didn't realize I had that much appeal for you."

He reached out and slid his fingers beneath her hair to cup her neck. Abbie felt heat scurry down her spine.

"You make me forget what a disaster we were, Abbie. What a helluva mistake you made when you married me. You should've married one of those other guys you'd been dating. Today you'd probably have a marriage that works and a son sleeping in his room instead of hanging out in Sade Court."

Abbie brushed her fingers across his cheek. "Do you know this is the first time you've ever said this much about what happened between us?"

"Call it regret that I screwed up your life."

"But you didn't. I was there, too. I made mistakes."

She swallowed, realizing the magnitude of all the missed opportunities, all the anger that in the past had flared out of control.

Now this mutual regret, this respect for each other, was too fragile to handle, too easily breakable to dwell upon. Abbie wanted to tiptoe away and leave the pieces they'd touched upon alone. Whether it was a shield for hope or a guard against pain, by the time Burke opened her car door, she felt immensely better.

He took her arm as they crossed the street. "If you want to pass on going to the Merry-Go-Round with me, it's okay." He glanced at his watch. "It's only three-thirty, so you've got a few hours to think about it."

"No. I want to go."

"It's not going to be a picnic."

"I know. But Justin and Candy might be there."

He tightened his hold on her. "God, I hope so."

As they walked into their room at Johnny's, Abbie realized that even if their own relationship never worked out, their love and concern for Justin would always be strong and solid. In a quiet way she took strength from that.

AT SIX FORTY-FIVE they left Johnny's and walked toward the Merry-Go-Round. Anyone who happened to glance in their direction would have said they fit right in.

Abbie never would have believed that Sade Court had a fashion standard, but it clearly did. Grungy and sloppy were the keys, and anything that didn't conform would've stood out mightily. Burke wore black leather boots, tight, faded jeans and a torn denim vest over a T-shirt. His hair was brushed back, the earring visible, and despite the fact that dusk had fallen, he wore dark glasses.

Abbie had had to do more of a make-over. From Pammie, she'd gotten a pair of red tights. Over those she wore a long sweater with an open-weave geometric pattern and a deep V-neck. The sleeves were pushed up just above her wrists. Huge silver hoops dangled from her ears, and her hair had been arranged by Pammie. Burke had told her it looked as if she'd been electrified.

Abbie had peered in the mirror while Pammie grinned behind her.

"I kind of like it," Abbie had said, feeling the anticipation of doing something more productive than waiting and hoping.

Glancing at Burke, she'd noted his frown. Except he wasn't looking at her hair, but at the front of her sweater. When Pammie went to find another can of hairspray, Burke moved behind Abbie.

"You're not wearing a bra," he'd said flatly, but there was something edgy in his tone.

"How can you tell? This sweater is huge."

"I can tell."

"Well, I figured since I'm playing the part of some sex-starved female who can't wait to get you into bed, I may as well dress for the part."

Scowling, he'd muttered, "I can see the swell of your breasts, and if you move just right, I can see your nipples."

Abbie had walked closer to the mirror and stared intently. All she could see was the geometric pattern. In fact she thought it helped to disguise the braless look. She owned a couple of evening outfits that couldn't be worn with a bra. In her opinion they were much more revealing than this tentlike sweater.

"I think you're seeing things, Burke."

He'd moved behind her and boldly cupped her breasts. Abbie sucked in her breath. His fingers instantly found her nipples. Their eyes met in the reflection.

"I don't want anyone else seeing what I can see," he'd said gruffly.

She'd taken a tiny step backward and found herself tight against his body. At the base of her spine she'd felt the slight swell behind his zipper. Not what she would have called a raging arousal, but then Burke had always been good at keeping himself controlled.

She'd had no doubt he'd planned tonight with all his control antennae up. She knew him too well to believe this was some sort of convoluted way to turn them both on so that afterward they could have sex.

"I want you to put on a bra."

"Burke, don't be silly. I told you . . ."

He'd dropped his hands and turned her to face him. "Do it for me, Abbie."

"For you?" Her mouth had been so dry she could barely swallow.

"I don't want the distraction."

She'd blinked in surprise. "I distract you?"

"Everything about you distracts me," he'd muttered, but she could tell it was not an easy admission. "Just put the bra on, okay?"

She'd done as he asked, but mostly because she found herself so inordinately pleased he considered her a distraction.

Now, as they approached the Merry-Go-Round and Burke took her arm he felt her breast press into him. "You did what I told you?" he remarked.

"Yes."

"Then how come it doesn't feel like it?"

"Maybe it's just your imagination."

"No, sweetheart, when it comes to you, my imagination needs no encouragement."

Determined not to attach any significance to his words, she said, "Since we're supposed to be playacting, do I hang on to you now or should I build up my arousal and pant a lot when we get inside?"

He gave her a mercurial glance. "For someone who was so outraged last night when you found me on your couch, this is a change."

"It's all an act, Burke, remember?" she said breezily.

"I'm beginning to think I was safer with Kaufman," he grumbled.

Inside, as the name proclaimed, was an old-fashioned merry-go-round. The music, the horses moving up and down the poles, the spinning lights and mirrors, all reminded Abbie of the old amusement park where her parents had often taken her when she was a child.

The noise pounded right on through the waves of shouting and hoots of laughter between friends who arrived or departed.

A bar lined one wall, and Abbie's immediate reaction was that it should've been serving snow cones, cotton candy and cups of cold soda. But if the bar made her frown, the drug dealing astonished her.

It was flagrant and boldly accessible. Cash changed hands, wads of it, as if it was just play money.

To Burke she whispered, "Is there some unwritten code against stealing in here?"

"Yeah. Steal and you're dead."

"Oh."

"Let's get a beer."

Abbie stayed close to him as they made their way to the bar. After ordering two glasses of draft, he drew her to an empty stool. He sat so that his back was against the bar. With the dark glasses in place, he could easily look around without appearing to do so. By the number of people in shades, Abbie guessed that wasn't a novel idea.

She stepped close to him so that her body appeared to be plastered against him. She pressed her mouth to his neck and then took the liberty of giving him a very wet kiss.

Burke groaned.

"I'm trying to be authentic," she whispered, her mouth brushing his chin.

"Guess what. It's too authentic."

The beers were left by a skinny bartender with hair to his shoulders. Burke pushed the cash toward him with barely a second look.

Still against him, she whispered, "Do you see anything?"

"Nothing yet."

They stood looking like two lovers in between sessions in the sack. Burke kept his arm around her, his hand on her hip. Abbie leaned into him, kissing his neck occasionally and at the same time glancing from beneath lowered lashes for any sign of Justin.

She pushed her glass of beer away, settled against Burke and slid her fingers down his shirtfront to the waistband of his jeans.

He clamped a hand around her wrist. She pulled back, but she hadn't forgotten what she and Burke were supposed to be doing, and her eyes were watchful for any sign of Justin. She gave Burke her best flirtatious smile.

He scowled. "You're enjoying this, aren't you?"

"What can I say? You're a real turn-on, Mr. Wheeler."

He studied her for a long moment. "In case you're worried I might act later on all this passion, I left the condoms at your house."

"Ah, but I found them and brought them with me."

Abbie would have loved to have a camera to capture the shocked look on his face. His next words made her eyes widen.

"What in hell did you do that for?" he snapped.

"Really, Burke. We both know that things can happen and have happened between us. This way there won't be any surprises. Neither of us is a fool. Besides, I'm more mature now than when I tried to save our marriage by getting pregnant. I'm certainly not so irrational that I'd chance a pregnancy in the hope of getting you back. And if I did get pregnant, I'm sure you'd conclude I had some ulterior motive."

Burke didn't respond but just stared beyond her, his scowl deepening. Then to her surprise he tugged her against him.

With her anchored close, he said in her ear, "Let's work our way to the merry-go-round. That way we can get a better view of the crowd."

"Something's happened, hasn't it?" She could feel the tension in his grip, hear the edge in his voice.

"Stay close," he whispered, ignoring her question.

"Justin? Candy?"

"Maybe."

She tried to see through the dense crowd, but it was impossible. The carousel came to a stop and new riders clamored to get on. Holding firmly to her hand, Burke hauled her to one of the horses just as a lanky teenager approached it. Burke pushed in front of him.

"Hey, man, this one's mine."

"Yeah? Didn't see your name on it."

The teenager, who had an acne-riddled face, snorted. "You ain't lookin' in the right place."

Burke gestured toward the entrance. "You know a squid named Justin?" Burke gave him a direct look. "Heard tell Glassy was the kid to see for info."

The name brought the teenager's head up fast. "How d'you know Glassy?"

"Jeep sent me."

The kid's eyes darkened and he began to fidget. "Never heard of no Justin, man."

The merry-go-round began to turn while the boy's eyes darted toward the door. The rising and falling horse was between them. As the music became louder, the kid suddenly bolted.

Holding Abbie's hand, Burke took off after him. The crowd had thickened and Burke knew that once Glassy hit the street there were a thousand directions he could go in. Abbie dodged hands and lascivious looks.

Burke halted at the doorway, swearing as he saw the kid race down the street. "Let's go," he said to Abbie.

He released her hand and the two of them ran after Glassy. The kid turned down another street. Abbie and Burke dodged garbage cans and two men huddled together sharing a bottle.

Then they heard a door slam somewhere.

Burke stopped, hands planted on his hips, eyes scanning the area.

Breathing fast, Abbie said, "Where did he go?"

"Good question."

"That door we heard slam . . ."

Burke glanced in the direction he thought the sound had come from—a building a hundred feet or so down the street. He took Abbie's hand and drew her close to him. "I'll take you back to Johnny's and then go take a look in that building."

"No way, Burke."

"Abbie, I haven't got any idea what's in there. I'm not going to chance anything happening to you."

"But it's okay if something happens to you."

"It's not the same thing. I'm a cop and—"

"Don't give me that," she interrupted. "You're not going in there as a cop and you know it. I know you think Justin is in the area, and I'm not going to stay at Johnny's and worry myself sick about you. I'm already worried sick about our son."

He scowled at her. "I'm not taking you in there when I don't know what in hell is going on."

"Burke—"

"Don't waste your breath arguing with me," he said, reinforcing his words by taking her elbow and directing her back down the street.

But they hadn't gone more than a few feet when a gunshot rang out from the area of the building where the door had slammed.

Abbie's face drained of color.

Burke swore and started toward the building, then stopped when a door burst open and a teenager raced down the steps.

For a fleeting moment the boy stopped, looked around as if aware he was being watched and then turned to run in the opposite direction.

It was Justin.

CHAPTER TEN

BURKE AND ABBIE both shouted his name. Then they took chase, fully expecting the fleeing teenager to duck out of sight at any moment. A bus rumbled up the street and Justin waved his hand frantically at the driver.

The bus stopped, and before Burke could get close enough to do anything but swear, Justin had boarded and the vehicle had lumbered off, belching fumes. Burke made a mental note of the time and the bus number, although he knew it wasn't likely to be much help. Justin could get off the bus anywhere.

Abbie gulped, her breathing ragged, her body limp as she sagged against Burke. She tried to force back the tears of frustration but failed miserably. They streamed down her cheeks in a steady flow.

Burke knew he should take the logical step and pull her into his arms and murmur soothing words, yet he stood unmoving, allowing her to lean against him but unable to offer any solace.

God knew, he understood her frustration and pain, but his emotional wariness around her had steadily increased in the past few hours. He was mystified as to why he'd thought he could keep their relationship strictly focused on their shared concern for their son.

A crazy assumption.

Now, watching Justin run from them, Burke was left feeling more than uneasy; he felt totally inadequate as a parent and as a cop. Somehow, despite his efforts to keep the two roles separate, in these past few moments they had solidly merged.

He took his dark glasses off and scowled. Abbie sniffled and wiped her eyes. Still he didn't put his arms around her; he didn't like the link that seemed to be forming between them. Their step into a sexual relationship, he realized now, wasn't just a mistake, it was a disaster. He'd played with fire and got more than singed; he'd gotten burned and branded.

Touching the small of her back, he said, "Let's go."

"Where?"

"Back to Johnny's."

"But—"

"He's gone, Abbie, and standing out here isn't going to help."

She stared at him, refusing to move. "Why did he run, Burke? My God, he must have heard us call him. He must have known it was us."

And why, Justin, Burke wondered, *didn't you realize how terrified I am that you're in some major trouble?*

To Abbie he murmured, "He ran *because* it was us. I think the gunshot may have been a signal. Remember, he hasn't been kidnapped. He's a runaway." Shaking his head in self-disgust—how could he not have moved fast enough?—he muttered, "Goddammit, this shouldn't have happened."

She halted and stared at him, puzzled. "What do you mean?"

"I'd hoped the contact would lead to Justin, but I hadn't counted on him bolting."

"Wait a minute..." she began, but he took her arm, and set off in the direction of Johnny's. "I want to know what's going on," she demanded, effectively stopping their progress by tugging her arm free and planting her feet apart.

"Isn't it obvious? Justin just got on a bus for God knows where."

"I don't mean that. You said 'contact.' Are you saying you set up that meeting with the kid beside the carousel horse?"

"I was told a kid named Glassy would be there at that particular time. At Raffles, before I hauled Kaufman out, I learned that Glassy's a small-time dealer who supposedly knows who the newest arrivals are in Sade Court."

"So you just boldly asked about Justin?"

He shrugged. "Sometimes being straightforward produces the best results. In this case it did. We know now for sure that Justin is here, because we've seen him." He gestured at the building they'd seen Justin come out of. "And my guess is that by morning he'll be back here."

"For Candy?"

"Yeah, unless I've missed my guess and they're not together."

"They are."

"Probably. Our suspicions plus the pregnancy-test kit..." He paused and frowned at her. "Why are you shaking your head?"

Abbie wouldn't look at him. "If she's in there, we have to try to find her."

"You think whoever is in there will roll out the welcome mat? Forget it. Better not to alert her if we want to see Justin again."

"You believe that if Justin learned Candy was with us, he would run even farther?"

"I don't know, Abbie, but since we don't know why he ran away from us just now, or why he ran away at all, I don't want to take that chance."

She nodded. "Neither do I."

He stared at the building. "But you're right about taking a look to see what we're dealing with." He urged her into the shadows of the building directly across the street. "Stay here. I mean that," he warned.

Burke was gone ten minutes, and by the time he returned, Abbie was shaking with anxiety.

"Well?"

"Two exterior doors, front and back. Looks like lots of tiny rooms or apartments. That makes a lot of interior entrances and exits. Light's dull inside like it's from candles or flashlights. I don't want to go busting in there without some backup. If Candy's in there, she'll hide or possibly get away. The element of surprise is best, but I can't pull that off myself."

"You're probably right," she said, but he guessed it was difficult for her to be patient. He, too, wanted to move, but a reckless move now would not be to their advantage. Besides, Justin might come back and then they could have both kids safe.

Burke gave Abbie an intense look. "Earlier you said you knew Candy was with Justin. Is there something you haven't told me?" he asked, deliberately ignoring the fact that he'd regularly tried to and succeeded in keeping things from her. But that had been cop stuff, the part of his life no one could touch but him.

He didn't miss her quickly shifting gaze. She wasn't as quick or as able to mask her feelings as he was.

Gently he cupped her chin, pressing his thumb against her lower lip, urging her to look at him.

"Ah, I thought so. Did Justin tell you something you haven't told me?"

"No, not Justin. Ginger."

"When you drove them home?"

"Yes."

"Let me guess. She has a socially correct scenario to account for why her daughter would run off with riffraff like Justin."

"She knew they were having sex."

Burke stared at Abbie. "She knew? For sure?"

When his eyes narrowed, Abbie took a deep breath as though gearing herself for his anger. Softly, as if it was a secret, she said, "Ginger saw them in bed at her house."

Burke didn't say anything. He wasn't shocked. Hell, he wasn't even surprised, but he felt a line of raw tension spread across his neck and down his spine.

Abbie hadn't told him. Even if he was a total sap, he

wouldn't buy that she'd forgotten. No way. She'd kept it from him, and that made him furious.

Perhaps because it made her a mirror image of himself.

For years he'd kept silent about things until forced into revelation. And there'd been damn little that forced him. Had Abbie learned that doing as he did was the way to deal with him?

Burke made himself stay calm. "Are you going to give me the details, or is this some goddamn guessing game?"

Abbie stiffened but then filled him in on what Ginger had said.

"And she told you this during the ride back to Rhode Island?"

"Yes."

"Why in hell did you wait until now to tell me?"

"Might I remind you that a lot has happened since then, including your surprise visit to my house?" she snapped. "And you felt no urge to tell me about your plan to see Glassy. Besides, since we'd already concluded Justin and Candy were together—"

He gripped her shoulders and shook her. "These kids have been humping in the afternoon instead of studying for chemistry tests at the library and you didn't think it was important enough to tell me?"

"You make me sound so calculating."

"Bingo."

She looked as if he'd punched her, and Burke instantly regretted his anger. There was no excuse for dumping all the blame on her. And yet he felt left out and more than a little deceived.

Abbie lifted her chin, her eyes guarded.

"It wasn't calculated, Burke. I intended to tell you. I just didn't see how it would change anything."

"Well, we'll never know, will we?" He turned away from her, his face grim.

The color washed out of her cheeks, then just as suddenly she went on the offensive. "Maybe you were a good teacher," she shot back. "You've certainly never had any qualms about keeping things from me. In fact, if I hadn't insisted, you would've left me home from the very beginning."

"You're goddamn right I would've."

He closed his eyes and tried to make himself calm again. Abbie's apprehension was evident; his own exhaustion threatened to swamp him. They were both frustrated, worried and scared. Good excuses for short tempers and painful words. None of these back-and-forth jabs were helping them find Justin and Candy.

"All right, Abbie. Let's acknowledge we both have faults. One being that we're too damn good at keeping things from each other." He waited a few seconds for her to agree or argue.

She kept silent, the tenseness in her body beginning to give way. Finally she nodded.

"Now, as for Ginger," he said carefully, "did she tell you all this in front of Harvey?"

"No, he was asleep."

"Asleep! How in hell could he sleep when his daughter is... Never mind. Poor bastard is lucky he doesn't know just how bad a situation his kid is in.

Am I correct in assuming Harvey is the reason she didn't say anything at her house?''

"Yes. She was afraid of what he might do."

"Then he'll really be in high gear if Candy is pregnant."

"I didn't mention the pregnancy kit. Since we don't know for sure if Candy is, I didn't want to alarm Ginger."

Burke frowned. "Don't alarm Ginger. Don't tell Harvey. Why in hell are we protecting them from the truth? We're doing the worrying for *four* parents."

"Maybe we're stronger, Burke. And you're a cop. You know when to worry and when to act. I don't think either one of them has a clue what to do."

"I'm not sure I do, either," he said grimly. "If I did, Justin wouldn't have made it to that bus and left us here like a couple of dopes."

Sighing, he dragged a hand down his face. "Come on, let's go back to Johnny's and—"

He halted his words and stared, then wrapped his arms around her and held her so tightly she could barely breathe.

"What is it?"

"Shh." He pressed her head against his neck. "It's Justin."

She tried to wriggle free. "Oh, my God—"

He held her fast. "Stay still."

He felt her tension and knew if he released her she'd run toward her son.

To Burke's amazement his own usual restraint was wobbly. He, too, wanted to race out and grab the boy.

With Abbie tucked close to him, her head pressed beneath his chin, he whispered, "He must have gotten off the bus and doubled back between the buildings."

"What are we going to do?"

"Nothing. I want to see if he goes back into the same building."

Burke watched as his son moved along the shadowed fronts of the buildings with the cautious alertness of someone poised to break into a run at the first sign of trouble. Even from this distance, Burke knew the boy was scared. Yet the fact that he'd come back to the same place proved something was in there he needed or wanted or, as Burke suspected, was responsible for. Candy.

Burke was gripped with an odd feeling; here he was watching his kid in the same manner he would in a stakeout, gauging and analyzing a suspect's moves.

"What's he doing?" Abbie whispered.

"Moving toward the building we saw him run out of. Slowly, looking around, jumpy, I'd say. His habit of rubbing his fists against his hips is in good form."

Abbie tried to move. "Please, just let me see him."

Burke loosened his hold but didn't release her. He still didn't trust her not to give in to her maternal instinct and either cry out for Justin or run toward him.

To Burke's surprise she gripped his arm as she watched her son. Justin had moved up the steps and was pushing open the door. Within seconds he was inside and the door was closed behind him.

"Burke?"

"Yeah?"

"You know what I'm thinking?"

"That we better move now before he and Candy disappear."

She nodded.

Burke didn't want to go back to square one, which is what would happen if Justin slipped out of their grasp.

He didn't like taking Abbie into that building, but his other choice was to take her back to Johnny's. She would balk at that, and if she did stay there, it wouldn't be for long. She'd be out and following him in no time. And he sure as hell couldn't leave her here on the street.

"I'm going with you," she said firmly.

"Now, why doesn't that surprise me," he muttered, but his thoughts were already on what they might find in the building. "Let's go."

Moments later Burke pushed open the wooden door without knocking and walked in with Abbie close beside him. He paused to get his bearings. They were in an entryway; a single bulb offered the only light. Suspended from a frayed electrical ceiling cord, the bulb illuminated badly cracked plaster walls where the dirt competed with the graffiti.

Muted conversations and rap music indicated the rooms were occupied by kids. Faint traces of marijuana lingered in the air, and as he took a step forward he felt the crunch of a syringe under his foot. He grimaced.

Four closed doors greeted them, and Abbie gripped his arm. "This is like that old game show—pick a door and hope it's the right one. How do we know which one?"

"We don't."

He moved forward and pressed his ear to the first one. Silence. Then the second. The music thrummed and he could hear two people talking. The third and fourth sounded similarly occupied.

Burke was relying on instinct and his past experience with closed doors hiding the unknown. Back at the first door, he determined from the silence that the occupants were either asleep or waiting for him to enter. It was this last possibility that had all his senses on alert.

"Stay behind me," he whispered to Abbie.

He tried the knob. The door was unlocked. Bracing himself for a giveaway creak or squeak, he pushed the door, and it opened as though an oil can had greased its hinges. Not a sound. His heart thumped and his forehead broke out in a cold sweat.

Slowly he eased the door wide, praying the place was empty. Abbie was so close to his back he could hear her rushed breathing.

The light from the street trailed through the window, revealing enough of the depressing room to show it was empty. Burke relaxed.

Still he kept Abbie behind him. He didn't venture in, but shoved the door back against the wall.

Finally, after ensuring that even the darkest corners weren't occupied, he grimaced at the too-familiar sight of desperation and hopelessness. He'd seen, busted into and shaken down a hundred rooms just like this one in his years of working the drug detail.

Dirty mattresses had been thrown on a floor littered with crushed beer cans, plastic bags and empty capsules. A pair of torn sneakers had been left behind, as well as some porn magazines that made those he'd found under Justin's mattress wholesome by comparison. An innocent-looking milk carton and a half-finished box of chocolate cream-filled cookies added innocence to the dismal sight.

Abbie glanced around. "No one's here, Burke. Are we going to check the other rooms?"

Burke stared at the cracked wall, but in particular at a grimy sheet that hung suspended on a rod. Graffiti and numbers were scrawled on the wall in different colors like some sort of community bulletin board.

What was behind the sheet? he wondered. A window? Since it was an interior wall, probably not.

"Burke?"

"Yeah, just a minute."

He walked to the sheet and without drawing it aside flattened his hand on the cloth. It felt solid but not as steady as a wall. He repeated the motion a few more times at different spots.

"What is it?"

Carefully he slid the sheet aside and found a piece of plywood the size of a car door. Burke closed his eyes and cursed. He was fairly positive some sort of hiding place was behind the wooden slab. What he didn't know was how extensive it was and how many kids it concealed. If his hunch was right, Justin was probably among them, but there was also the possibility the other rooms had similar setups or exits. Should he and Abbie stumble in there without his first checking out the apartment's layout, the kids could run and they might never find them.

He made his expression neutral and turned back to Abbie. "We can't do any more. There's obviously no one here."

"Not in this room, but what about the others?"

"No. Let's go." He took Abbie's arm, and when she tried to say something more, he clamped a hand over her mouth. He hustled her outside, down the steps and walked her a few yards down the street.

He said, "Keep your voice down. The street's too quiet."

"Why did we leave? We only checked one door. Justin went into the building, so he has to be there."

"I know what we saw, but since the other doors have occupants behind them, the element of surprise is impossible and dangerous. Knocking and asking questions would alert Justin."

"But we can't just leave!"

"If he doesn't think he's in danger of being found, he'll probably stay where he is."

"Probably? Then he could also leave. Burke, we know he's here. I can't go away, knowing—"

"Don't argue with me," he said in a low voice.

Then, as if finally realizing this was not the place to argue, she said, "What are you going to do?"

"Go back to Johnny's and get some information, for starters."

"Information about what?"

"About the underground network of runaways."

ABBIE SAT in Johnny's office with a mug of coffee in her hand and listened with growing astonishment to Johnny fill Burke in on what was under the apartment building.

They talked about tunnels, a beeper system that hooked one tunnel to another and hundreds of kids. All were runaways, and their reasons were anything from rebellion or neglect to looking for a family or just cruising for some action.

Abbie had said nothing, mostly because she was trying to fit Justin into one of the categories Johnny mentioned. Never had she felt so helpless or so confused. Justin certainly hadn't been neglected or lacking in family, despite the divorce. She and Burke had both been mindful of his need for two parents.

Rebellion might account for some of his actions in the past, but most kids went through those stages without running away. No, she guessed that Justin's reasons had to do with Candy—and with the pregnancy-test kit.

"Burke?"

He turned around, the phone clamped on his shoulder. He'd called the local police precinct to get a fix on whether they'd ever investigated the apartment building.

He held up his hand to indicate she should wait until he was off the phone. "Two months ago, huh? Did you go in through the first apartment?" He listened, his mouth set in a grim line. "Then it's new. No, my wife was with me, so I didn't investigate. Yeah. Okay. I'll meet you here in twenty minutes."

He hung up without looking at her. He began poring through the notes he'd taken of what Johnny had told him.

As if on a second thought, he turned to her. "Did you want to ask me something?"

"If Candy is pregnant…" She swallowed and closed her eyes, finding that verbalizing her thoughts wasn't easy. "If she is, then perhaps Justin thought we'd be so upset this seemed the best way."

"Running away is not the best way. It's the dumbest way."

"We know that, but at sixteen, he probably doesn't see it as dumb."

"Obviously he's justified his actions, but he's also put a lot of people through a lot of worry. You, especially. And Candy's parents."

"And you."

"Yeah. And me."

Abbie scowled, but he turned away, tossing his notes on the desk.

Johnny stood. "The unmarked car should be here in a few minutes. I'll give y'all some privacy."

On his way out he stopped and rested a hand on Abbie's shoulder. "Don't be too hard on Burke, Abbie. When you work with these kinds of problems and situations all the time, the way he does, it's tough to see the logic when it happens to you personally."

She nodded. Johnny gave her shoulder a squeeze of encouragement and left the room.

She turned to her ex-husband. "You're blaming yourself, aren't you, Burke?"

"I don't want to talk about it."

She went over to him and touched his arm. "You accused me a little while ago of being deceptive. I'm trying to be up-front with you about what I feel. This isn't your fault. And I realize you're doing the best that can be done."

He shrank back from her. "Better not say that till Justin is found and safe. I just might botch this up."

"No. That's impossible." She knew it as surely as she knew her own name.

He stared at her, his intense green eyes barely masking the pain of that possibility. "Is it? I botched up our marriage. It's not hard to imagine that I could botch up trying to stop my kid from running even farther away." He shook his head in disgust. "Look. Forget I said anything. We got enough problems to worry about."

Then he stood, stepped past her and left the room. Abbie blinked, taken aback by his belief that he might botch up finding Justin. She knew Burke too well. He'd move heaven and earth if necessary, but he would locate their son.

His admission that he'd botched up their marriage stunned her. Not because he'd ever denied it, but because he'd always refused to talk about it.

When she'd asked for the divorce, he'd said he'd been expecting it. Then he made sure she got alimony she didn't want, gave her a glowing recommendation for custody of Justin, insisted she have the right to return to the court for more child-support money if she thought she needed it. Her lawyer had been slack-mouthed with astonishment, and Burke's attorney had told Burke he was insane. Still, Burke's instructions had stood.

Abbie had never taken advantage of his generosity and had been more than willing for him to maintain a strong father-son relationship with Justin.

In retrospect, she realized they'd gotten along better after they were divorced than when they were married. An obvious reason why any thoughts she might have entertained about renewing their relationship were stupidly naive. Burke had never liked the restraints that marriage had put on him.

But Abbie knew, too, that there was a limit to her willingness to understand him. She'd never known Burke to talk and cajole and try to explain. Too many times he'd simply expected her to know what he would do, what needed to be done; his attitude had left a wide gap in their relationship.

Abbie drew a long breath. If nothing else, she'd allowed herself to be naive, perhaps even willingly deceived by Justin. He'd been living a double life and she'd been blissfully unaware. Well, no more. Watching Justin run from them tonight as if they were two strangers bent on hurting, instead of helping, him had opened her eyes.

Perhaps if she'd been more aware months ago, instead of putting on those rose-colored glasses . . .

She got wearily to her feet. Suddenly she felt older, a little wiser and sadder. Hope had been easier when she'd been ignorant.

CHAPTER ELEVEN

"ABBIE?"

Burke stood impatiently in the doorway of Johnny's office, tugging on his leather jacket. He'd changed from the vest and T-shirt to a black sweatshirt. His hair was mussed and he shoved it back with impatient fingers.

"Yes, I'm coming." She tried to pass him, but he gripped her arm. "What's wrong?"

"Nothing."

"Are you scared of what we might find?" she asked.

That was an understatement. "Just uneasy. Look. You don't have to go. In fact, I'd rather you stayed here."

"No, I want to be there. Justin and Candy will be terrified seeing all you men."

He nodded, urging her forward, but she balked.

"Now what?" he said.

"What'll happen after we get home?"

"Don't you think you're getting a little ahead of yourself?"

She knew that perhaps she was, but she had to think beyond these next moments to the time when Justin was home.

"I meant with Justin," she said. "Something is obviously very wrong, whether it's Candy being pregnant or something we…" She hesitated and then went on, "Or something I've been unaware of. Otherwise he wouldn't have run away."

"Has it occurred to you that he's the one doing something wrong? Parental neglect might be a factor in some runaway situations, but Justin wasn't and never has been neglected."

"This is your son, Burke, not some case file."

He bristled. "Are you saying I'm not acting guilty enough? Not upset enough?"

"No, of course not."

"Then what do you want from me, Abbie?"

"I want you to show me that you and I can work together after this is over."

He sighed heavily. "Look. I want to spend more time with Justin, but I think you're missing an important point. It's not only you and me working together. Justin is going to have to cooperate. Just because he has a disagreement or a problem with one of us is no excuse to bail out."

"Maybe he thought that was the best way."

"At the risk of stating the obvious again, running away is never the best way. Whatever his problem is, it hasn't been solved, just gotten more complicated."

Just like our own relationship, she thought. She and Burke were still at odds. There were times when they agreed and a thousand times when they didn't. But she couldn't deny that she'd added to the disharmony. Her inability to trust Burke to put her and Justin before his work had severely damaged their relationship.

Burke said, "Abbie, don't try to figure him out until we've had a chance to talk." He cupped her chin and tipped it up so he could see her eyes. "It's going to work out. You just have to give it some time."

"Time isn't the answer, Burke. Trust is."

He studied her briefly, then without agreeing or disagreeing, he held her head steady while he brushed her mouth with his.

She let her eyes close, savoring the touch, the sweetness of it, the sense of connection.

She flattened her hands against his chest and wished he would pull her into his arms and comfort her, reassure her, tell her that once Justin was safe at home they would all live happily ever after.

Sighing, she slid her hands from Burke when he released her.

Never again would she be that naive. The reality of the past few days had forever destroyed any lingering idealistic illusions.

Outside in the cool night, she stood silently as, a few feet away, Burke consulted with two undercover police officers. This was the first time she'd been this close to Burke while he was working.

Never in a million years would she have thought that an opportunity to be with him in a professional capacity would be because their own son had run away.

She shivered, the chill deeper than a physical cold.

She dreaded what they might find, while at the same time knew there was nowhere else she wanted to be.

She heard one of the undercover men say to Burke, "We've been trying for months to find the connection between Sade Court and this underground. Too bad it was your kid who had to be involved."

"Yeah."

The officer lowered his voice, which made Abbie all the more determined to hear him. "Look, I don't want to be a pessimist, but your having located one of the entrances is no guarantee."

"I'm aware of that."

"It might even be a grim discovery."

"Look," Burke snapped impatiently. "I'm no stranger to grim discoveries. You think I haven't considered the most horrendous scenario? You think his mother hasn't? Hell, there's no way to prepare for this if—" his voice grew hushed "—Justin and Candy aren't there . . . or worse."

The officer nodded, obviously aware of what "worse" meant. "I got kids, too, so maybe what I'm trying to say is if you and your wife want to skip the raid, then no one here is gonna think anything about it."

Burke shook his head. "I appreciate the offer, but I have to be there because I'm his father not because I'm a cop. As for Justin's mother, well, Abbie's tough. Besides, all my efforts to handle this alone haven't worked. Now that we're moments from actually finding Justin, she's not about to bail out."

"Okay, then let's move."

Burke opened the back door of the dark sedan for her and then slid in beside her. She folded her hands and tried to remain calm, despite the jumpy fear in her stomach.

They drove the few blocks to the apartment building, parked across the street and settled in to wait. For what, Abbie didn't know. The car radio cut into the silence, and the two men in the front seat exchanged comments that Abbie decided were coded, because she couldn't understand a word.

Burke paid little attention to them or to her, but instead stared out the window at the building looming a few yards away.

Abbie touched his arm and he whipped his head around as if he'd forgotten she was even there. Then in a move that startled her, he put his arm around her and pulled her close. Abbie felt a deep relief and she wasn't sure why.

"Scared?" he asked.

"Anxious. I want him to be glad to see us."

"Given that a couple of hours ago he ran when he did, that might not happen."

"Burke, what if . . . ?" She let her question trail off, unable to put this new terror into words.

"If he doesn't want to come home?"

"Or if he runs away again . . ."

His face was troubled. "It gets back to the reason why he did it in the first place."

Two more cruisers arrived, killed their lights and waited.

On the car radio, she heard an officer say, "Madison and his men have it covered on the other end. Whenever you're ready, Lieutenant, say the word."

"Just about, Duncan," the officer in the front seat replied.

Their radio conversation continued while Abbie said to Burke, "What do they mean, 'the other end'?"

"The other end of the tunnel. This underground living is popular with runaways. Once I told them where the apartment building was, they checked their maps. It seems that an old tunnel built during Prohibition winds beneath the streets. It was used to smuggle bootleg whiskey into the local restaurants. The city had it sealed off, but some kids discovered it a few years ago, and it's become a home for a lot of runaways."

Abbie swallowed, unable to stop her instinctive revulsion. "God, that's like rats in a sewer."

Burke paused a moment. "Yeah, not a comforting thought, is it?"

The lieutenant in the front seat turned and said, "Burke, Abbie, we're just about set. Here's the plan. Duncan and his men will enter first and take control of the situation. Since you heard a gunshot, we know they've got weapons. We just don't know how many or even how many kids are there."

He gave Abbie a concerned look. "Burke knows the score, but this could be unpleasant. If you want to wait here until we bring your son out, that's understandable."

She shook her head. "I'll be all right. I want to go."

The lieutenant shrugged. "Burke, keep her with you."

Burke nodded.

They got out of the unmarked cruiser and she forced herself not to clutch at him. She knew she'd done far too much of that lately. Once Justin was safe, they'd be divorced parents again with all the rules of that nonrelationship back in force. Yet Abbie felt a huge measure of relief. Whatever they found, Burke being there for her and for Justin was very important.

The police moved up the building's wooden steps, shoved open the door and then entered the room Burke and Abbie had entered earlier.

Before Abbie could blink twice, they'd removed the sheet that covered the plywood. There was a set of hinges at the top. Without a second's hesitation they tore the flimsy wood away. Beyond lay yawning darkness from which emanated waves of damp, chilly air. Instantly Abbie heard shuffling, frantic motion and swearing.

"Hell, it's the cops!" a voice yelled.

"Run!"

"Freeze!" an officer shouted.

Most ignored the order and began running, the sound of their steps fading into the distance as they headed for the other end of the tunnel. The police didn't try to stop them.

There were four rickety steps down to a stone-and-dirt foundation. The graffiti-covered walls and ceiling were rounded, with little head clearance for anyone over six feet.

Abbie was behind Burke, and he halted just a few feet beyond the steps. Along the wall to his right hunched the kids who'd chosen not to run, the kids who *couldn't* run.

About ten teenagers were huddled together. One girl was very pregnant and another so glassy-eyed Abbie knew she was high on something. One boy grinned, then scowled, a bottle of liquor nestled lovingly in his arms. The others stared blankly at the adults.

The pathetic sight sent a punch of raw emotion into Abbie; she had to cover her mouth to stop herself from crying out.

The police moved, not particularly gently, and made them all stand up. Burke swept his flashlight across the kids looking for Justin and Candy.

Abbie clutched his arm. "They're not here," she whispered in a choked voice, while at the same time she searched each young face a second time. "Oh God, Burke, do you think they were with the ones who ran?"

That wasn't hard to imagine. After all, Justin had certainly run when he saw them earlier.

Burke stepped away from her to shine his light into the deeper recesses of the tunnel. To Abbie, he said, "Stay here."

The officer named Duncan said, "Burke, one of the men can check things out."

"No. I'll do it."

Abbie started to follow, and Duncan grabbed her arm. In a voice that sounded far too knowledgeable, he said, "Better do as Burke says."

But she twisted her arm free. "No, I have to see. I have to know."

She stepped in front of the ragtag group of teenagers, her revulsion eclipsed by her sadness and outrage that her son had chosen this to living at home. She couldn't help but wonder what these kids had experienced with their families that would make them prefer living in a dank tunnel.

She felt her way along the wall, her eyes finally adjusting to the gloom of the winding hole.

Up ahead she heard a muffled curse and she picked up her pace. Rounding a curve, she came to an area that had been hollowed out as if the tunnel's original builder had started in one direction and then changed his mind.

There, in that triangle of space, she found Burke hunkered down, his body blocking what the flashlight had revealed. She moved up behind him.

Her eyes widened and she felt slightly nauseated. "Oh, my God."

Justin was crouched there, and tears he no doubt had tried desperately to control slid down his cheeks. Candy was curled up on the ground beside him, moaning piteously. Her long blond hair was dirty and matted, and she was holding Justin's hand in a grip so tight Abbie guessed she was using most of her strength.

Burke whipped his head around, his face so grim and white Abbie was taken aback. He shoved two fingers in his mouth and gave a piercing whistle. Then he turned back to Candy and Justin.

His whistle brought an immediate response. The ground trembled with the pounding of running feet.

Duncan came to a halt, assessed the situation, then shook his head as if he'd seen it all too many times.

Into his portable radio, he snapped, "We need a rescue. Fast."

Duncan squatted down where Burke was trying to make Candy comfortable. He'd taken off his leather jacket and wrapped it around her. She curled into its warmth gratefully.

Finally her strength seemed to give out, because she dropped Justin's hand. Justin swiped at his tears and met his mother's eyes. Abbie could see his fear, his terror, his shame, and her own eyes smarted with the tragedy of what lay before them.

Burke glanced at Justin as if seeing his son for the first time. In a brittle arctic voice, he asked, "What in hell happened?"

Justin blanched, and Abbie stiffened at Burke's harshness. She put her arm around her son and found him shivering.

"Burke," she said, "there's plenty of time later for questions. Can't you see how upset—"

"Shut up, Abbie."

She stared at him as if she was seeing a stranger, but he ignored her. "I asked you a question, Justin."

Justin gulped. "I don't know. She was okay until tonight. She isn't going to die, is she?"

"When tonight? After you ran away from us?"

"No, sir." He squirmed. His eyes were fixed on the huddled figure of Candy. "Before."

"She was like this when you ran?" Abbie asked, astonished. She couldn't conceive of Justin's leaving Candy alone in this much pain.

"Not this bad. She was just having some cramps. I was running because—"

Burke cut him off. "She's pregnant, isn't she."

Justin folded his arms and refused to look at either Burke or Abbie. His expression closed down as if he knew that no explanation would satisfy his father.

"Answer me, goddammit!" Burke roared.

"Burke, for heaven's sake," Abbie pleaded.

"Stay out this, Abbie."

"I will *not* stay out of it. You aren't going to browbeat our son with blame when he's obviously terrified."

Burke glared at her so fiercely she shut her mouth. Justin said, "Yes."

"Yes, what?"

"Yes, she's pregnant . . . or she was . . ."

Abbie's legs threatened to give out from under her, but she fought the dizziness.

Burke narrowed his eyes and stared at his son so hard, so accusingly, Abbie could feel Justin retreating. She gripped her son's arm, furious at Burke for laying all the blame on him. Candy deserved to take some responsibility for this. God, she and Burke and the Kaufmans all deserved to take some responsibility.

She shook off those thoughts. Blame was secondary right now. The main thing was getting Candy to a hospital so she could be treated. Later, Abbie was sure, they would all do plenty of finger-pointing.

Suddenly there was the sound of footsteps hurrying toward them. Two EMTs appeared, and Burke, Duncan, Justin and Abbie moved aside so they could do their work.

They did a preliminary check on Candy, then moved her carefully onto a stretcher. One of them handed Burke his leather jacket, then Candy was covered with blankets. But when they brought the straps up to keep her secure, she whimpered in pain.

Her head lolled to the side, her eyes wild, searching. "Justin..."

Justin reached out and touched her cheek. "I'm sorry, Candy. Please, you gotta be okay."

So softly Abbie doubted anyone but herself and Justin heard it, Candy murmured, "Love you, Justin. Love you always."

Justin gulped, and then the stretcher was being lifted and carried away. One EMT notified the local hospital, saying they were bringing in a sixteen-year-old with a possible miscarriage or botched abortion.

Duncan followed the stetcher out through the darkness of the tunnel, leaving Abbie and Justin and Burke.

Abbie braced herself for Burke's fury, or at the very least more harsh words. He said nothing.

Burke had no words, but his silence didn't match his inner turmoil. For all his years in police work, for all the devastation and pain, the horror and regrets he'd witnessed, the scene he'd just encountered couldn't be measured in words and platitudes.

A young girl who might die, his own son deeply involved.

Abbie needed him to reach out to her and to Justin. The situation called for comfort and soothing, for bonding together as a family; this was a moment to unite, not separate.

Yet Burke didn't move. He remained at a safe distance, his guts as tight as steel, his heart like a stone.

When he should be the comforting husband, the concerned father and family man, something inside him closed down.

Instead of being supportive, he could only stand frozen at a distance, gripped by his own inadequacies as a parent and a husband, even while a desire to be both clamored inside him.

When he'd seen the terror in Justin's eyes, he'd felt his own heart break. Yet he felt ill equipped to reach out to his own son and offer support when the near-tragic events had been so unnecessary. In all honesty, what he felt was fury, not sympathy.

And so he hadn't tried to understand, but had judged Justin as harshly as he would have any punk kid who'd hurt someone else. And he knew his anger was defensive; he was afraid of losing control of himself, and anger threw up a protective barrier.

Anger was safer than emotional involvement. Yes, he'd comforted Candy, but that was different. She was young and scared and in pain—and she wasn't his own child. He wouldn't fall apart comforting her. He could remain detached.

He shuddered now. If Justin had been lying there, or Abbie... God, he'd have killed whoever was responsible.

Burke glanced at his watch, aware suddenly of the eerie silence that thickened in the small space. It wasn't much larger than a walk-in closet, yet the distance between him and his son and Abbie could have been miles. Justin stared at the place on the tunnel floor where Candy had lain just moments before. Burke stood less than a foot from his son, and yet neither reached out to the other. Abbie stood rigid, as though trapped between two magnetic fields of tension.

Burke stepped to one side, gesturing that his son and ex-wife should precede him out of the tunnel. "Come on, let's get out of here."

Abbie didn't move. "No. You go ahead. Candy needs to be checked on and the Kaufmans notified. Justin and I will be right along." She wanted a few minutes alone with Justin. He and Burke were so far apart she hoped to get some answers on her own. As Justin's mother.

Burke hesitated as if to argue, then, apparently deciding not to, he nodded and left.

Once Burke was out of hearing, Justin let out a long, shaky breath. "He hates me, doesn't he?"

"Sweetheart, there's plenty of time—" She tried to touch him, to comfort him.

But he pulled away from her. "No. He's right to hate me. I hurt Candy. I didn't mean to, but she was so freaked out... Her old man would've made her...and she didn't want to...I couldn't tell...Dad would've been so pissed off. Jeez, it seemed like the right thing to do and then it was too late..." He shuddered.

Abbie felt a growing horror at his words, not only at what she could decipher, but at the gaps in his rambling sentences. The EMT had said miscarriage or botched abortion. My God, had Justin taken her to some back-alley abortionist or had he...?

She wet suddenly dry lips. No, he wouldn't have tried to do it himself. A shiver of abhorrence gripped her.

Justin, however, stared into the darkness, his fists balled and tight against his hips, his expression one of pain and rejection.

In that moment she knew that her son believed she, too, had judged him the way Burke had. Aghast, she reached out her hand to him again, but he stumbled back. Then, apparently having made a decision, he pushed her out of his way and raced into the dark tunnel.

"Justin!"

He didn't answer. Abbie started after him, but he'd run in the opposite direction from which she and Burke had come. Automatically she looked that way, hoping Burke might still be within shouting distance.

"Burke!" No response.

She tried again, but still no answer. He must have already exited the tunnel.

In that instant, Abbie could have kicked herself for not taking Justin's arm and going with Burke. They'd be outside now and on their way to see Candy.

She glanced from the dim light in the direction Burke had gone to the gaping darkness into which Justin had run. She really had no choice unless she wanted to risk losing Justin again. It would take too much time to find Burke first. Her decision made, she headed into the tunnel Justin had taken.

Burke had left the flashlight, thank God. Moving quickly, she started to feel light-headed. The air in the tunnel was close and fetid. Her breathing came in gasps and halting gulps. Her throat ached both from the assault on her lungs and the held-back tears.

The tunnel grew narrower and damper. In places the smell of sewage penetrated the walls. She kept moving forward, thankful there weren't a lot of side exits.

Five minutes passed.

Ten.

Fifteen.

Twenty.

She was growing tired, stumbling, her breathing now reduced to ragged pants.

Faint noises filtered back to her from beyond. Voices, footsteps, but oh, so far away. The flashlight flickered, dimmed and then gave out completely. Blackness consumed her, but she couldn't turn around now. She'd gone too far. She stepped carefully forward, working her way deeper into the darkness.

"Justin, please come back!" she called, but the endless gloom swallowed her voice as effectively as it had swallowed her son....

CANDY WAS BEING carefully loaded into the rescue vehicle when Burke approached. She was unconscious, but the EMTs assured him her vitals were strong.

To Burke, one of the rescue men said, "She's underage, so parental permission is going to be needed, Mr. Wheeler. You got a number the doc can call?"

Burke turned around, expecting to see Abbie a few feet behind him. "Abbie . . ."

He frowned as his eyes scanned the crowd of people the raid on the tunnel had brought to the streets. Kids, pedestrians, rubberneckers in cars, all swarmed the area. No sign of Abbie and Justin. He swore under his breath. He'd thought they'd followed him.

Duncan was still in the building, and when Burke had come through the room, the cop had been questioning the kids before allowing them to be taken to the precinct. Maybe Duncan had stopped Justin to question him and Abbie had stayed with him.

Burke had decided that since he'd screwed up so royally in the tunnel, the least he could do was be there for Justin when he faced the police.

Quickly he gave the EMT Harvey Kaufman's name and address. The man nodded, closed the doors, and the van sped off with sirens blaring. But as Burke started up the steps to the building, the lights went out, and in a few seconds Duncan appeared. Burke glanced back at the police cars. Could Justin and Abbie be in one of them?

Duncan stopped. "That about wraps things up, Burke. I have to make a stop at the hospital. Hey, you okay?"

Burke felt a growing concern. "Have you seen my wife and son?"

"Not since the tunnel. Didn't they come out with you? I was busy with the other kids, so I didn't notice."

"They were behind me. I thought you might have stopped them to ask Justin questions."

"Yeah, well, I'm gonna have to do that, Burke, given the condition of the girl, but I wanted to wait till later. You know the law, so I know I can count on you to bring him to the precinct. Maybe they're in the lieutenant's car."

"Maybe."

Burke and Duncan checked, and when that drew a blank, asked an officer who was standing nearby. He said he hadn't seen Abbie since she went into the tunnel with Burke.

The last of the kids had been put into a police wagon, and Burke saw the lieutenant step back after saying something to the driver.

"You seen Abbie?" Burke asked.

"I thought she was with you."

"I thought so, too," Burke replied, cursing himself for not waiting for them.

"Could she and your son have already gone to the hospital?"

Burke shook his head. "No one saw them come out."

The two men headed back into the building. They went into the room, and Burke descended the rickety steps that led into the tunnel.

Why in hell hadn't they come out? From behind him, the lieutenant asked, "Want me to go with you?"

"No, stay here." Burke knew he had to do this himself.

"Take my flashlight." The lieutenant handed the light to Burke, then added, "It's about three miles of tunnel. I'll give Madison a shout and have him send some men in at the other end."

Burke frowned. "She wouldn't have gone to the other end."

"Not deliberately, but she may have gotten confused with all the turns. She could have headed in the wrong direction."

"I might buy that if she was alone and Justin hadn't lived in this dump. He must know the way out."

But the lieutenant's words had hit a nerve that had nothing to with the twists and turns in the tunnel and everything to do with how he'd treated Justin earlier. In an instant of insight, Burke knew that now he faced the very real consequences of that. He'd closed out his son when Justin needed him, and now not only Justin, but Abbie, too, had disappeared.

He moved deeper into the tunnel, shivering from more than the chill. He flipped on the flashlight, the illumination meager in the pitch-black hole. He walked quickly, his steps sure, his heart not so steady.

He passed the hollowed-out area where they'd found Justin and Candy and moved on, ignoring the above-ground sounds of civilization muted by the barrier of earth and cement.

He cupped his hands around his mouth and called, "Abbie! Justin!" Then he stood silently to listen.

A faint noise floated back to him, but he couldn't tell what it was. He moved forward again, his ears attuned to any sound.

The deeper he got into the tunnel, the more he began to wonder what Abbie and Justin had been thinking. If they'd taken a wrong turn, surely they would know it by now. Burke had already walked three times farther than the distance they'd walked to find Justin and Candy.

He trudged on, the cold eating through him, the fetid air making him nauseated.

"Hey, Burke!" a voice called, and a beam of light approached.

He stopped and waited. The light got brighter and in a few seconds a police officer appeared.

"Did you see anyone?" Burke asked.

"Abbie's with us."

Burke closed his eyes in heartfelt thanks. "Is she all right?"

"Cold and in a panic, but not hurt."

"In a panic?"

"Yeah. We don't know where your son is."

CHAPTER TWELVE

"PLEASE, I HAVE TO FIND Justin," Abbie said. She was at the far end of the tunnel, having been led out by a couple of police officers. "He was just a few feet ahead of me," she went on desperately. "He can't have gone far. He's upset and angry and..."

Her words faltered and she stopped for a breath. She wanted to set off immediately in search of Justin, but the grip the police officer had on her arm didn't allow her to go anywhere.

"Your husband will be right here. He'll help."

Abbie stiffened, anger rushing through her. She managed to contain it; she'd save any invectives for Burke.

This time she had no intention of cringing from his icy stares; she had no intention of backing off from the rage she felt. She was angry, too, at herself for depending on him, for believing in all his solicitation, his worry about Justin and, yes, even in their intimacies. She'd foolishly allowed herself to assume that loving him was the one thing that could bind them. But in the lengthy and complex area of their relationship, and in light of the present circumstances, simply loving him had proved of little value.

It hadn't been enough. Not nearly enough. She saw things more clearly now than ever before.

Burke emerged from the dark, his eyes haunted, his face grim.

He gave her a long look, but when he attempted to touch her, she shrank away. He narrowed his eyes and she guessed he was furious with her.

Well, she decided, that was fine. She was just as furious with him. Thanks to him, their son had now run away for the second time.

Burke asked the officer about Justin. "Any ideas on where to look?"

"We've notified the cars in the area. I talked to Duncan and he said your kid was pretty shaken by what happened with his girlfriend. The hospital might be a good place to start." He gave Burke the name of the hospital.

"Yeah, by now they'll have notified her parents," Burke said. "We'll check there."

The officer suggested to Burke that he take them back to Johnny's so they could get their car and go on to the hospital.

"But what if Justin's still here?" Abbie asked Burke when he agreed to this plan. How could Burke walk away so easily?

"Justin can take care of himself," he said tonelessly.

Given his attitude in the tunnel, she shouldn't have been surprised by his answer. Nevertheless her fury rose.

"You're a bastard, Burke Wheeler."

His hold on her arm tightened. "Let's go."

"No."

"Abbie, don't argue with me," he said through gritted teeth.

"Why? Are you going to close me out? Holler at me and blame me? I can't even think of a good reason why I should be talking to you, never mind rushing off with you as if you're a worried parent."

He pulled her aside and in an ice-coated voice said, "I have no intention of standing here on a public street arguing with you. You can scream to your heart's content when we're alone."

"Our son has run away! Again, Burke! Does that even bother you?"

"Hell, of course it bothers me."

"Then why were you so cruel in the tunnel? I know you were worried about Candy—I was, too. But Justin needed to know you cared for him. He needed you to act like his *father,* not some damn cop doing his duty."

Burke tugged her close, his mouth mere inches from hers, his voice a bare rasp. "Because doing my duty is a hell of a lot easier than being a husband and father."

She stared at him openmouthed, thrown totally off balance by the enormity of his confession. His duty was easier? My God, had she stumbled on some vulnerable facet of him that in the past she'd thought was nonexistent? Was his struggle to be a family man more perilous for him than she'd ever imagined? Had the problem all this time been not that he didn't trust her, but that he didn't trust himself?

"Burke?"

But he released her, backing away as if he'd revealed more about himself than he'd intended. She got only the briefest glance at his face, yet it was long enough to know that he was definitely unnerved.

"Burke?" she tried again.

"Forget I said anything."

"It's not what you said, it's how you feel."

"I feel like hell, okay? Is that enough? And given this godawful mess, does it matter a damn how I feel?"

"It matters. It matters to me and to your son," she said forcefully.

He gripped her upper arms and shook her. "Let . . . it . . . go."

His emphasis only made her more certain than ever that he regretted his self-revealing outburst. Something had scared him, and although his reaction might be mostly because of Justin, Abbie tucked it away in a corner of her mind to examine later.

Taking her by one arm, he urged her toward the police cruiser.

"Burke, I can't just leave here." She wrenched out of his grasp.

He planted his hands low on his hips. "What in hell are you going to accomplish here?"

"There's a good chance Justin's still around here. He might—"

"Might what? Rush out from behind some building and into your arms? Not likely."

"But if I leave and he needs me . . ."

She gulped and turned her head away, swallowing the sudden emotion. The truth tumbled through her despite her efforts to close her mind to it.

Their mistake had been in looking for Justin together, she believed. Their son was no fool and he must have assumed that if his mother was with his father, then his parents must be in accord; his mother must be just as angry as his dad. And if that was how he felt, then God knew where he'd gone.

In a starkly pain-filled voice, she said, "He doesn't want to need me, does he, Burke? He ran because when he sees me, he sees you, too. He probably thinks I'm judging him as harshly as you are." She lifted her chin, the anger in her eyes now turned to regret. "But none of that really matters, does it? I've been unfair to you, blaming you when this is just as much my fault."

Without speaking, Burke put his arm around her, and she leaned against him, glad for his support and strength. They climbed into the cruiser and were driven the short distance to Johnny's, then got into Burke's car and drove to the hospital.

At the front desk, they were told Candy was on the fifth floor.

Abbie prayed to God that Justin was there, but what if he wasn't? As she and Burke rode the elevator, she thought she'd never felt so useless. Her hopes had been high through this entire arduous process, but now she could barely find a glimmer of faith.

This time Justin had run because he believed his father hated him, and heaven only knew what he believed about her.

She shuddered. What had Burke said? That it was easier to be a cop? God, that was an understatement. For her it was far easier to give instructions on dress fabrics and the newest styles than to try to work her way through the trials of parenting a teenager.

The elevator doors opened, and she and Burke stepped out.

As they rounded the corner and walked toward the nurses' station, Burke said, "The Kaufmans were notified, so they're probably on their way."

"I'd forgotten all about them."

"I gave the EMT their name and address, but I didn't have their phone number."

"I had it."

"Yeah, when they were putting Candy in the rescue van, I thought you were right behind me."

And if Justin and I had been, he would be here right now.

If only Burke had glanced back when they were in the tunnel, he would have seen they weren't following.

If only she'd taken Justin's arm and followed, not stayed behind to try to comfort him. Then if he'd balked she could have called out for Burke.

Now Burke got the attention of the nurse seated behind the Plexiglas petition and asked for information about Candy.

The nurse glanced at a chart on the wall. "Are you her parents?"

Burke shook his head. "No. My wife and I found Candy."

She frowned at them. "You're the Wheelers?"

"Yes."

"You have a son named Justin?"

Abbie's pulse sped up and Burke gripped the edge of the desk. "Yes, we do."

The nurse peered at them as if they represented the very worst in parenting. "Your son has been very...difficult," she said, the accusation in her tone impossible to miss. "I had to threaten to call the police to get him under control."

Abbie grimaced at the word "difficult," but she was deeply relieved. Candy and her condition was Justin's concern; he hadn't run away again—he'd come to find out about Candy. A wealth of pride in her son filled her.

"Thank God he's here," Abbie said, smiling despite the nurse's stern look.

"Where is he?" Burke asked, his own relief obvious in his barely audible question.

"In the waiting room. I told him if he didn't cooperate, he would not be allowed to see his girlfriend."

"Then Candy's going to be all right?"

"Yes, but if you want any details, you'll have to talk to the doctor," she said, turning away.

For Abbie the good news about Candy was enough for now.

Burke let out a breath that sounded as if he'd been holding it for some time. Then he took her arm and they walked toward the waiting room.

Stopping outside the swinging doors, he said, "You go on in alone and talk to Justin, Abbie."

She started to argue. After all, they were a family; they should all be there. Yet insisting Burke go into the waiting room to see his son when clearly he didn't want to might only ignite a further explosive situation between father and son.

"The Kaufmans will want all the details," she said, giving him a good reason to delay seeing Justin.

He nodded. "Yeah, good idea. I'll wait here, and when they arrive I'll fill them in."

They stared at each other for a few tense seconds.

Abbie had never seen him look so empty.

Burke had never felt so inadequate and hollow.

He turned away and walked back toward the elevators.

Abbie entered the waiting room. Justin was sprawled in a chair, eyes closed, reminding her so much of Burke she felt a little dizzy.

She moved forward cautiously, not wanting to startle him, although she doubted he would bolt now. The nurse probably hadn't told him anything about Candy, so to Justin the girl's condition was still in question.

Standing beside him, she curled her hands into fists to keep herself from trying to hug him or treat him like a little boy with a skinned knee. After a moment she uncurled her fingers and reached out to gently brush back the wave of dark curly hair that fell over his forehead.

His eyes flew open and he jackknifed into an upright position as if scalded. Abbie withdrew her hand. His wariness was understandable.

He folded himself forward, head down, knees apart, his eyes studying his unlaced sneakers. "Hi," he mumbled.

"Hi yourself." She sat down in the chair beside him.

He glanced toward the closed doors. "Do you know anything about Candy? I mean, is she okay? I asked that nurse, but she made it sound like a big secret."

"Candy's going to be okay."

He visibly relaxed, then started to rise. "I gotta see her."

"We asked, but the nurse said her parents have to visit first."

"Her parents are jerks. Especially her old man." Then, as if his mind was just catching up with what Abbie had said, he looked at her directly. "You said *we* asked. You and Dad? He's here?"

"He's waiting for Candy's parents."

"Oh."

"He didn't come in because he was afraid you'd get upset."

Justin gave her a dubious frown. "Him? Afraid? Yeah, sure."

"Your father has a hard time saying what he feels."

"No, he doesn't. He made his feelings very clear in the underground." Then, as if he'd given the past few days a lot of serious thought, Justin said, "I don't blame him. I even hate myself."

Abbie's heart contracted. "Sweetheart, he doesn't hate you."

The boy shrugged, then reached into his shirt pocket and pulled out a slightly crushed pack of cigarettes. He got to his feet and, moving a couple of yards away, he shook one out and stuck it in his mouth.

"Uh, Justin, there's no smoking," Abbie said, pointing to the sign.

"Oh, yeah. Right." He scowled, replaced the cigarette and shoved the pack back in his pocket, then began to pace restlessly.

Abbie hadn't realized he smoked, but she wasn't surprised. Running away with a pregnant girlfriend, shoplifting, running from her and Burke... Smoking was little more than a blip of concern.

She laced her hands together and cleared her throat. "At the front desk, the nurse said you were difficult."

Justin stopped his pacing and looked at her. "She wouldn't tell me how Candy is or let me see for myself. I should be there when she has to face her parents."

"Honey, her parents aren't monsters."

"Yeah, sure. Her old man'll call her a tramp for running off with riffraff like me."

"You're not riffraff."

"He thinks so. He thinks the only guy good enough for his daughter is some geeky nerd who's on his way to some big-time college." Justin resumed pacing.

"Is her father's disapproval the reason you and Candy ran away?" Abbie braced herself for the answer.

He stopped again and fixed his gaze on her as if judging the amount of truth he intended to tell her by the distance between them. "Sort of. She was afraid her father would make her get an abortion."

Abbie nodded. "Your dad and I suspected she might be pregnant."

He lowered his head, and for the first time, Abbie heard his voice falter. "Yeah. With my baby..."

Quickly, so that he wouldn't think she was sitting in some deep moral judgment of him, she got up and went to him, touching his arm. He flinched but he didn't shake off her hand.

"Sweetheart, why didn't you come to us?"

His face went pale at her question. It was as if she'd suggested he walk on burning coals.

"Are you kidding? Dad would've freaked out." He paused, and the silence in the room suddenly felt crushingly close. Taking a step away, he muttered. "I remember what happened before..."

Abbie blinked. She felt a sudden sense of dread and had to force herself to ask, "Before what?"

Justin shuffled his feet, obviously embarrassed. "Before you guys split. One night I heard you arguing when Dad came home real late. It was about when you got pregnant with me."

Abbie closed her eyes and braced herself. Oh God. Surely Justin hadn't heard the accusations she and Burke had flung at each other.

"Justin, people say things in anger—"

"Dad was really pissed off and said a lot of stuff about you deceiving yourself if you thought a kid would make things better between you. I kept thinking . . ." Justin turned away, but not before Abbie saw the genuine pain in his eyes.

She knew her own face had gone pale. Her throat contracted so tightly she had to struggle to get her next words out.

"Justin, you should've come to me. In an argument, in the heat of the moment, a lot of hurtful, angry things are said, but often they're things people don't really mean. There are explan—"

"I heard what I heard," he interrupted sullenly. "Don't try to goop it up with dumb excuses. Just because I was a little kid didn't mean I didn't know that you and Dad never loved each other and you only had me to keep him from leaving." He turned away.

Abbie wished Burke was here. He had a way of cutting through all the words and getting to the point. And the point that worried Abbie was what Justin had concluded.

That his father hadn't wanted him.

"Justin, you were about ten years old and—"

"Did you, Mom?" he interrupted again. "Did you get pregnant to make Dad stay with you? Am I the reason you didn't get divorced right away?"

"No!"

"She's telling the truth, Justin."

They both swung around. Burke stood in the doorway.

Not moving, he continued. "I admit I wasn't enthusiastic about having kids, but after you arrived I never once didn't want you. I've never, not even for an instant, regretted having you for a son."

"Then why did you accuse Mom of using me to save your marriage?"

Abbie started to say something, but Burke stopped her, saying, "I think he wants the answer from me."

Abbie nodded, and after a long pause Burke began slowly, "This isn't easy for me, Justin, because I don't have a simple answer. I guess it was easier to blame your mother for trying to save our marriage than it was for me to admit I never should have married her in the first place. Having you scared me because I didn't have a clue what a father was supposed to do to raise a kid right. Just as I didn't have a clue how to be a husband."

He glanced at Abbie, then back at Justin before going on. "I made some major mistakes, going so far as believing that divorce might fix things. If I'd been around, you might have come to me and your mother about Candy instead of running away." He took a deep breath. "Then again, you may have inherited that from me. I'm a real pro at running from what I don't want to face."

Abbie gaped at him, astonished at his admission.

Not once had he mentioned his obsession with being the perfect cop.

Not once had he spoken of his own horrific childhood, his father's illegal activities, his lack of a mother.

Not once had he laid blame on anyone but himself. Yet as pleased as she was by his honesty, her heart sank at his one glaring omission.

He'd said nothing about loving her. Nothing about *ever* loving her.

In the lengthening silence Justin stared at his sneakers.

Burke was looking at her.

Finally, to Justin, she said, "What did you think we would do if you'd come and told us about you and Candy?"

He shrugged.

Burke crossed to him. "You thought I'd freak out the way I did when you overheard your mother and I arguing."

"I guess."

"You're right, Justin. I would've been angry. Damn angry."

"Burke!"

He turned to Abbie. "Enough of treating Justin like a child. He's not. He knows the score, and to pretend I would've been cool and detached is ridiculous. I would've been furious."

Justin looked at Burke with an expression that seemed to show acceptance rather than rejection of Burke's honest words. Perhaps the gritty truth was best. Burke wouldn't coddle him as if he was an ignorant kid refusing to take responsibility for his actions.

With a maturity in his voice that Abbie had never heard before, Justin said, "Candy isn't just some girl for me to get it on with, Dad. I love her."

Burke studied him a few seconds, then, apparently accepting Justin's explanation, he asked, "Why weren't you using birth control?"

"We were. Uh, most of the time."

"That's all it takes—that one time. Did you know that Ginger Kaufman saw you one afternoon in Candy's bed?"

The slump of his son's shoulders said it all.

"Pretty bold and arrogant, don't you think?" Burke glanced over at Abbie as if to say *He comes by those traits naturally. We were bold and arrogant, too.*

Abbie agreed. She recalled all the places she and Burke had made love in those eager early days when Burke was trying to convince her he was all wrong for her and she was telling him she didn't care, she wanted him anyway.

How simple it all seemed back then, she thought wistfully. Kisses and touches that soon had them lost in the heat of desire. If her guess was right, Justin and Candy had experienced that same overwhelming passion.

Abbie sighed and found Burke staring at her. His eyes asked, *You remember all those places, don't you, Abbie?*

She did. Besides the back seat of Burke's car, they'd made love in the sand dunes that lined the beach, in the hayloft of a neighbor's barn, in the pantry at her mother's house on Christmas Eve a few weeks before they were married. Yes, she remembered them all.

Justin looked from one parent to the other. "Jeez, we were just lookin' for a place to be alone. We would've gone to my house, but Mom would've found out. Mrs. Kaufman didn't check up on Candy, but after school Mom was always calling or coming home to check on me."

"That's because she worried about you," Burke said. "Now we know she had good reason. So when you thought Candy was pregnant you didn't go to her parents because you were afraid of her father. And you didn't come to us because you were afraid I'd be furious. That leaves your mother. Why didn't you tell her, Justin?"

His cheeks flamed red. "Jeez, Dad..."

"Embarrassed?"

"Well, telling your mother you've been having sex is tough."

"Especially when you like it so much you have no intention of quitting."

He mumbled a "yeah."

Burke put his arm around Justin and the two stood quietly for a few moments.

Abbie dabbed at the dampness in her eyes, hardly able to believe that a renewed relationship with their son had come out of all this.

Then from the corridor outside the waiting room came raised voices.

Abbie walked to the door and opened it. Ginger and Harvey Kaufman were having a heated argument.

"Dammit, Ginger, let go of me," Harvey said angrily, trying to pluck his wife's hand off his wrist. "That kid hurt my little girl."

"Harvey, please. The doctor said Candy is going to be fine."

"Fine!" He spat out the word and glared at her. "How can you say *fine*? She's lost her virginity, she could have died because he knocked her up—"

Ginger clamped her hand over his mouth. "Keep your voice down. You want everyone in the hospital to hear you?"

"I don't care who hears me."

"Harvey, listen to me. We should be grateful Candy is alive and no permanent damage has been done. She says she loves Justin, and you're talking as if this was all his fault."

"Damn right! It *was* all his fault!"

A few passersby in the corridor glanced in their direction. Ginger stepped in front of Harvey as if to shield the sound of their argument.

Abbie was about to interrupt and tell them to come into the waiting room when Ginger said in a tone that was tight and pointed, "Harvey Kaufman, you're acting like a narrow-minded puritanical idiot."

His jaw dropped at her accusation.

But before he could summon a response, she continued, "Candy is just as much to blame, and she admits it. Why can't you put away those silly blinders and accept that your daughter is going to make her own decisions? She's no longer a little girl with apple cheeks and pigtails just waiting for Daddy to come home. I'm warning you, Harvey, if you continue to treat her that way, she's going to get in real trouble."

"And you don't call this real trouble?" he sputtered indignantly.

"I call it a mistake that got out of hand. Perhaps if she'd thought you wouldn't act like Attila the Hun, she would have come to us instead of running away with poor Justin."

"Whose side are you on, Ginger?" he asked, appalled.

"There are no sides here, Harvey. This isn't a war. This is about our daughter growing up, and we can make that a lot easier by supporting her and helping her make choices instead of running away for fear of how we're going to act."

"But she wants me to like this little bastard and I want to kill him!"

Abbie stepped back into the room and let the door swing shut. She was not entirely unsympathetic to Harvey. She might not like hearing her son called a little bastard, but he was reacting as any frightened parent might. And her respect for Ginger had climbed considerably. The woman was standing up to her husband and viewing what had happened with Justin and Candy as a serious mistake, not as some disaster from which they couldn't recover.

At last the Kaufmans came into the waiting room. Harvey was scowling and muttering under his breath, and Ginger had hold of his arm, as if she feared he might try to do something lethal to Justin.

Justin started forward, his fists clenched at his sides. But Burke clamped a hand on his shoulder and held him back.

In a low voice he said, "Why don't you go and see Candy? I have a feeling she'd like to know you're here. Your mother and I will talk to the Kaufmans."

He gave his father a grateful look, then glanced at Abbie. She nodded for him to go ahead, then turned her gaze to her ex-husband.

Burke had handled Justin better in the past twenty minutes than he ever had, she thought. Nothing was as important for kids as their parents' being willing to be open and truthful with them.

Burke had shown honesty by admitting to Justin that if he'd told him about Candy's pregnancy, he would have been furious.

Justin had guessed his father's reaction would be anger; having overheard his parents' argument when he was ten had destroyed any faith he might have had that his father's anger didn't mean rejection. That, coupled with Candy's fear of her own father, had made the two teenagers frightened enough to see running away as their only choice.

Abbie watched as Justin made a wide turn around the Kaufmans. Harvey glared at him, then swung to face Burke.

"Now see here, Wheeler. That kid of yours—"

"Knocked up your daughter, ran away with her, and now you're blistering mad."

"Yes, but—"

"I know just how you feel."

"You do?"

"Fathers tend to get pretty upset when their kids are in trouble."

Harvey gave Ginger a superior look. "See, he knows how I feel even if you don't."

Obviously exasperated, Ginger glowered at Burke. "Mr. Wheeler—"

"Burke." He grinned so engagingly that Abbie lowered her head to hide her own smile. "May I call you Ginger? Given the circumstances, the formalities seem a little silly."

Ginger gaped at him, whatever argument she'd been about to raise apparently forgotten.

"Why don't you and Abbie get some coffee?" Burke suggested. "And I know Abbie wants to see Candy. Harvey and I will work things out between us."

Abbie crossed to Burke and touched his arm, indicating she wanted to speak to him alone.

They excused themselves and walked to the windows, which were at the far side of the room. They stood with their backs to the Kaufmans, partially hidden by a couple of pillars. Burke draped his arm around her neck as if they were in deep consultation, and they were so close together she could hear him breathing. She caught the too-familiar male scent of him and had to stifle the impulse to throw herself into his arms.

Haltingly she said, "I owe you an apology."

"Accepted."

"But you don't know for what."

"It doesn't matter. Right now, all that's important is Justin and Candy. Let's just concentrate on them and getting them home."

He reached into his pocket and pulled out a crumpled ten-dollar bill. "Here, this should cover the coffee for you and Ginger."

She started to refuse it, but then, scowling, she peered at the bill he'd pressed into her hand. She looked up at him. "How did you know I didn't have any money?"

"Abbie, you never carry money when you're with me."

Her thoughts scrambled for a time she could have cited to refute his claim, but there wasn't one. My God, he was right! But what settled deep inside of her was the fact that her action had been natural and automatic; totally subconscious. She'd depended on Burke and counted on him for something as incidental as knowing she didn't need money because he always had it.

She had depended on him, counted on him, trusted him... Abbie shook away the direction of her thoughts. This was ridiculous. Counting on him to have money was hardly in the same league with counting on him to be there when she needed him.

He dipped his head and kissed her, his mouth warm, his hand tightening around her nape as if he wanted more than just a marginal response.

"You're a dangerous woman, Abbie Wheeler. I'm almost sorry this is all about to be over."

"We could . . ."

"Find someplace private and dark?"

She met his gaze; her heart was weakening. "I should be appalled at the suggestion and say absolutely not."

He grinned. "But you want to say yes, so let's do it."

"This is all your fault," she said, exasperated at her own instant reaction. "If we hadn't made love the other night, I wouldn't be feeling like this."

He brushed his fingers across her breasts. "It's called a taste of the forbidden."

"You're not easy to forget, Burke."

"We always did have great sex. What about it? Once more before we get on with our lives."

She searched his face. "You're serious, aren't you?"

He took her hand and pressed it to the front of his jeans. "Serious. Name the time."

She shivered, her good sense at war with the love she had for him—a love she knew now she'd never gotten completely out of her system. It was insane; all she stood to gain was more hurt. And yet...

"I don't know, Burke. Once we get home, Justin'll be there...."

"He'll be at your place. We'll go to mine."

She hesitated, then shook her head. "I can't. I'm sure other women have been there and—" Feeling foolish, she cut off her words and lowered her gaze.

"Abbie, look at me."

Slowly she lifted her lashes. "This is a dumb idea," she said. "Let's just forget we even considered it. We both have our own lives. Having some fling with each other will just complicate things.''

Burke, however, wasn't going to let the issue drop. "I want you, Abbie. Badly. And you want me. Just as badly. True?"

She could only nod.

"Then let's skip all the reasons why we shouldn't."

He kissed her again, this time deeply, his tongue tangling with hers in an erotic dance she couldn't and didn't want to deny.

He lifted his head a fraction. "Next week. Tuesday morning after Justin goes to school.''

She swallowed.

She should say no.

She really should.

CHAPTER THIRTEEN

BURKE, ABBIE AND JUSTIN all stayed at Johnny's that night.

The next morning, after their bags were in the car, and while Justin used Pammie's desk phone to call the hospital and talk to Candy, Burke and Abbie went into Johnny's office to say goodbye.

Burke extended his hand. "Johnny, what can I say but thanks."

"Hell, I didn't do anything but give y'all a home base," he replied, shaking Burke's hand warmly. "You and Abbie did the legwork."

"But the home base was a godsend. If you need any help from down my way, just give a shout."

"Fair enough." Johnny glanced toward the door. "Where's Pammie gotten to? She wanted to make sure y'all didn't leave before she saw you."

Abbie glanced out at Justin, who had leaned back in Pammie's chair, propped his feet on the desk and had the phone anchored to his ear.

After she and Burke had talked in the hospital waiting room, Abbie had visited Candy. The girl had been pale but alert—and happy Justin was with her. The Kaufmans had agreed when the hospital suggested Candy stay for a couple of days just to make sure she didn't develop any further complications. The doctor had determined that Candy had not suffered from a botched abortion, but had had a natural miscarriage which had resulted in hemorrhaging.

Later Burke took Justin to the local police precinct, but no charges were filed. Running away wasn't a criminal offense, and from Abbie's observation of Justin and Candy last night, she doubted they would try that again.

Justin blamed himself for Candy's losing the baby. He should have gotten her emergency help or at the very least not run when he'd seen his parents, but panic and fear and not realizing how badly Candy needed medical attention had all worked against that.

Burke had asked him directly about the roll of cash Pammie had seen him with at the Merry-Go-Round. It turned out Justin had simply been securing a place for the two of them in the tunnel. As for the shoplifting, they'd had so little money to spare that Justin felt they *had* to steal the pregnancy-test kit; they'd wanted to make sure Candy was pregnant.

Justin told Burke he'd never shoplifted anything before, and judging by his failure to notice the in-store security camera trained on him when he slipped the kit into his jacket, Burke was inclined to believe him.

With his questions answered, Burke had looked exhausted, and Abbie had admitted to not feeling all that energetic herself. She'd just been relieved and happy that Justin and Candy were all right. The past few days had not only been filled with crisis, but she'd been forced to face her unwieldy and complicated feelings for Burke, as well as face the future, once more, without him.

She'd been unable to deny what her heart was saying.

She still loved Burke.

She'd thought that anything as profound as that realization would have come by way of some romantic gesture, or at the very least occur when she was deliriously happy to be with him. It hadn't.

In those moments when he'd drawn her aside in the hospital waiting room and said he wanted her one more time, Abbie had known. Known without a doubt that she still loved him, and known that love would once again hurt her.

And loving him was the reason she'd almost refused his suggestion of making love, just as loving him was the reason she'd finally agreed.

Circumstances, the tension of not knowing where Justin was and then working together to find him had been the glue that had kept them close these past few days. But now that Justin was safe, all that remained was sexual desire. Not a lot different from those days when their marriage was crumbling.

Abbie shivered. Why had she agreed to make love with him one more time? Had she no pride? No sense of outrage that he could just whisper and touch her and she'd melt into a puddle of sensation?

Justin hung up the phone, and Burke went out to talk to him. They seemed totally at ease with each other now, and why, Abbie thought, shouldn't they be? The two had pretty well cleared up the issues between them—unlike Burke and her; ease was the last thing they had between them. Here she had stupidly fallen back in love with her ex-husband, and all he wanted was a morning of sex.

Good move, Abbie. This is definitely not the road to everlasting happiness. She pressed her fingers to her temples. Maybe she was more exhausted than she realized.

Nevertheless, she stood up and brushed her hands down her jean-clad thighs. As much as she wanted to see Pammie to say goodbye, she also wanted to get home.

She walked out of Johnny's office and into the reception area. "Burke?"

He turned and nodded. "Yeah, we should get moving."

Johnny stepped out of his office, too, a puzzled frown on his face. "I can't understand why Pammie isn't here."

Then, as if she heard her name being called, Pammie rushed in the front door. Her hair was flying, her cheeks flushed, her eyes alive with excitement—and a touch of something else. Fear? Self-protectiveness? Clutched to her chest was a folder bulging with papers.

Breathlessly she said, "Sorry I'm late, but I wanted to gather all these up to show Abbie..." Her voice trailed off as if suddenly she wasn't as sure of herself in front of Burke and Justin. She was surrounded by silence as everyone waited for her to speak.

Wanting to ease the teenager's awkwardness, Abbie walked over to her and slipped an arm around her waist. "What did you want to show me, Pammie?"

The girl fumbled with the folder, laying it carefully on her desk. Her hands shook nervously, and Abbie glanced at Burke. He picked up her signal and said to Justin, "Let's you and I go get doughnuts and coffee and wait in the car."

"And I have some calls to make," Johnny said. "In my office." He went back in and closed the door.

Justin headed for the door to the street, but Burke turned to Pammie before he left. "Sweetheart, it was great seeing you again, and I'm glad things are coming together for you."

Spontaneously she threw herself into Burke's arms. He caught her, returning her hug fondly before setting her away.

With a catch in her voice, Pammie murmured, "I'm glad Justin is okay, but if he hadn't run away and you hadn't come and I hadn't met Abbie..." Her voice dissolved into a gulp and a sniffle.

Over Pammie's head, Burke mouthed a "What's going on?" to Abbie. She shrugged, spreading her hands in confusion.

Finally Burke dropped a kiss on the girl's forehead and grinned. "Well, Abbie's dying of curiosity about what you want to show her, so I'm gonna split and let you two talk."

Pammie nodded, but then added fervently, "You're so lucky to have her, Burke. I mean she's just so super."

Burke gave Abbie a long look. "Yeah, she's pretty sensational."

By the time Burke left, Abbie was more confused than ever. Other than spending a bit of time talking about fashion consulting with Pammie and encouraging her to think about taking some college courses, she didn't know what she'd done to garner all these compliments.

She had to admit to curiosity, but she prayed Pammie wouldn't ask her for modeling advice. Despite Abbie's intention to mention the scar on the other occasions they'd talked, she hadn't had the heart.

Pammie was nervously sorting through the papers. Not looking at Abbie, she took a shaky breath. "You remember I said I wanted to be a model?"

Abbie nodded, dreading the thought of shattering Pammie's illusions. If Pammie asked her directly, she wouldn't lie to her.

"Well, I know that won't ever happen." She touched the scar on her cheek. "I think I've always known, but it was so hard to let go of that dream. Sort of like wanting to see everything in a positive light."

"Rose-colored glasses," Abbie murmured, pleased and relieved that Pammie had figured out the reality all by herself.

"I guess. I think, too, that modeling was kind of safe to want. You know, like wanting to go to Hollywood and be an actress? Lots of girls talk about that, but they know it won't ever happen. It's sort of a fantasy kind of thing, you know?''

Abbie nodded, impressed.

''Anyway, after we talked that day about clothes and you told me what you did, I pulled out some sketches I'd done.''

Pammie took some of the pages from her folder and laid them out on the desk.

Abbie moved closer and studied the charcoal drawings. Her eyes widened at the talent they revealed.

Although rough in technique, they demonstrated an impeccable fashion sense, an intriguing sweep of individual style and the kind of bold neo-classic patterns that Abbie hadn't seen drawn with such flair in years. So many students of fashion simply copied or tried to enhance already established styles. Pammie's were innovative and dramatic—qualities Abbie knew were gold in the fashion world.

''These are exceptionally good, Pammie.'' Abbie went through the sketches one more time, even more impressed by the girl's use of subtle detail. ''You definitely have a promising career ahead of you in design.''

Pammie dropped into a chair, noticeable relief spreading across her face. ''I knew I had to show them to you, Abbie. Since you work with designs, I knew your opinion mattered. But I was so scared you'd think they were awful.''

Abbie fully understood just how fragile Pammie's faith in herself was, but she also realized how much courage it took to risk criticism.

Once more Abbie sorted through the array of sketches. "Then thank God I can tell you they're terrific."

Pammie's eyes were sheened with tears. "I don't know what to say. I don't even know what to do with them or where to go or who would want to look at them."

Abbie grinned. "Then let me help."

"You mean it?" the girl whispered, her words more awed than questioning.

"Yes, I mean it."

For the next few minutes they discussed Pammie's future in fashion design, and Abbie offered to show the sketches to her friend Celada. As a fashion designer whose collection had recently won critical praise, Celada had achieved success, Abbie knew, partly because she was always on the lookout for new talent. Talent such as Pammie's. Her work would make Celada delirious.

"*The* Celada? You really know Celada?" Pammie's eyes were as round as saucers.

Abbie smiled. "Yes, I know her very well."

From euphoria Pammie fell into sinking distress and collapsed back in the chair. "Omigod, I can't. What if, well, if she...Celada...*the* Celada...No, no, I can't."

Abbie touched her shoulder. "Pammie—"

"I used all my courage to show you. And you're a friend. I couldn't deal with *her* seeing them and hating them."

She started to gather up the sketches, but Abbie stopped her. "Listen to me, Pammie. Do you think I would offer to show these to Celada if I didn't think she'd like them?"

"I don't know. If you didn't want to hurt my feelings, you might."

"Wouldn't it be crueller for me to raise your hopes knowing someone else would dash them? What kind of friend does that? If you trust my judgment, then you must trust that I wouldn't expose you to Celada's expert eye if I didn't believe she would see the same talent I see."

"I'm scared."

"I know. These sketches are filled with your heart. And when we risk our heart it's scary. The alternative is never knowing if you've passed up a wonderful career opportunity because of fear."

"I don't know..."

"Pammie, you've beat drugs. You've gotten away from an abusive boyfriend, and you've faced the reality that your scar has closed the door on modeling for you. All of those are big accomplishments. Think of showing these sketches to Celada as your next accomplishment."

The girl nodded slowly. "You really think she'll like them?"

"Yes," Abbie said firmly. "I know she will. She'll have suggestions and she'll point out where they still need work, but that's all part of learning and getting better."

"Okay..." Pammie hesitated, her worry not quite gone. "But you'll call me and tell me the moment you hear something, even if it's bad news?"

"I promise."

Carefully Pammie placed the sketches in the folder and handed the entire thing to Abbie as if she were relinquishing her soul.

"How long do you think it'll take?" she asked.

"A few days." Abbie gave her a big hug. "While you're waiting, get busy and do some more designs."

By the time Abbie climbed into the car a few minutes later, she felt wonderful. Besides finding Justin and Candy, she'd maybe helped a young woman launch a career. Someone once said that good things can happen in the most unlikely places. Who would have thought that Justin's running away would result in the discovery of a new talent in a rat hole like Sade Court?

She glanced over at Burke. Too bad the risk she was considering with her own heart wasn't as simple.

"So what's up with Pammie?" Burke asked. "What was it she had to show you?"

Abbie explained, leaving out nothing.

He nodded, a smile forming. "You really think Celada will go for them?"

"You sound like Pammie, but yes, I think she will. I know Celada's taste, and discovering talent she can personally nurture and guide makes her look good. Pammie will go far. I know it."

She put her head back and closed her eyes. God, she wished she herself only had to make a career decision. That seemed easy compared to a relationship decision.

Should she keep the appointment with him on Tuesday?

Should she take the less risky path and refuse?

How she wished she could have it both ways.

ON TUESDAY MORNING Burke walked out of the Providence police station and climbed into his car. Since he'd returned to duty, his mind had been so unfocused he'd taken himself off a new investigation so as to avoid the chance of making some fatal mistake.

Will Gagne, the Walcott detective who'd introduced Burke to Harvey Kaufman, walked up to the car and leaned down, his hands gripping the open window.

"Had to come up here to ID a prisoner. I was hoping I'd catch you." He paused. "Hey, you look tired. Everything okay?"

Burke shrugged, his thoughts as sluggish as his body. "I don't know. Maybe I'm getting old."

"Hell, aren't we all," Will muttered. "How's Justin doing?"

"Good. Still seeing Candy, but he's back in school with his mind on grades and college."

"School must be a helluva lot more exciting than when we went. But then, these past few days have probably been a better teacher than all the sex-education classes in the world."

Burke nodded. "Yeah, despite what happened with Candy, I think both kids have come out of this stronger."

"And Abbie?"

He shifted in the seat, suddenly aware of all the ways Abbie was on his mind. So much so he could barely think about anything else.

He'd tried to tell himself it was the planned sex, and of course that was part of it, but the myriad other stirrings had nothing to do with sex. And these other stirrings scared him because he didn't know what to do with them. Sex was easy, the satisfaction rewarding, but also predictable. The deeper emotions that rolled and tossed in his gut weren't as easily explainable.

"I haven't seen her since we returned from Boston."

"I got filled in on what happened in Sade Court, but there were also a lot of blanks. The chief told me you've been preoccupied and restless since you got back. Now this is just a suggestion from an old friend, Burke, but maybe a vacation..." Will ventured the word as if he was suggesting an illegal operation.

"Then what?"

Will shook his head. "You *are* in a bad way. You're supposed to say, yeah, be nice to get drunk and get laid."

Burke scowled. "You know what, Will? I couldn't be less interested in either. You do it and it's over with, and the awful emptiness just comes back even worse than before. A vacation is supposed to refresh you and give you a new outlook. If I took one I'd just be coming back to the same old life.''

"Then do something to change it.''

"I could retire and take up something exciting like basket weaving or horseshoes,'' he said wryly.

"You could think about getting married again, too.''

"No, thanks. I tried that once and managed to screw it up royally.''

Will straightened, muttering, "I have a feeling this is a no-win conversation. So, where you off to?''

"An appointment.''

"You don't look too anxious to keep it.''

Burke stared out the windshield for long moments. Will was right. Now that he was less than an hour away from ringing Abbie's doorbell, he had cold feet.

He glanced down at the car phone. He could call and cancel. *Sorry, Abbie, I just don't want to make love to you.* Or he could go and do it and end it and that would be that.

He turned to Will and managed a half grin. "I better go. You and I should plan to get together and toss back a few beers.''

"Yeah, let's. I'll call you.'' Will reached in and clamped a hand on his shoulder. "Get some rest, buddy, and think about what I said about marriage. It's not always blissful, but it's a helluva lot better than being alone.''

Burke started the car after Will walked away. His friend's words sounded ordinary, clichéd almost. The sort of thing one says because it can't be refuted. Yet he, Burke, had chosen to be alone even when he'd been married.

He'd kept much of himself locked away from Abbie for fear she'd find out he had feet of clay. He'd been scared of being too honest with her because of an ingrained terror that what would emerge would be all the bad characteristics his father had paraded like badges of honor. Greed, lust, vengeance . . .

And yet Burke had been guilty of all three with Abbie; in fact, he was about to commit them again in a very short while.

Greed—he could never get enough of her.

Lust—no woman had ever made him so hard, so hot—and seemingly without trying.

Vengeance—maybe seeing her again now was partially vengeance against his old man, a way to prove that Burke Wheeler didn't have to lie, connive, cheat and steal to get what he wanted.

He could be up-front, honest and still have what he wanted.

A day in bed with his ex-wife.

BURKE TURNED onto Abbie's street. It was close to ten in the morning. The April sun was bright, and daffodils added bursts of vivid yellow to a number of yards. Two mothers pushing strollers walked side by side down the sidewalk.

Next door to Abbie's, a woman was hanging flowered curtains on a clothesline. A telephone-repair truck was parked a little farther up the street.

Surveying the scene, Burke realized how normal and invitingly familiar it all looked. It was as if he'd been hurled back in time to one of those mornings early in their marriage when he'd had a couple of hours free and stopped at home.

He would catch Abbie on the phone or sewing or taking care of the baby; he would kiss her and tease her and within minutes they would be on the bed in a tangle of half-shed clothes.

Nostalgia, he mused grimly as he pulled into the drive and shut off the engine. Sitting in the silent car, he reminded himself he'd had such memories of their lovemaking before, and though pleasant, they'd never been more than that.

So why in hell was he hesitating? Was he afraid that the next few moments together were all there would be? They'd make love and he'd get up, get dressed and leave as if she was just any woman? Greed, lust and vengeance?

Wasn't that exactly his intent? a tiny voice inside him asked. Hadn't he even said it that way to her at the hospital?

I want you one more time, Abbie. Not forever, but one more time as if she were just an itch he needed to scratch.

He knew better. He knew she'd always been more.

She'd always been the vulnerability he hadn't wanted. The distraction that could, at the oddest or most inappropriate moments, make him want to chuck off all his control-freak tendencies and unlock those separate compartments that made up his life.

Instead, he'd methodically and deliberately shut himself out of Abbie's life.

If what he wanted was to continue down the lonely road he'd been on most of his life, to avoid creating more complications for Abbie and himself, then he shouldn't be here.

Finding Justin and Candy safe should have been enough.

No question he'd made a major mistake when he followed Abbie the night she drove the Kaufmans home. He'd stepped over the line and allowed himself to indulge. Once he'd had a taste of her, she'd been like a double shot of bourbon on an empty belly; he was still intoxicated.

Yet beyond the enticement of lovemaking Burke was caught now by a badly frayed determination to keep himself separate from her emotionally, to keep total control over his life so that he'd have the mental resources and stamina to—

Burke was brought up short.

The stamina to do what? Be a good cop? Continue with his obsessive belief that anything or anyone who distracted him from his purpose had to be set apart?

Compartments.

He'd put Abbie in the compartment called marriage.

He'd given her great sex.

He'd more than adequately provided for her and Justin.

Only when something came along that he couldn't control did they have major problems.

Those problems had culminated when she'd set up that meeting to discuss the divorce.

He shoved a hand through his hair. With wrenching insight, he knew he had no one to blame but himself. He could have made it to that meeting with her. Celada's arrest could have been handled by anyone Burke assigned to deal with it. But, no, he'd handled the problem because he didn't want to meet with Abbie.

He couldn't and didn't have the guts to flat out tell her the truth. He knew why; he'd always known why. Burke grimaced in disgust at this new view of himself. *You're a real hero, Wheeler.*

He was about to restart the car and leave when he glanced up and saw her standing in the front doorway. She wasn't running out to greet him. Perhaps she was giving them both a chance to change their minds. If he chose to drive away, she could simply close the door.

Burke felt his body tighten. She looked sensational. A black silky robe, her hair loose about her shoulders. Had she used that erotically scented lotion he always noticed when he got really close? Had she rubbed it between her breasts, in the small of her back, down her thighs?

His mouth was dry and his hands clammy. His gut was tight, his arousal straining his jeans. God, twenty feet separated them and his body was already jumping with need.

Damn.

As ABBIE WATCHED HIM from the doorway, the intensity of her need frightened her. She'd been waiting for him and had seen him turn into the drive, then remain in the car. It appeared he wasn't any more sure of the wisdom of coming here than she was about letting him in.

If she'd kept the front door closed, he wouldn't have known she'd seen him, then he could have easily changed his mind and driven away. But Abbie wanted him to know she was waiting. Maybe not a wise decision, but definitely a heartfelt one.

She loved Burke with a need so achingly strong she could no longer deny it. As difficult as it was to allow herself to be vulnerable, she had to take this step. She could not spend the rest of her life wondering what if. Whether he wanted to hear it or not, she intended to tell him she loved him. Needed him in her life.

She'd carefully prepared for this, taking care to put in her trusty old diaphragm—so much better than a condom. She'd showered and applied the musky lotion he'd once told her would make a saint have dirty thoughts. She'd fluffed her loose hair with her fingers to give it a wild tangled look.

As she stood in the shade of the doorway, her restlessness grew. Her breasts felt heavy, her body damp and hot and naked beneath the black silk robe. She'd loosely knotted the thin tie at her waist. She leaned against the wall for support and closed her eyes as he drew closer.

BURKE GOT OUT of the car and slammed the door, then shoved his hands deep in his pockets. Now that he'd made the decision, neither his body nor his unsettled thoughts were going to allow him to run away.

Quickly he crossed the yard. He was a few steps from the door when he caught the scent of her.

Burke reached her, urged her into the house, then closed the door behind them. He stood still for a few seconds to give himself some moments to slow his breathing, to clear his head.

Something let go inside him, spilling like scalding lava, running white-hot, so that no part of his body wasn't burned.

"You knew I couldn't stay away, didn't you?" he asked in a whisper that sizzled and sparked between them.

"I'd hoped you couldn't."

"This doesn't settle anything between us, Abbie."

"But it would seem the divorce didn't, either."

He stood still for a few more seconds, then slid his hand around the back of her neck, drew her close against his body and without any further hesitation, kissed her.

CHAPTER FOURTEEN

BURKE DRANK from her lips like a man dying of thirst. Abbie slid her arms tightly around his waist as if fearing he might change his mind, move away and leave.

He eased her back against the wall, moving his hands from her shoulders and skimming them down the sides of her breasts, soaking in her softness. He allowed himself the ease and pleasure of touching the slight fullness of her hips from childbearing and taking delightful note of the way she fit against him as if she'd been made especially for him.

Abbie gave in to the instant kindling of sensation that fluttered down her spine. Her heart overflowed with love for him, and she was determined not to let him leave here without telling him.

She had no idea how he would react or even how she would express herself. For still bound in her feelings for him were threads of concern that she was once again setting herself up for pain and disappointment.

As much as they'd shared physically in the past few days and their mutual worry and relief over Justin, Burke remained emotionally distant when it came to their personal relationship. The fear she would never know him totally was both a challenge and a curse.

Yet now, as she blossomed under his touch, she told herself that for these moments her love for him was enough. Coming together in a blending of bodies and souls and timeless satisfaction was what she needed, what she wanted.

Burke, too, knew this joining would be different. Her passion and the way she drew them together as if they were endlessly entwined made this moment distinct. Love and making love; that instinctive swirl of everlasting satisfaction always crowded out all logic and reason when it came to Abbie. That interminable sensuality now pitched him into a need so great he shuddered with it.

He deepened the kiss, tangling their tongues, absorbing her taste and the sweetness of her passion. The scent of her drenched him. Not just the exotic lotion, but anticipation, the seeping heat of desire and a binding need for this woman. Not purely in a physical way, but a connecting of hearts and feelings for her and with her.

Only with Abbie.

Burke lifted his mouth and gazed into her eyes. He saw vulnerability there, an openness, a soft and languid willingness. Without breaking his hold, he reached behind him and turned the lock on the door.

Abbie sighed, relaxing slightly with the knowledge that at least he didn't plan to just kiss her and leave. Her cheeks were warm, her lips slightly parted.

Without taking her eyes from him, Abbie reached up to touch his mouth, her fingers trembling either from anticipation or uncertainty, Abbie wasn't sure.

They drifted across his lips with a feathery lightness that made him catch his breath.

"Abbie—"

She pressed her fingers firmly against his lips now, as if to hold back any questions, still his objections. "Shh, don't tell me. At this moment I just want to make love to you."

He pushed aside the unresolved discord that lay heavy on his soul. He had to deal with it, and yet here, with her touching him, allowing herself to trust him for this next little while, he mentally pushed his worry into a dark corner of his thoughts.

In the softest of voices, as if it was their secret, he said, "Not near as much as I want to make love to you."

Then he lifted her into his arms. The folds of her silk robe were slippery on his hands, and the warmth of her skin sifted through the fabric and invited his exploration. The satiny lapels that closed across her breasts gaped open as he strode quickly toward the bedroom.

When he got there he gave up all attempts to resist and dipped his head to kiss the swell of her breast. She sifted his hair through her fingers, holding his mouth against her as if his touch was the most precious of gifts.

The room was large and airy, and Burke saw more than he had that night they'd slept here after making love. Then, they'd been in the midst of worry over Justin and their rediscovered passion. Now, he felt a distinct welcoming.

This wasn't just a tryst, a few moments of sexual satisfaction after which he could simply get dressed and walk away. The profoundness of that thought disturbed him.

Before when they'd made love, he'd kept the emphasis on the physical, on the heat each could generate in the other. He was no fool; he knew her desire as well as he knew his own. In the past that desire had been a compartment of its own where he could concentrate on the pleasure and not the promises of love and trust.

Abbie had turned the covers back on the crisp blue cotton sheets. Her queen-size bed stood in an alcove of windows framed with lacy striped blue sheers. The matching shades were carefully lowered. The sunshine eased through the open wedge to dance across the bed in a kaleidoscope of patterns.

Burke lowered her to the bed, kissed her deeply, lingering to touch his mouth to her cheeks, her eyes and finally to press his lips into the inviting V between her breasts.

Straightening, he couldn't drag his gaze away from the alluring magnet of her body. She lay before him, watching him, her hair fanned across the sheet in delightful disarray. Her hands lay relaxed and palms up at her sides.

She, too, watched him as he pulled off his shirt and reached for the button on his fly. She lifted her hand and touched his bare stomach, running her fingers down the arrow of hair that disappeared into his pants.

Burke sucked in his breath, and taking her hand, he pressed it to his arousal. She kept her hand there, moving slowly, caressing him through the denim.

He squeezed his eyes closed, both loving and damning his need for her. In some ways he felt like a fraud. Wanting her, knowing she wanted him and yet achingly aware she was doing this without any promises from him, without any hope he wouldn't use their divorce and the complications of an ongoing relationship as a reason to walk away.

Hell, he'd either walked away or, worse, simply stayed away when they'd been married. Taking that step now would not only be easy, it would be practical.

Except for one basic fact. Something inside him had been exposed in the past week. He wanted to think it was Justin's running away, a crisis that had brought them together, just like in the movies.

But it wasn't Justin or the crisis or even the constant clamor of desire he felt for Abbie. No longer did he just want her willingness to make love; he wanted her willingness to make love and be his love tomorrow and the next day and the next.

All those separate compartments where he'd so carefully slotted the so-called priorities of his life sud denly spilled into one another. They'd become individually weakened and now were virtually indistinguishable from one another.

Being the supercop, proving that he wasn't like his old man, that he wasn't a thief, a liar and a bastard underneath a facade of honesty, now seemed vastly overrated in his mind compared to losing Abbie. But in many ways all those things were true.

He'd stolen Abbie's chance for happiness by his unwillingness to share all of himself with her. He hadn't been pleased when she told him she was pregnant with Justin, but in reality the problem hadn't been her pregnancy, but his own fear of having a child, of being a lousy father.

At that point, he'd already realized their marriage wasn't working. Her need to be part of every aspect of his life and his need to close her out had rubbed against each other with the abrasiveness of sandpaper. Burke's obsession to be the best cop on the force had isolated him from the most important thing that had ever happened to him.

Abbie. Only Abbie.

He straightened and moved away from the bed.

"Burke?" Her expression was confused.

"I can't do this, Abbie," he said, feeling as empty and hollow as he'd ever been.

For a damning stretch of silence, she just stared. Then she sat up cautiously and in an incredulous whisper asked, "You don't want to make love?"

He shoved both hands through his hair and swore. "I can't let lust and greed for you be the reason." He sat on the edge of the bed, near her, not touching her.

"Greed and lust? Those aren't just feelings *you* have, you know. I've felt them, too. Greed that I didn't want to share you with anyone or anything. And lust, too, Burke. Sometimes I've just wanted you with a purely physical ache."

He watched her, his eyes darkening, his head nodding in understanding. "Like that time in my car," he muttered.

"Yes, it was wonderful. Messy and not very comfortable, but it had been so long and..." She ducked her head when his eyes probed intensely.

He reached out his hand and tilted up her chin so that she had to look at him. "It had been a long time for me, too, sweetheart."

Then he leaned over and angled his head to kiss her. She slid her arms around his neck and melted into the kiss. His tongue curled around hers, sweeping up her taste, investigating every crevice.

Finally he whispered, "You're distracting me."

"It's just good old lust, remember?" she teased as her heart swelled with excitement.

She knew it was more; she knew that for her this was love with all its problems and pain and, like now, an almost heavenly perfection.

"Just partly. Lust never had the power to do to me what you do."

She wriggled closer and he kissed her again, this time pulling her into his arms.

He brushed his fingers down her cheek, wondering how she could be so smooth, so soft. "One of the things that became clear to me these past few days was that parenthood works best when the parents are equal partners. During our marriage, I always indicated in a hundred different ways that I expected you to handle everything that had to do with the family. Sleep with me, raise my kid, take care of anything emotional by yourself. I might just as well have hung a sign around my neck that read, 'Cross this line and I won't be there for you.' ''

Burke eased away from her, mostly because touching her distracted him from what he needed to say. He got to his feet and took the few steps to the window, raised the shade and watched a cardinal flutter at the sill.

He felt somewhat like that bird—hovering on the outside and looking in.

In a halting voice he said, ''The night we were supposed to meet to discuss getting divorced ...''

Abbie wanted to scramble up and throw herself into his arms. She couldn't let him take all the blame for that. But she stayed put and, winding her fingers into the folds of her robe, said softly, ''I was horrible to you the next day when you came to the shop.''

''Your anger toward me was deserved, Abbie. I made the name bastard sound angelic.''

''Burke—''

''No, let me finish.'' He turned and faced her. ''When Celada called me, my first reaction was to do nothing. I had to meet you and I didn't want to get involved with her problems. Then she wanted to call you because you'd always been there for her. You know how volatile she can be. She started to cry about how the arrest was all a big mistake. I kept thinking that, because you were her friend, if she needed you, you'd go up to Boston to be with her, and I didn't want you to do that. All I could think of was that you had enough with Justin and our problems. You didn't need to take on Celada and her hysteria, too."

He hesitated a moment before finally adding, "But beyond Celada's problems was my own reluctance. I didn't want that meeting with you."

Abbie blinked. Didn't *want* to meet her? That was different than viewing the meeting as unimportant.

"But why? We weren't happy. Even the attempt at marriage counseling . . ."

"That didn't work because I thought it was no one's business but our own what was going on in our personal lives. Looking back, I think I was more afraid of being married to you, and that's why I balked." He waved his hand, indicating that was all in the past. "We'd agreed that a divorce was best for us, and certainly best for Justin."

She rose to her feet and pulled her robe tightly around her. "I was hurt and furious when you didn't come to meet me. I believed I'd become so irrelevant in your life that even meeting me to get rid of me was too much trouble."

He stared at her for a long incredulous moment. "Get rid of you? God, no. In fact, it wasn't until I arrived in Boston and got Celada taken care of that I realized why I didn't want to meet you. But what *really* bothered me was that I had willingly gone there to do something I swore I'd never do as a cop. I pulled strings to get Celada freed and the charges dropped. Me, who had this obsession about never doing anything that even sniffed of something unethical. Yet doing that for her was easier and more palatable than meeting you to discuss a divorce.

"I didn't want you to leave me, while at the same time I knew you'd be better off and happier because I'd managed to make you so *un*happy. Even the next day, when you were so furious, I couldn't tell you. I stood there and watched everything I cared about go up in smoke, and I didn't say a damn thing."

Abbie walked over to him and put her arms around him.

"Twice you did something questionable rather than expose your real feelings. You helped Celada and you bribed that drugstore owner who told us Justin had stolen the pregnancy-test kit. Remember you wanted him to call us at Johnny's if he saw Justin again?"

At Burke's nod, she laid her head against his heart. "You know, Burke, most people would see what you did as minor, but I know you. For you those things were major, because they pitted that obsession to be the perfect cop against how you really felt in your heart."

He hugged her fiercely. "It all sounds so simple now. Yet back then I didn't have a clue about trusting my heart. Maybe because it was telling me that *you* were what I needed. I didn't want to hear it, so it was easier to let you divorce me than give up my determination to prove I wasn't like my old man."

After a long pause he said, "Only *you* could pull absolution out of the dregs of what I did to you and Justin."

"As long as we're heaping blame," she said, "don't forget I made that awful remark about uncomplicating your life by getting out of it."

"Yeah." He stared down at her. "As hard as this is for me to say, at the time I didn't disagree. You were a complication, but not because we were married."

He paused again, and Abbie's pulse sped up in both fear and hope.

"It was because I was afraid I'd fallen in love with you."

Her heart pounded with relief. "You were afraid you'd fallen in love with me? Oh, Burke..."

He ran a finger down her cheek, his gaze drinking in all that she was, all that he'd let go and now found again.

"Don't you see?" he said. "I couldn't tell you. I was completely blown away by the emotion, and if I admitted it, told you how important you were to me, how much I needed you—" he took a deep breath "—I was afraid I'd lose focus on what I wanted and what I'd sworn I would accomplish with my life. It was very disconcerting to know I would pull strings to get Celada out of trouble so I would have an excuse not to meet you."

"But you never even told me that was the reason. You never gave me any reason at all for not showing up."

He laughed, but without humor. "Yeah, I could've said something like I just broke the law to avoid you. Would you have believed that?"

She stared for a moment, then shook her head. "No. I guess not."

"Yeah, well, I figured that, too. Besides, it made me feel too vulnerable. I couldn't have told you then if I'd wanted to."

"But you have now. Why?"

Again, he stared at her, realizing that now there was no turning back. Being honest with himself meant being honest with Abbie. Yet he was still scared. Scared she wouldn't say she'd give them another chance. But he'd come this far...

Holding her and looking into her eyes so he didn't miss any nuance of expression, he said softly, "Because you and Justin are all that matter. Last week, with Justin missing, being the perfect cop became vastly unimportant. Sure I used the tools I'm trained for, but the realization that Justin had run away because he believed he couldn't come to us made me take a hard look at the kind of father I'd been. In my attempt to be unlike my own father, I made some crucial errors in being a father myself."

Abbie's heart turned over with love. "Burke, Justin adores you. I know if he were given a choice of a thousand men to be his father, he would choose you."

"How about you?"

"Of a thousand men, would I choose you to be his father?" She looked at him in confusion, as if waiting for some profound comment.

Burke didn't have anything profound, just the truth of how he felt and what he wanted with her, which was more than he'd ever wanted anything else.

Cautiously, he eased the question out. "Would you choose me to be your husband?"

She knew from the laserlike stare of his eyes that he wanted the truth.

No glossing over it.

No answers because they could settle for just making love. No rosy outlook because they'd functioned as parents those few days last week so could simply slip back into that role.

Abbie knew she could say yes or no to his question; he would accept either.

Instead, she stretched up and kissed him, tasting his fear, his trepidation that he might have exposed too much and would get little in return. A vulnerable Burke, she knew instinctively, was very serious.

Abbie said, "I chose you once, Burke, and yes, I would choose you again. Despite all our problems, I never really stopped loving you." She wanted to be honest so there was no misunderstanding. "Sometimes I hated you. A lot of the time I was furious with you, but I also know that those strong emotions don't happen unless there's an unbreakable connection. I loved you, but I was sure you didn't love me. No matter what I tried or how understanding I was, we always ended up farther apart."

Burke released her and crossed to the other side of the room, as if the physical distance would give her a chance to change her mind if she wished. Her heart filled with love when he turned toward her. His expression had softened, his vulnerability evident yet obviously frightening to him.

"This could be a helluva mistake, Abbie," he said with a tinge of anxiety. "I know I love you. I know I don't want to live without you, but..."

"You're afraid that once the bloom or newness wears off, we'll realize we made a mistake."

"Maybe I want a guarantee."

"I have one."

She went to him, took his hand and pulled him back toward the bed.

In a determined voice she said, "Here's the guarantee. When we have a problem, we're honest with each other. We don't close down and make assumptions without discussing things. Just like we're doing today."

"Hmm, you mean you'll lure me home for some great sex and wait till I feel guilty and spill my guts?" He grinned, his fingers tangling in her hair.

Abbie smiled, her eyes bright with promise. "And I'll be sure to watch for any ethical slips on your part," she teased. "That should be a good way to gauge how you feel."

He kissed her soundly. "It was a tough thing to face. To know that to have you I might have gone to any length, but the most damning was my refusal to admit that you were more important to me than anything else, that I loved you so much."

His hands slid over her bottom as he backed her up to the edge of the bed. She squeezed her fingers into the waistband of his jeans.

Burke pushed her robe off her shoulders and brushed his thumbs across her breasts, teasing the hardened nipples until she thought she'd explode with desire. Then, his hands inching down her belly, he eased her back onto the sheets. Their bodies hummed with a delicious tension. Burke adored the softness of her skin, its beautiful glow, loved the way her tangled hair spread out on the pillow. Abbie welcomed the warm weight of his body, the tightening of his muscles as she ran her hands caressingly over him.

He stroked the most feminine part of her, feeling her heat, her moistness. When she could bear it no longer, she parted her legs farther and urged him to sheath himself deep inside her.

Burke groaned. "Guess this means I'll have to marry you again." He kissed her mouth, her throat, as he moved in her. "I love you, Abbie."

"I love you, too." She arched her hips and had the pleasure of feeling him shudder. "Love and marriage are definitely the most ethical things to do."

"Definitely..." he murmured.

Burke kissed her deeply as she arched up again and again and brought their bodies to one final peak. Their pleasure spilled, and then seemed to go on and on...

LATER, AS THEY LAY entwined talking of the events of the past week, Abbie said, "If anyone had told me that Justin's running away would've resulted in us getting back together, I'd've said they were—"

"Looking at life through rose-colored glasses?" he asked, and then tucked her closer to him.

She tipped her head up so she could see him. "Yes."

"Then, since I couldn't be happier, you have my permission to polish up every pair you have."

She hugged him, her eyes smarting with tears of joy. "What happened to that cynicism of yours?"

"Would it sound too corny if I said your love chased it all away?"

"Oh, Burke..."

And as he wrapped her in his arms, they both knew that their future together would bring them a happiness to last a lifetime.

EPILOGUE

"YOU MAY KISS the bride."

Burke placed his hands on Abbie's shoulders and lowered his mouth to hers in a gentle but poignant kiss. Abbie sighed. Her happiness knew no bounds.

"I love you, sweetheart," he whispered.

"And I adore you," she returned.

With a mischievous wink, he asked, "Do you think our guests would notice if we slipped out the back and skipped all the congratulations?"

She grinned. "I think we should stick around for a little while."

"Yeah, I was afraid you'd say that."

The minister, his glasses sliding to the end of his nose, beamed at the wedding guests who filled the pews "I'd like to introduce you to Mr. and Mrs. Burke Wheeler."

Abbie and Burke turned and faced their friends and family, then, with her arm through his, they walked down the center aisle amidst smiles and wishes of luck and happiness.

It was late May, longer than Burke had wanted to wait to marry, but Abbie had insisted. She'd wanted her mother here, and she'd needed to arrange for time off from her job in California as tour guide to the stars. Abbie had wanted Celada to come, too, and the fashion designer had been in Europe for the spring fashion showings and an extended vacation. Others, from Will Gagne to Candy Kaufman and her parents, to Johnny Rebel and Pammie—Abbie had wanted them all there, and that meant a few weeks' notice.

But the day had finally arrived, and the small white clapboard chapel with its New England charm and abundance of wisteria bushes had made the entire event storybook perfect.

As they stood outside greeting guests, Celada approached. Impeccably dressed in a banana yellow fitted suit and matching hat, the black-haired designer drew Abbie into her arms.

"I'm so glad you came," Abbie said warmly. She'd worn an ecru lace-and-silk dress. Around her neck was a triple strand of pearls Burke had given her.

Burke excused himself from her side and went to chat with Will Gagne.

Celada said, "After I heard what happened with Justin, I'm sorry I wasn't here. But I'd say *some* good came of it. He and his girlfriend look pretty happy, and those sketches you sent me are very promising."

Abbie smiled. "When you say 'promising,' I know that means they're outstanding. Pammie is standing over there watching us. She's nervous and believes you're untouchable."

"Hmm, well, let me go and introduce myself. I'll see you at the reception."

The reception was held in a private dining room of one of the more popular restaurants in Walcott. Abbie and Burke moved among their guests, chatting and laughing. A buffet was served and the four-tiered wedding cake was decorated with silver roses and the same bride and groom that had topped their cake the first time they were married.

Justin claimed a dance with his mother, and Burke danced with Abbie's mother. Hours later, after the guests had departed, Burke and Abbie got into their rented chauffeur-driven limo for the forty-five-minute ride to the airport.

"At last I have you all to myself," Burke said as he tucked her close to him.

"I know. It seems like forever since you kissed me."

"Not a tough request, Mrs. Wheeler," he said, brushing his mouth across hers and then groaning as he deepened the caress.

Their honeymoon would be short—four days in Bermuda—but both knew that a long honeymoon wasn't nearly as important as a long and happy marriage. Abbie's mother happily volunteered to stay with Justin, taking advantage of her visit to catch up with old friends she hadn't seen since she'd moved out West.

Celada and Pammie had hit it off and made plans to meet and work on Pammie's designs. Justin and Candy were dating and still in love, according to Justin, but their experience in Sade Court, despite the horror and sadness, had taught them a lesson in not trying to handle problems on their own when advice and help were needed.

Now, in the back of the dimly lit limo, Burke poured two glasses of champagne and presented one to Abbie.

"To my bride, the most beautiful and wonderful woman in the world," Burke said, touching the delicate flute to hers.

Abbie's smile was full of love and joy. "To us. This time, my rose-colored glasses predict a long and blissful future."

"I love you, Mrs. Wheeler," he said.

And after they finished their wedding champagne and extinguished the dim lighting, they fell into each other's arms. The airport was still some distance away, and Burke and Abbie didn't want to waste even a single moment getting started on their own private forever after.

HARLEQUIN SUPERROMANCE®

If you've always felt there's something special about a man raising a family on his own...
You won't want to miss Harlequin Superromance's touching series

He's sexy, he's single...and he's a father!
Can any woman resist?

THE TROUBLE WITH TEXANS
by Maggie Simpson

Jake Evans knows exactly what his late wife's sister is doing in Sotol Junction, Texas. She's checking to see what kind of father he is. Michelle Davis will no doubt be reporting back to her mother in Boston about how eight-year-old Brooke is being raised. And Jake had better keep that in mind, despite the attraction developing between him and Michelle. If she thinks for one moment that he'd allow the Davis family to take Brooke away from him, she'd better think again.

Available in August

Be sure to watch for upcoming FAMILY MAN titles. Fall in love with our sexy fathers, each determined to do the best he can for his kids.

You'll find them wherever Harlequin books are sold.

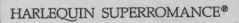

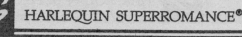

HARLEQUIN SUPERROMANCE®

SHOWCASE

Special Books by Special Writers

Under One Roof
by Shannon Waverly

The Author: Two-time RITA Award finalist and
Romantic Times Reviewer's Choice winner, she's
got fans worldwide. Shannon wanted this, her tenth
book for Harlequin, to be a very special one. *It is.*

The Characters:
Spencer Coburn. Overstressed physician, divorced father.
He's currently the sole emotional and physical support of...
Stacy Coburn, his teenage daughter—his *pregnant*
teenage daughter.
Gina Banning. Hardworking, divorced schoolteacher and
only child. She's currently the sole emotional and physical
support of...
Joe Banning, her eighty three-year-old father—her seriously
ill father.

The Story: One of the most moving, honest and *uplifting* books
you'll ever read. And it's just plain *romantic,* too!

Watch for *Under One Roof* by Shannon Waverly
Available in August 1996, wherever
Harlequin books are sold.

SHOW10

HARLEQUIN SUPERROMANCE®

RETURN TO
CALLOWAY
CORNERS

Remember the Calloway women—
Mariah, Jo, Tess and Eden?

For all the readers who loved *CALLOWAY CORNERS*...

Welcome Back!

And if you haven't been there yet or met the Calloways...

Join us!

MEET THE CALLOWAY COUSINS!

JERICHO
by Sandra Canfield
(available in August)

DANIEL
by Tracy Hughes
(available in September)

GABE
by Penny Richards
(available in October)

HARLEQUIN®

Don't miss these Harlequin favorites by some of our most
distinguished authors!
And now, you can receive a discount by ordering two or more titles!

HT #25663	THE LAWMAN by Vicki Lewis Thompson	$3.25 U.S.☐/$3.75 CAN. ☐
HP #11788	THE SISTER SWAP by Susan Napier	$3.25 U.S.☐/$3.75 CAN. ☐
HR #03293	THE MAN WHO CAME FOR CHRISTMAS by Bethany Campbell	$2.99 U.S.☐/$3.50 CAN. ☐
HS #70667	FATHERS & OTHER STRANGERS by Evelyn Crowe	$3.75 U.S.☐/$4.25 CAN. ☐
HI #22198	MURDER BY THE BOOK by Margaret St. George	$2.89 ☐
HAR #16520	THE ADVENTURESS by M.J. Rodgers	$3.50 U.S.☐/$3.99 CAN. ☐
HH #28885	DESERT ROGUE by Erin Yorke	$4.50 U.S.☐/$4.99 CAN. ☐

(limited quantities available on certain titles)

	AMOUNT	$
DEDUCT:	**10% DISCOUNT FOR 2+ BOOKS**	$
ADD:	**POSTAGE & HANDLING**	$
	($1.00 for one book, 50¢ for each additional)	
	APPLICABLE TAXES**	$_____
	TOTAL PAYABLE	$_____
	(check or money order—please do not send cash)	

To order, complete this form and send it, along with a check or money order for the
total above, payable to Harlequin Books, to: **In the U.S.:** 3010 Walden Avenue,
P.O. Box 9047, Buffalo, NY 14269-9047; **In Canada:** P.O. Box 613, Fort Erie, Ontario,
L2A 5X3.

Name:_____

Address:_____ City:_____

State/Prov.:_____ Zip/Postal Code:_____

**New York residents remit applicable sales taxes.
  Canadian residents remit applicable GST and provincial taxes.

HBACK-JS3

Look us up on-line at: http://www.romance.net

Sabrina   It Happened One Night
Working Girl   Pretty Woman
While You Were Sleeping

If you adore romantic comedies then have
we got the books for you!

Beginning in **August 1996** head to your
favorite retail outlet for
LOVE & LAUGHTER™,
a brand-new series with two books every
month capturing the lighter side of love.

You'll enjoy humorous love stories by favorite
authors and brand-new writers, including
JoAnn Ross, Lori Copeland, Jennifer Crusie,
Kasey Michaels, and many more!

As an added bonus—with the retail purchase,
of two new Love & Laughter books you can
receive a **free** copy of our fabulous
Love and Laughter collector's edition.

LOVE & LAUGHTER™—a natural
combination...always
romantic...always entertaining

HARLEQUIN ®

BRIDE'S BAY RESORT

UNLOCK THE DOOR TO GREAT ROMANCE AT BRIDE'S BAY RESORT

Join Harlequin's new across-the-lines series, set in an exclusive hotel on an island off the coast of South Carolina.

Seven of your favorite authors will bring you exciting stories about fascinating heroes and heroines discovering love at Bride's Bay Resort.

Look for these fabulous stories coming to a store near you beginning in January 1996.

Harlequin American Romance #613 in January
Matchmaking Baby by Cathy Gillen Thacker

Harlequin Presents #1794 in February
Indiscretions by Robyn Donald

Harlequin Intrigue #362 in March
Love and Lies by Dawn Stewardson

Harlequin Romance #3404 in April
Make Believe Engagement by Day Leclaire

Harlequin Temptation #588 in May
Stranger in the Night by Roseanne Williams

Harlequin Superromance #695 in June
Married to a Stranger by Connie Bennett

Harlequin Historicals #324 in July
Dulcie's Gift by Ruth Langan

Visit Bride's Bay Resort each month wherever Harlequin books are sold.

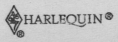

HARLEQUIN ®

BBAYG